MW01026436

WINTER'S RESCUE

WINTER BLACK SERIES: SEASON TWO
BOOK TWO

MARY STONE

This book is dedicated to all the mommas out there, who love fiercely and still feel like they're never doing enough.

DESCRIPTION

Nice girls finish last. Bad girls finish dead.

When Private Detective Winter Black-Dalton receives a slew of messages from a mother desperate to protect her children after a traumatizing divorce, she takes the case without hesitation. Not only is it a welcome distraction from unpacking boxes, but Winter hopes to assuage the guilt still fusing her to her past.

She should have known better.

A crayon drawing of guns and "nakid notty girls" by her client's five-year-old daughter hints at the wealthy and powerful father's depraved activities. When the man in question warns Winter off the investigation, he reeks of cunning. But she has no hard facts, only impressions. And with no FBI badge to open doors, she needs to get creative.

But the more Winter investigates, she fears something far more sinister lurks beneath the surface. And when local call girls mysteriously disappear, Winter must risk it all to save other young women from the same fate.

The mystery and suspense continue with *Winter's Rescue*, the second book in the Winter Black Season Two series, a thrilling ride that will make you realize things aren't always as they seem. Sometimes they're much worse.

1

Bridget Augusta had never intended to take her clothes off for a living. But one thing she learned in her nineteen years on Earth was that life was full of surprises.

Like now.

Here she was…alone…on a Saturday night…at a remote gas station near Middle of Dang Nowhere, Texas. Of course, she'd been in similar places for years. For a runaway, home was often anywhere and nowhere at the same time.

Her life changed once she found work—such as it was—dancing at seedy dives. An offer to work at private parties for rich men eventually came along, and Bridget now had a place she could legitimately call home. It had been a while since she kissed her old life goodbye. She liked money and planned on never being without it again.

And for the moment, her clothes were firmly in place.

Which was a good thing, since an icy January wind whipped off the adjacent highway. She held back her long brown hair with one hand and pulled her coat closer with the other while she watched the gas pump numbers tick nearer to full.

"C'mon, c'mon," Bridget urged, as if she had the power to do anything but wait for the tank to fill. Finally, the pump chimed, and she spared a hand to remove the nozzle from her Volvo. She pulled her coat tight again as she headed to the station to collect her receipt—this was a business expense, after all.

"Maybe next time, I'll get a nice hotel room instead of heading home after work."

Her clients rarely offered her lodging once her job was done, even if they did offer lots of other opportunities. She had rules, though, and never went for the offers, no matter how tempting. Plus, she'd been warned about watching out for guys who promised to *take her away from all this*. Safer and better to just head out on the road, even if it sometimes meant topping off the tank late at night.

"Demands of the job, girl. You knew that when you signed up."

After getting her receipt, Bridget hurried back to the comfort of her warm car and reached for her sports drink. Only another half an hour on the road before she could crawl into bed and sleep. She started the engine and yawned before heading out onto the deserted highway. The lights guiding her to the interstate on-ramp were few and far between, but she was less than a quarter mile away.

Damn.

She took another sip, hoping it would help the dull headache crawling up the back of her head. She blamed her discomfort on the long night. The money she made dancing for the wealthy partygoers was great, but the groping, the encouragement to drink more than she knew was safe, and the endless invitations *to go somewhere else* always bugged her.

Bridget was a dancer, not a whore, but men could never tell the difference.

The dark expanse beyond her headlights added to her

unease with the remote location. Maybe she should have pushed her car to reach Austin before stopping. As the road bent right, coming around the curve, the glare of flashing hazard lights caught her attention, and she let up on the gas a bit.

A black Mustang coupe convertible sat parked on the shoulder. Someone leaned against the side of the car.

It was dark and a long walk back to the gas station if this person was on empty or needed some other kind of assistance. Against her better judgment, Bridget slowed her car. Not too much, though. She was fully prepared to take off if it turned out to be a guy, or *guys*, but she'd become curious about who was stranded on the desolate road. Curious enough to at least give them a moment of her attention.

She'd been stranded before and knew the feeling.

Bridget squinted to make out the person's features, and as her car eased closer, she caught the profile of a young woman in a fancy designer outfit and high heels gripping a handbag that would've cost Bridget a full night of dancing for her wealthiest clients. She debated passing by, until the glint of tears on the woman's cheeks moved Bridget's foot off the gas pedal.

This is the last thing I need.

Bridget wanted to be tough and keep driving, but she thought of herself in the same position. Stuck alone on a deserted road in the middle of the night wasn't a situation any woman wanted to be in. She understood the stranger's tears. They would have been her own.

She eased the car closer to the Mustang and stopped. Lowering her passenger window, Bridget looked up at the woman, still sticking close to her driver's side door. She seemed afraid.

Who could blame her?

"You need some help?" Bridget anticipated a glimmer of relief in the woman's face, but there was nothing.

"My phone's dead." The young woman sniffled. "And I'm out of gas. My husband didn't want me to go out with my friends. He always tells me I'm careless and irresponsible. This will make him so pissed. I'm afraid of what he might do to me."

The tough, independent woman Bridget strived to be shuddered at the memories of her father's blows and the feel of his hands between her legs. The endless torture had driven her from the trailer park she'd called home. She'd hoped her nightmares would end after the sick bastard blew his brains out. They didn't. The bruises might not have lasted, but the abhorrent pain remained.

Bridget eased across the passenger seat. "I can give you a lift to the gas station. I'm sure they have a gas can you can use to fill up your car." She offered the woman a friendly smile. "With any luck, you won't have to mention a thing to your husband."

The tension in the stranger's shoulders eased, and she loosened her grip on her fancy handbag. "Oh, I can't tell you how much I'd appreciate that."

She hurried to the passenger door as Bridget sat back in her seat. It felt good to help another woman, even if the atmosphere of the empty road gave her the creeps.

Bridget waited for her passenger to buckle in, then checked her mirrors. Not a car in sight on the dark highway.

She did a quick U-turn and headed back to the gas station. Bridget got a better look at her passenger under the occasional passing streetlight.

The woman looked young to her, but what did she know? Barely nineteen, Bridget couldn't buy beer without a fake ID.

She was about to ask the stranger her name when a loud pop came from the front of the car, and the steering wheel jerked in her hand. Bridget's heart shot to her throat as she gripped the wheel, fighting the pull of the vehicle to the right.

The unmistakable *thunk, thunk, thunk* of a flat tire made her groan.

Son of a bitch. Of all times...

Bridget checked her rearview mirror and peered out the windshield, wondering what she'd hit. There was nothing on the road.

She pulled over, skidding as gravel pinged and bounced along the car's undercarriage. They drew to a stop, tilting slightly to the right.

Bridget reached for her car door to check out the damage, and her passenger gripped her arm.

"Please, don't go."

The wide-eyed terror in the woman's pale face made Bridget wonder just how dire her situation was. A woman in a good relationship didn't fear every little thing. She should know. The PTSD that lingered from her days with her father still reared its ugly head from time to time.

She patted the woman's forearm, loosening her grip. "It's okay. I've got to see what I hit. Then I can call roadside assistance."

"My husband's going to know I screwed up now."

Bridget held the woman's tiny hand, wanting to relieve her anxiety and offer a suggestion of getting her a hotel room for the night, but decided not to say anything for now. First, she needed to take care of her car. After that, she could deal with the skittish stranger.

She climbed out of the car, worried about the woman's situation. She wasn't one to go out of her way to help people, but this woman pulled at her heartstrings. Maybe her past had caught up with her. Who knew? At least she could try to do some good.

The bitter wind slapped Bridget's face, and she pulled her coat tighter. The idea of being stuck on the highway far away from her warm bed didn't sit well.

No good deed goes unpunished.

True that.

The right front tire, as she anticipated, was shredded. She stooped, getting a closer look at the wheel. Thank goodness for the bright moonlight. Without it, she'd be fumbling around in the dark with only the flashlight on her phone to aid her.

A few yards back on the road, a brown bag caught the moon's glow. Suspicious, Bridget walked over to check it out, praying she wouldn't find a kitten or puppy corpse inside.

"What is it?"

Bridget jumped at the young woman's cry. "I'm not sure," she shouted back. "Roll the window back up."

With trembling hands, she opened the filthy bag and peeked inside. A handful of thick, shiny, industrial nails glistened inside.

Rage mixed with fear coursed through her, immediate and hot. She gazed back down the road toward the gas station, thinking everything through.

Someone had placed this bag here on purpose. As a joke? Or worse?

Heading back to her car, she fumbled with her phone. How long would the roadside service take? Would she be better off walking to the safety of the gas station? Changing the tire herself and getting the hell out of there?

She didn't know.

A flash on the road just ahead disintegrated her internal debate. The gleam of metal made her take a step forward. More nails in case the first bag didn't do the trick? No...this was too big to be a nail.

A knife?

If it was, she could use a weapon right about now.

Bending to inspect it, she nearly fell over when a piercing scream rose from behind her. Before she could run or do anything, a hand covered her mouth and something sharp sank into her neck.

Her hand flew to the wound, and she stumbled forward. But the person behind her tightened their grip, pressing her against their chest.

Bridget tried to struggle, tried to pull the hand away from her mouth. At least she thought so, but her movements did no good. An odd sense of floating overwhelmed her, and she couldn't seem to control her legs. They wobbled and threatened to give way.

The air thinned, and she struggled for breath. Her mind raced for explanations.

What's happening to me?

The world spun, and she tumbled to the gravel-strewn roadside. The hand was gone from her mouth, but when she sucked in a breath to scream, only the smallest of whimpers escaped her throat.

In the distance, she spied treetops swaying in the chilly night breeze. The cold that had bothered her before didn't register anymore. A rock cut into her cheek as she fell, but she didn't care.

A blanket of calm enveloped Bridget, and her mind became a fuzzy mess of scrambled memories. She pictured herself back in her bed, cozy and safe.

Bridget closed her eyes, and the world instantly melted away.

A heady whiff of yeast drifted past Winter Black-Dalton's nose as she pushed a black lock of hair from her face with a flour-dusted hand. The sunlight pouring through the kitchen windows highlighted the butterfly posters, cabinet handles, and matching light fixture with Tiffany glass accents. The room had a warm, welcoming feeling that Winter hoped to recreate in her kitchen. Once she and her husband, Noah, finished unpacking it.

Winter's determination to copy Gramma Beth's bread recipe to the letter had taken up most of her Sunday afternoon. She punched the thick dough on the wooden cutting board, swearing the damn blob didn't feel the same as she remembered. The consistency was off.

"Dammit."

"Is there a problem?" A face framed by wavy silver hair popped up beside her.

Winter glanced at her beloved Gramma Beth. Her gingham-checked apron didn't have half the flour on it that Winter's did.

"It's not right." Winter punched the lump of dough again. "I did something wrong."

Her grandmother reached for the unmade bread, poking a finger into the side of it. "I'm sure it's fine."

Winter sagged against the counter, reveling in the aroma of the rump roast drifting across the kitchen.

Gramma Beth added a few more sprinkles of flour to the dough. "You just need to work it a little longer."

Winter folded her arms as she watched the woman work, not caring about her flour-coated hands and spreading even more dust onto her shirt. "I'm hopeless. I'll never be the wiz in the kitchen you are."

"You have other skills, dear." Her grandmother moved the dough to an oiled bread pan.

"I was hoping to impress you," Winter confided. "I wanted to make this week's Sunday dinner special."

Gramma Beth wiped her hands on her apron and cupped Winter's cheek. "It is special. You're here. Noah's here. That's all Jack and I wanted when we left Richmond. To be closer to you two."

Winter's heart squeezed. "Only after I twisted your arm to move to Austin."

The move had been a fresh start for everyone, especially after the horrors of dealing with her younger brother, Justin, and his psychotic rampages. Her grandparents, living only four blocks away and in the same neighborhood, ended up being a godsend.

Beth's airy laughter filled the kitchen. "You didn't twist my arm. Your grandfather and I wanted to come. I told you before, my only condition was our traditional Sunday dinners." Her grandmother winked. "You've held up that end of the bargain so far."

Winter dampened a towel and set it over the loaf of

bread. "Sometimes, I feel guilty. Like I took you and Grampa away from your life in Virginia."

Her grandmother returned to the stainless stove. "Nonsense. I have everything here I had there. I even get to crochet blankets for the Austin homeless shelter."

This was new. "Since when?"

Beth lifted the lid on her pot of bubbling brown gravy. "Oh, that started just recently. And you know how much I love to crochet." Her grandmother gave her a wary side glance. "How's the new job going?"

Winter had tried not to think about her first case as a private detective. Saving her first client from a murderous childhood acquaintance out for revenge had been a dark and gruesome task. Remembering how rats were used to consume the murderer's victims still gave Winter nightmares. She never wanted to see another rat as long as she lived.

"It's not what I expected." Winter plucked a green bean from a bowl on the counter and snapped off the ends.

Winter's good-looking, broad-shouldered husband, Noah Dalton, the type who looked like he belonged herding cattle on a local ranch, stuck his head in the door. "Smells great, darlin'. When do we eat?"

She frowned at him. "Not for another half an hour. Go back and keep Grampa Jack company. How's the game going?"

Noah's playful grin never faltered, even as he pressed a hand to his stomach. "I might faint before the last quarter. Just one nibble to hold me over?"

Winter liked the stubble on her husband's chin. He rarely went without shaving, but the grizzly look suited him. His brown hair had grown from his usual crew cut, and she could run her fingers through it at night when they were alone in bed. His forest-green eyes appeared more vibrant, thanks to his bright red shirt.

When she didn't answer, the smile fell away, and Noah stepped into the kitchen. "You okay?"

He knows me so well.

Gramma Beth raised her wooden spoon. "She's fine, now get your hide in the living room and make sure my husband doesn't nod off before he's had his supper."

Winter lowered her head, holding back a snicker as Noah hurried out of the room.

Beth brought the pot of gravy to the counter and set it next to Winter. "Is there something you're not telling me?" She nodded at the entrance. "He looks worried."

Winter wished her husband hadn't set off alarm bells for her grandmother. "He just thinks I'm working too hard. Noah's the one who suggested taking off for this three-day weekend. No work. Just us. He wanted me to relax after my last case."

Gramma Beth opened a cabinet and removed a white gravy boat. "Was it that bad?"

Winter rested her hip against the counter, mindful of her words. "Not bad. Just taxing."

Her grandmother studied her with a probing gaze. "Do you think you should be taking all this on before you settle into your new home?"

Winter peered into the dark gravy. "Unpacking is driving me insane."

Beth lifted her chin. "Yes, but you need a home before you can have a family. Set down your roots here before you go off looking for cheating husbands, missing people, or whatever it is you do."

Winter was about to enlighten Gramma Beth when her phone vibrated in her back pocket. Linked to her desk phone used only for Black Investigations, it signaled that her voicemail box was full. But how could that be? She'd set it to take up to thirty-two messages.

Retrieving her phone, she checked the screen. It *was* full.

What the hell?

"You were supposed to leave that at home." Gramma Beth waved a finger at her. "I asked you and Noah for a work-free evening."

Winter itched to be alone and check her messages. She hoped it was a new job—anything to keep her from having to unpack one more moving box.

She smiled at her grandmother, hoping to assure her all was well. "I remember. I'm going to the bathroom, but when I get back, we'll talk about what I do for a living. And it's not chasing cheating husbands."

Beth kissed her forehead. "As long as you aren't hunting killers like you did in the FBI. That terrified me."

In the paneled hall outside the kitchen, Winter wiped her eyes, glad to escape the kitchen before Gramma Beth could see the effect of her words. She slipped into the baby-blue powder room that smelled of lilacs.

Shutting the door, she rested her head against the cool wood, taking a minute to clear her mind. Then she wiped her fingertips clean on a towel and opened her phone screen.

The thirty-two voicemail alerts charged her with excitement. Thirty-two people wanted her services.

She swiped through the list of missed calls over the past three days. Winter had stuck to her agreement with Noah and diligently avoided her phone. But now, knowing the overwhelming list of potential clients waiting for her, she couldn't hold off anymore.

One number appeared on the list five times—that someone had repeatedly reached out to Winter sent a shiver of alarm through her. Only two kinds of people left repeated messages…the crazed or the desperate.

Winter listened to the voicemail to determine which one the potential client might be.

"*My name is Julia Eversmeyer.*" She rattled off her number. "*I'm calling because...because...I need to protect my children from my ex-husband. They've been massively traumatized by our divorce, and now I...well. I believe he's...sick. Please. Help me.*"

Winter hesitated before playing the remaining voicemails. The heightened fear in Julia's voice added to Winter's concern. If children were involved, she would have to take the case. That had become her weak spot as of late.

Ever since...

Visions of little Timothy Stewart played in Winter's head. His small form, lying on the RV floor, his mouth duct-taped shut, tears streaming down his face as he stared at his mother's lifeless body. How her despicable brother, Justin Black, escaped from his locked psych ward unit, drugged her, and forced her to kill Timothy's parents to save Little Timmy and his sister, Nicole...

With that gun pointed at the kids, Justin held all the cards. She was at his mercy. Failing to choose was the same as putting the gun to Tim's head and pulling the trigger herself.

Kill the father, or Justin would murder the kids.

"Ticktock, Winter. Four...three..."

A heartrending cry escaped little Tim. The noise ripped at Winter's defenses, shattering something inside her.

She battled the anguish that threatened to drag her under. She was an agent. Calm under pressure, cool under fire. Emotions couldn't help her now, so Winter locked them away, allowing clinical detachment to descend instead.

She had a choice to make.

The dad...or the kids.

"...two..."

Out of time.

When Winter glided forward, her legs didn't even feel like her own. Nor did her hands as they reached out to cradle Greg's head. She registered the warmth of his skin, and the stubble that prickled her palm.

"...one..."

There was no more thinking, only instinct and muscle memory carrying her through the motion. A sharp, forceful twist, and—

Crack!

Winter still heard that sound in her sleep, and often during her waking hours. To this day, she refused to even think about what Justin put the little boy through after kidnapping him. Timothy had spent months traveling the world with her psychopath of a brother because of her. She'd never been the same since that horrible day.

Even as she forced the images of Timothy and Justin from her mind, Winter knew who her next case would be...Julia Eversmeyer. The other twenty-seven messages could wait. Julia needed her first, and Winter felt compelled to help. Maybe in some small way, it would make up for the guilt that still gripped her after what had happened to Timothy.

Winter closed her eyes and held onto the sink. She wished she could clone herself and take on multiple cases simultaneously, but the science wasn't there yet.

Back outside the bathroom, she tucked her phone into the pocket of her jeans. She rounded the corner to the kitchen, freezing when she saw her grandmother staring into her bread pan.

"What is it?" she asked, rushing into the warm room.

Gramma Beth held out the moist towel she'd placed over the bread pan. "You might want to start over with that bread recipe, dearie. That mound of flour you made isn't going to *rise* to the challenge."

Good thing Gramma made a loaf earlier.

Winter pressed her lips together and marched toward the

counter where her unbaked loaf waited. "Just wait. I'll conquer your recipe if it's the last thing I do."

Her grandmother's lighthearted chuckle chased away the disappointment she felt in her cooking skills. "You do that, dearie." Beth returned to the oven and slipped on her oven mitts. "Just leave the rest of the cooking to me. Otherwise, you might burn my house down."

3

Rumble, rumble.

      Noah Dalton repositioned himself on the sofa, trying to focus on the football game blaring from the flatscreen and not on the noises coming from his empty stomach. The aroma of pot roast, the hint of new potatoes roasting in butter, and the heavenly essence of freshly baked bread made it impossible to keep track of the score.

Fifteen minutes. You can last that long. Discipline.

But reason told Noah that was what he'd told himself fifteen minutes earlier. He glanced over at Grampa Jack, wondering how the older man endured the agony of the savory smells coming from the kitchen, but the avid Patriots fan had his eyes closed, appearing far too relaxed.

Noah checked his watch once more, looking for a distraction. Lucy hadn't arrived yet, which didn't surprise him. His sister was always late, even though she swore she'd arrive in time for the six o'clock Sunday meal.

He debated if he should give Grampa Jack a nudge. Noah stood, about to tap Jack's shoulder, when the phone in his back pocket vibrated. He'd shut off the ringer at Gramma

Beth's insistence, but curiosity needled him. Who would call at this hour on a Sunday?

Noah stole a glance at Jack and checked the screen on his phone. It was his boss. Suddenly, the desires of Beth McAuliff paled in comparison to his duties as a federal agent. When SSA Weston Falkner called, Noah had to answer.

He hurried from the living room and eased the front door open, mindful not to disturb Jack. His thoughts jumped ahead to the reason for such a call. His job was twenty-four seven, and crime didn't rest on holidays, but this cut into his vacation time. It was an unwritten law on the force. Vacation time was sacred. You were left alone when you were out of the office.

Once on the porch, Noah hesitated before taking the call. Winter would kill him if she found out.

He cleared his throat before he spoke. "Yes, sir." Noah hoped Jack didn't wake up and find him missing. "Sorry for the delay. I had to step outside."

"We have a lead in an ongoing missing persons case linked to a sex-trafficking ring." Falkner's stern voice came through the speaker, grating on Noah's nerves. "I need you to pack tonight and prepare to head out tomorrow with Agent Taggart."

Well, good evening to you too.

Falkner reminded Noah of the gruff Supervisory Special Agent Aiden Parrish back in Virginia. Aiden also had a hard outer shell and had come across as a coldhearted son of a bitch at first. In the beginning, Aiden had been Noah's least favorite person, but now, he and the SSA had developed a friendship of sorts. He wouldn't admit it out loud, but he actually missed the man.

Would his relationship with Falkner take a similar turn? Noah wasn't holding his breath.

Noah looked up and down the quiet street, amazed by the

calm in the Destiny Bluff subdivision. He should have been used to his life in the Violent Crimes Division taking him away from the reality of suburbia, but sometimes it became hard to separate his work world from his domestic bliss.

Before, when it was only his hide to sweat over, he didn't mind the gruesome scenes, deaths, and depravity. But now, with a wife, a mortgage, neighbors with children who rode their bikes to school, and a peaceful, middle-class community, it had gotten a lot harder to remain impassive.

"Ah, yes, sir. I understand."

"I'll need you at VCD first thing. You can skip your usual coffee run." It seemed Parrish 2.0 remained as affable and outgoing as a clam.

"Any idea how long we'll be gone?" Noah winced as he asked the question.

It was never an agent's place to ask about the length of any assignment. The work ended when the unsub got arrested, but Noah couldn't go running off without giving Winter some estimate of his return. He might have been an FBI agent, but he was a husband first.

"Several days," Weston admitted in a dark tone. "So pack accordingly." The head of Noah's division hung up without so much as a goodbye.

Noah cursed softly, a pang of worry crowding his heart. He lifted his chin and stared at the pink Texas sky. Now wasn't a good time to leave Winter alone. His wife had just wrapped up a hellish case and needed him, but this was his job. Winter knew that. She wouldn't hesitate to leave him behind if she got called out. Why did he feel so restless about her staying behind?

He tried to brush his reservations aside, but leaving Winter alone to handle whatever debacle of a case she stumbled into didn't sit well with him. If she ended up with another Fitzgerald case, putting her life in danger, Noah would never forgive himself for leaving.

The hunger that hounded his stomach earlier turned into burning despair.

"You look like you have the weight of the world on your shoulders."

Noah turned to find his sister inching closer. Lucy's green eyes gave him a thorough once-over while the snake tattoo on her neck pulsed with each heartbeat, making her appear more detached than concerned.

A former Navy officer, Lucy had given up her sea legs and chased her passion…tattoos. Though she was a talented artist with a devoted following, he still had a hard time seeing his older sister hanging out with bikers and shady characters. Not that she couldn't take care of herself—she'd been beating him up since the age of two—or that anyone with a tat was shady.

Body art had surpassed trendy a decade ago, and more people than not now had ink on their person.

He pulled her into a quick hug. "Just work stuff."

Stepping back, Noah offered his sibling a friendly nudge as his gaze traveled to her snug black leather pants and high-heeled boots. "Make sure you don't share clothes with Winter. I might not survive it."

Lucy cocked a dark eyebrow. "Don't bullshit a bullshitter, little brother. You're worried about something. What is it?"

"Not now." He checked his watch as he guided Lucy toward the door. "I'm glad you're on time for once. Gramma Beth will be pleased."

Lucy opened the front door, halted, and inhaled deeply as the essence of pot roast wafted outside. "Oh, my god. That's divine."

Noah chuckled as he ushered her inside, glad for the

distraction from his distress over leaving Winter behind. "Yeah, if anything can make me forget my troubles, it's Beth's pot roast and a few glasses of wine."

4

_____

Winter sat at a dark-brown booth decorated with foam clouds at A Latte Love Café. Outside, Monday morning commuters rushed past her panoramic window, many appearing to be running late to their jobs. She hadn't touched the mocha latte she'd ordered, the morning with Noah still fresh in her mind.

"How long?" She trailed behind him as he carried his overnight bag to their front door.

He stopped and faced her, the lines on his brow giving away his apprehension. "I don't know. A couple of days."

She bit her tongue, not wanting to say anything that would make her sound like a needy wife. This was his job, and it had once been hers. Winter knew the rigors of working in the Violent Crimes Division, but what had changed was she couldn't go with Noah anymore. They couldn't experience the same highs and lows of the job together.

Or the same risks.

"I'll be fine." She forced a sincere smile. "I have enough voice-mails to keep me busy for weeks."

"I won't be gone for weeks."

"I know. Just a few days."

"That's right, darlin'. Just a few days."

The moment Noah shut the door behind him, though, Winter had started wandering the house like a ghost, flitting from room to room, trying to distract herself so she wouldn't race after him. The reality of what she'd given up with the Bureau hit her, but dwelling on those feelings would get her nowhere.

I did the right thing.

She'd busied herself with preparing for her next case, calling Julia Eversmeyer to set up the meeting at the Austin coffee shop. The quick phone conversation hadn't given her much by way of distraction, but when the woman didn't question her fee, Winter became intrigued. Terrified people didn't flinch when discussing the money needed to help.

During their phone conversation, Julia revealed that her five-year-old daughter had drawn a disturbing picture the week before. Gabriella's artwork had prompted the terrified mother to call Winter. Julia's harried tone made Winter wonder how disturbing any kindergartener's drawing could be. It wasn't like any child that age could draw more than stick figures, flowers, and a large yellow globe representing the sun.

She didn't need to wonder long. She knew very well the horror adults could thrust onto a child.

Winter rechecked her phone and took a sip of her latte while pondering what her prospective client had revealed so far. The paperwork for Julia sat beside the cup, waiting for a signature. Winter tapped the side of her drink, growing restless. She didn't enjoy waiting. There was so much to be done.

A stunning blond woman with a pale but frazzled expression and dark circles rimming blue eyes bounded into the coffee shop. Winter guessed this was Julia Eversmeyer. Her pressed pantsuit, designer handbag, and pointy heels screamed sophistication, but her frantic gaze gave away her desperation.

Winter stood, and the woman spotted her. She hurried across the room, carrying a piece of paper—likely the artwork.

"Ms. Eversmeyer." Winter held out her hand. "I'm Winter Black of Black Investigations. I'm so glad—"

The woman slapped the paper into Winter's palm. "Take a look at that."

Winter curtailed her response to the woman's abrupt action and repositioned the white sheet of paper in front of her.

At first glance, the array of stick figures was about what Winter would expect from a child so young. Some figures wore brightly colored but crudely drawn dresses, while others wore nothing at all, as if the drawing were unfinished.

She pivoted the page, focusing on the black objects in the hands of a few figures. The outlines of large guns seemed clear, but the words *nakid notty girls* scrawled at the bottom created a knot in her gut.

Winter flashed back to her Bureau days and the times she'd been forced to deal with young victims. She fought back the anger creeping up her throat. If this case was going to proceed, she had to maintain control of her voice and keep the conversation calm.

She motioned to the bench across the table and waited until Julia slid into the booth before retrieving her paperwork. Business before discussing a case. Julia wasn't her client until she signed on the dotted line.

"Well?" Julia's shrill tone was several octaves too loud for the small space. "Do you think that's pornography?"

Winter pressed her lips tightly together as she removed a pen from her handbag. Handling frantic people had been part of her job at the Bureau. She hadn't expected that to spill over to her private business. Although, she wasn't sure what made her think being a private citizen would offer her that protection.

"First, you need to become my client before I can discuss my impression of your daughter's artwork." She extended the pen and pushed the papers across the table.

The woman grunted and scrawled her name on the last page of the contract without reading a single word. She reached into her fancy leather handbag and pulled out a white envelope.

"Your retainer." Julia slapped the envelope on the table and tapped her finger on the child's picture. "Now, tell me what you think."

Winter retrieved the envelope and peeked inside to ensure the correct amount appeared on the check before slipping it into her messenger bag. She rested her folded hands on the table next to her lukewarm latte, collecting her thoughts.

Is it too early to tell this woman I think she's a little nuts?

Winter focused on the crayon drawing and went into interview mode. "Before I share my assessment, I'm very interested to learn what alarms you about this picture."

Julia tapped a naked stick figure. "What doesn't? My Gabriella drew this while visiting her father last week. We divorced nearly two years ago, and it was his time with our kids, according to the terms of our shared custody agreement."

Winter removed a legal pad from her bag. "What's your ex's name?"

"Frederick Schumaker, but I call him Freddie." Julia twisted her hands together. "He's always had a porn addiction. Christ, it's what destroyed our marriage. But I thought he would keep it from the kids."

Winter lifted the picture, showing it to Julia. "What do you see here?"

Julia tapped on the child's drawing. "Obviously, call girls. And what are they holding?" She pointed at the black objects in the stick figures' hands. "Weapons? Needles? And are they underage? Maybe even trafficked?" Tears welled in her eyes. "What has he exposed my daughters to?"

The poor mother's mind had clearly been tormented by this sketch, running wild with theories. Winter felt so sorry for her. But that didn't mean any of her imaginings were true.

Winter reexamined the drawing, searching for red flags. She'd spent enough time with young witnesses who had drawn their recollections of abuse or harm to know that it didn't appear that Gabriella had suffered either. The use of bright colors, like pink, gold, green, and yellow, denoted happy feelings. Children who had endured gut-wrenching horror didn't reach for the bright colors in the crayon box. They stuck with black and red to tell their stories.

Usually. Winter also knew that every single child was different.

What if red and black hadn't been a color option at the time? She needed to consider every possibility before drawing a conclusion.

On the surface, the only thing noteworthy about Gabriella's rendering were the objects that appeared to be guns and the writing at the bottom.

Winter clicked her pen, looking for an angle to pursue. "What does your husband do?"

Julia released a long breath and rolled her shoulders, seeming relieved to have someone listen to her tale. "He owns Schumaker, Finlock, and Reid Trucking. It's a big corporation based out of Austin. Freddie lives the high life in a twelve-bedroom mansion surrounded by gates and tons of cameras. Even his office downtown is riddled with security. You must get a pat down and practically pee in a cup to get to his place on the fiftieth floor."

Winter made a notation about the office building and company name. "He sounds paranoid. Any idea why?"

Julia repositioned her bag on her lap. "Pissed off colleagues, burned business partners. Orgies on every floor. Take your pick. Our marriage ended when he found out about my affair, but he's the depraved one who's made a bunch of enemies."

Winter offered a gentle, nonjudgmental smile. "Tell me about the affair."

Julia's eyes filled with tears, and she grabbed a napkin from the dispenser to keep them at bay. "He was a friend who shared my interest in organizing charity events. I only hopped into bed with another man because Freddie was more interested in porn and prostitutes than having sex with me."

Oof.

That last part was more than Winter needed to know. The cheating might have been relevant to the case, but the minutiae of her client's sex life was knowledge she could live without. "He asked for a divorce after he learned of the other man?"

Julia removed another napkin and dabbed her upper lip. "Yes. News got out quickly about my betrayal. It tore through his business world, embarrassing the shit out of him, which I never minded. He deserved it. But…" She choked on a sob and pressed the napkin against her eyes.

"But…?" Winter prompted.

Composing herself, Julia met Winter's gaze. "What it did to my children kills me. My kids were brought up in a veritable fairy tale. The kind with lavish birthday parties, ponies, more toys than they could count, and an endless amount of their father's affection. The divorce traumatized them. Everything they once knew in their perfect, peaceful world has been taken away."

Winter's heart ached for the woman. The strain of the divorce and how it had affected her children must have been weighing on Julia every day, but it didn't mean her husband was a criminal. Just an asshole. Not that the woman could throw stones.

"I could do some simple surveillance of your ex-husband's activities. Monitoring him at home and work will let me know if he's up to anything nefarious. That might quickly narrow down the mystery of why your daughter created this picture."

The pink on Julia's cheeks turned chalky. "That won't be easy. Freddie will figure out you're following him. And if he realizes you're working for me, my situation will go from bad to intolerable."

Was Julia physically scared of her ex-husband?

"Why is that?"

Julia snorted. "Because the son of a bitch hates me. Ever since he caught me with his former golfing buddy, he's been out to get me."

"That's not unusual," Winter assured her. "Ex-spouses rarely harbor the best feelings for their former partners, especially when infidelity's involved. But you make it sound like that was an issue for both of you."

Julia crumpled the napkin in her hand, waving away Winter's comment. "You don't understand. Freddie's a vindictive bastard. If you cross him, he will not stop harassing you. If you steal from him, he will hound you, and if you cheat on him, he will not let up until you're buried under a mound of bullshit." She tossed the balled-up napkins on the table.

Winter took a second to let the tension in the air settle.

Wow. Why the hell did you marry this guy? Or give him a reason to turn against you?

That didn't matter and was water under the bridge. Only one thing mattered. Julia was clearly terrified of her ex. Not physically. If Winter was reading her right, the mother worried that, no matter the number of drawings her daughter produced, it wouldn't matter. Schumaker's wealth and connections would crush her...and anyone intent on helping her.

Julia reached for Winter's hand. "You don't understand. I can't afford to end up back in court with Freddie fighting over alimony, custody, or whatever else his attorney can think of. Freddie has threatened to take the children from me completely...and he can do it. Until I have real evidence, that drawing, for example, I can't do a thing. The police would laugh me out of the station, and Freddie would sic his attorneys on me. That's why you must be careful."

Winter shivered as the mother's fear transferred to her. Julia was terrified of losing her children. Winter pulled her hand away, intent on focusing on the details instead of the emotion of the case. "When was the last time you were in court for custody?"

"Six months ago." Julia's cheeks pinkened. "My oldest two are teenagers, seventeen and sixteen, and now that they're mobile, they want to have lots of pool parties and things like that. Freddie's mansion gives them more space than my little house does." She lowered her head. "He can give them the lavish things I can't. I barely see them these days. Teenagers."

Money. Why did so much in the world come down to this?

"I promise I'll be as discreet as I can while doing whatever's necessary to obtain the information I need." Winter traced a stick figure, debating how to proceed. "What do you need me to collect, Ms. Eversmeyer?"

Julia jutted out her chin, and the harrowed woman she'd

presented when first entering the coffee house vanished. Her face became like a stone.

"I want rock-solid proof that Freddie's involved in deviant activity to have some leverage. He has the money and high-priced attorneys to shut me down in court, but I can turn the tables if I have leverage. After the affair, all I was left with was my word, which isn't worth much to anyone. But this isn't about me. It's about my children." She dropped her face in her hands.

Winter reached for another napkin and handed it to her. "I can't imagine how difficult it must have been for you."

Julia dabbed her eyes. "I don't matter, but I'll never forgive myself for disappointing my kids. And I'll die before their sick father poisons their lives."

Flashes of Timothy Stewart lying in a pool of brain matter and blood came back in a heated rush. Winter tried to push down the ugly images, but they didn't retreat this time.

She tented her hands, reining in her guilt. "Don't be so hard on yourself. You're human and make mistakes. Even the huge, ugly ones are unavoidable."

Julia nodded and dropped the napkin on the table. "Mistakes are like wolves. You have to watch your back after making them, or they'll sneak up and tear you apart one day."

Winter offered a comforting smile. "I'll get to the bottom of Gabriella's drawing as quickly as I can to alleviate your anxiety over this issue, and so you can feel safe."

Opening her purse, Julia removed a small compact. She checked her face, wiping away the remnants of mascara beneath her right eye. "Safe is something none of us will ever be again."

We'll see about that.

Winter picked up her pen. "Now, tell me about your children."

While Julia went on about the two daughters and one son

she valued more than life, Winter pondered the mother's earlier words.

"Mistakes are like wolves. You have to watch your back after making them, or they'll sneak up and tear you apart one day."

Lord knew that Winter had made plenty of mistakes in her life. The sound of Andrea and Greg Stewart's necks breaking resounded in her memory, raising the hairs on her arms.

Would she ever find forgiveness for all her ugly mistakes, even the ones she had no choice but to make? Or would the wolves also be hiding in the dark, waiting for her to turn her back so they could pounce?

5

The damp air kissed my face as I shoved open the heavy metal door of the old basement storm shelter. Updated to function as a panic room, with soundproofed walls and electronic equipment to monitor the entrance, the space worked perfectly for my plans. As I descended the cement steps into the darkness, my fingers twitched with excitement.

Knowing each inch of the space, I reached for the switch on the wall, and a flood of warm, yellow light bloomed to life. The room, no bigger than a jail cell, was icy cold. A shiver traveled through me as I spied my prize.

The beautiful Bridget Augusta—her hands cuffed behind her, and her ankles bound with duct tape—remained curled in the corner, her hair fanned out around her. The hatred in her eyes was good. I liked hatred. It was motivation.

"Why am I here?" Bridget demanded in a croaky voice. "Help me. Someone help me! Please help me!"

The screeching went on for nearly a full minute before her voice gave out. I didn't bother to shut her up. It was better to let her come to realize that nothing she did mattered.

When all was quiet, I moved toward her, relishing the panic contorting her features. The smeared mascara I could have done without. I wanted her less comical and more petrified.

But she made me feel powerful, nonetheless.

"Scream all you want." I stopped at her feet, checking the restraints. "I told you no one will hear you."

Bridget wiggled on the floor, fighting her bindings, but with less enthusiasm than when she'd first arrived. "How long have I been in here?"

I liked the way she struggled. "Twelve hours, give or take."

The shock registering on Bridget's face was amusing. *Time flies when you're bound and held hostage in a black hole.*

"People will be looking for me." Bridget put a lilt of firmness in her croaky voice.

Why do they attempt to put on a brave face?

Not bothering to hide my amusement, I inspected the growing bruises on her wrists, signs of her continued effort to get free. "Who is going to miss you? That alcoholic, trailer-trash mother of yours? She doesn't even know you're alive."

The mention of her mother increased Bridget's squirming. "Who are you? Why are you doing this to me?"

"Why? Why? Why?" I clucked my tongue. "Everyone asks why, but what do we ever do about it?"

I was new to the trafficking game, but she didn't need to know that.

"Please let me go."

I moved toward the wall, tracing my finger along the rough surface of the cinder blocks. "I was like you once. Trapped in Hell and waiting for someone to save me. No one ever did. That's how I learned about the real world. It's a place where people hurt each other. Some even learn to enjoy it."

Like me.

"I never hurt you." The tears began, carefully orchestrated with intermittent sniffles. "I tried to help you."

It was an attempt to lower my defenses, but I was immune. I'd heard all about the tricks, all the games a captive used to convince her tormentor that she was worth a pittance of emotion. The simple truth was this…no one possessed an ounce of empathy. The only genuine feeling any of us had was hate.

Walking the perimeter of the small room, I listened to the echo of my footsteps. The rhythm soothed and empowered me. "You fell into my trap is what you did. Nothing else. You're just a tool. Something I need to get what I want."

Bridget shuddered as another sob racked her body. "But why?"

Exhilarated by how her mahogany hair glistened in the low light, I moved closer and stroked her long mane, enjoying the silkiness. I wrapped a few soft locks around my fingers, keeping a firm grip. "You're not like me. You aren't in control. You see," I dragged her hair across the floor, "you don't have what it takes. Control over your emotions, over yourself, is key to survival in this world. No one can ever hurt or torment you again because you simply do not care."

Bridget winced as the pull on her hair grew more painful.

I enjoyed watching her suffer. It made me feel better about everything I'd endured. All the pain I'd been through. And they would pay for their crimes. Everyone would pay.

"Please don't."

I yanked harder. "I've conquered my pathetic human emotions."

Bridget screamed, jerking her head toward my hand to lessen the pain. Her agony was my fuel. It made me feel invincible. In control. No one would get the better of me again.

When I let go, my victim relaxed on the floor, but her trembling increased. That was good. She now understood nothing she did mattered.

"That's the difference between us. I'm in full command of my emotions. I don't cater to love or jealousy or despair. All I feel is loathing. It's like white fire pulsing through me, giving me the will to do what must be done." I stood, looking down at the worthless woman. "You, unfortunately, have a long way to go."

Bridget's sniffling filled the room, turning my stomach. *Why did they have to be so weak?*

"I don't understand," she got out between whimpers.

I moved to the door, turned, and folded my arms, staring at her soon-to-be broken shell. "Of course you don't. How could you? You haven't reached my level of emotional release. To be free of all the burdens life gives us is like nirvana." I chuckled. "And I'm not talking about the band."

Bridget glowered at me.

That was good. One last act of defiance was a sure sign the end of resistance was near.

"You're sick!"

I charged the few steps to her side. "No, you little idiot. I'm free. It doesn't matter why you were taken or what will happen to you. Can't you see that? You'll serve a greater purpose than anything you could accomplish alone."

Bridget turned her face to the floor as more tears stained her cheeks with the last traces of her mascara. "Stop."

"You're a speck of dust on the heap of humanity. No one cares about you or that your father abused you and then shot his brains out. No one cares that you ran away at seventeen, danced in shitty strip clubs until you found your current gig of, um, *catering* to rich men."

"Please." The word was barely recognizable.

Kneeling, I put my face closer to hers. "All that means is

that you're disposable. You're nothing but a two-bit hooker who won't even end up as a footnote in the obituaries. You can disappear, and the world will never notice."

Already bored with my new toy, I checked my watch. It was almost noon.

Damn, I have to go.

I stood, wiping the dust from my pants. No need to let anyone know where I'd been. In a few minutes, I had to meet up with Ken, my partner in crime. Even though having someone to assist in my extracurricular activities turned my stomach, it was essential to my plans.

Getting rid of the evidence, dumping Bridget's car, and disposing of her phone and purse required access to resources I didn't have. At least Ken, the sniveling idiot, remained useful—though my trust didn't extend very far.

I could never trust anyone with my secrets.

6

Winter sat at her desk, her second mug of coffee in her hand since meeting Julia Eversmeyer earlier that morning. Her stomach protested after she gulped back another caffeine rush, but lunch would have to wait. She had work to do.

The first step in any investigation was to gather information. Lots of information. Winter ran a background check on Julia based on everything she'd learned at their meeting.

Julia was an open book on social media. As a former charitable event organizer, there were hundreds of images to investigate. Pictures of her in stunning clothes, side by side with Austin's most glittering socialites, filled news sites as well as multiple social media pages.

Winter could see why Schumaker had married the beautiful blond. She glided through parties with an effortless grace without a hair out of place or a smudge of her lipstick. In all the pictures Winter scoured, there was never one of Julia frowning or unhappy.

However, the photos taken within the last year were different. Following her scandalous affair and subsequent divorce, the glamour girl had disappeared. Her wrinkles appeared more prominent, and her natural smile vanished. She'd become a social pariah, with her charitable work disappearing from the society pages.

And, boy, Winter couldn't blame her.

A damn sex tape?

Public court documents mentioned Schumaker finding a sex video of his wife during her extramarital dalliance. Julia failed to mention the video to Winter, which she would bring up to her client. Full disclosure was essential for any investigator. It kept her from walking into a shitstorm later, as her first case had so aptly demonstrated.

Winter could only guess Julia's humiliation after the tape's release.

No wonder she's so protective of her children.

Thankfully, the video never made it online, but rumors of its existence had caused "undue emotional distress" for Mr. Schumaker. Winter suspected that, because of his extreme wealth, it was more likely that Schumaker had paid to keep the tape under wraps, or threatened anyone who had the means to release it.

And use it as leverage against his wife.

His lawyer had claimed insupportability under the state's no-fault laws. Schumaker could have just filed for divorce without grounds and left the tape a secret. But no. It seemed Julia wasn't lying when she denounced her husband as a *vindictive bastard*. Whether his actions were based on revenge or hurt, Schumaker had severely tarnished his wife's stellar reputation while his conduct, if her stories were true, didn't make it into the papers. No local companies wanted to work with Julia or be associated with the disgrace and social scandal of such an elite couple's demise.

Frederick "Freddie" Schumaker was a lot harder to figure out.

The senior partner at Schumaker, Finlock, and Reid Trucking Corp., Schumaker kept a low profile and avoided social media and the camera at most social events. He'd seemed to let his wife get all the glory while he worked behind the scenes.

Without her FBI credentials, accessing Schumaker's bank accounts was impossible. But getting an idea of his net worth was relatively easy by running a check of Texas-based corporations filed in his name. Property assets came after another search of titles and liens within the surrounding counties of Hays and Williamson.

After finding the one mansion outside Austin, Winter stumbled on vacation homes in Miami, Florida, and the Hamptons. He had eleven cars, three motorcycles, and two boats registered in Texas. Several full-time staff popped up in searches, and Winter felt safe assuming they ran his estates.

The man was as powerful as Julia described, but Winter still didn't have a sense of him. Most people left a footprint on the internet through social media or news sites. The information on Schumaker's character, beyond being rich, remained slim.

Julia's children appeared more prominent than their father on database sites. A portrait taken before the divorce showed Grace, Gilbert, and Gabriella Schumaker smiling— adorable knockoffs of their blond parents. The girls favored their tall, attractive mother, inheriting her delicate features, while the boy was the spitting image of his serious, stern-looking father.

Winter recalled Julia's mention of the children's trauma following the divorce. She could only imagine how their lives changed after their father took their dreamlike existence away—at least, when they stayed with Mom, it was gone. Kids always paid the price for adults' messy decisions.

The empty eyes and shaggy brown hair of Timothy

Stewart crept into her thoughts again. Winter wondered if the young man would ever know peace. Had his young mind become so warped by her brother's indoctrination that he'd never recover from his past?

As Timothy's face faded from her mind, another problem occupied Winter's thoughts. Julia didn't want Schumaker to find out that she'd hired an investigator. It would limit what Winter could do, but that didn't mean she couldn't snoop around the Schumaker mansion. She just needed a cover to get her inside the home's massive gates.

That shouldn't be too hard.

She hoped.

7

The bright sun perched high in the sky as Noah veered the Bureau car into the parking lot of Helton Gas. He glanced at his partner in the passenger seat before turning off the engine. Special Agent Eve Taggart scrolled through her phone, never looking up at him.

"You've been quiet the entire drive. What's up?"

Eve's blue eyes were flecked with sadness. "I'm missin' my youngest's piano recital today." She slapped her phone on her lap. "You know how pissed that child's gonna be with me? She's been practicin' for months."

The pain his partner felt, Noah understood. The timing of their case wasn't the best for him either. Winter needed him, and he needed her. Spending time apart wasn't good for a marriage or a child.

"I get it." He kept his voice gentle. "The job sucks, most of the time. At least you don't have to worry about Pokey missing you. You and that damned bamboo plant are inseparable."

Eve smirked and glanced through the windshield at the

rundown gas station. "Not exactly the hot spot of Helton, Texas."

He took in the surrounding town. The storefronts nearby had a layer of dust across their display windows, the vehicles parked along the street were mostly pickup trucks that had seen better days, and the only residents out and about appeared to move slower than molasses in winter.

Across the street, the local diner named Ed's appeared to be the hub, with the most vehicles in its parking lot.

"Yeah, Helton sure is a lively place."

Noah could just picture the flea-trap motel booked for their stay. He just hoped it had hot water and an ice machine.

Eve pulled out her tablet and reviewed the information SSA Falkner had forwarded. "We're looking for a gas attendant named Tuck Hatcher. He claimed he saw *'some weird things that jus' din't seem quite right.'*"

He raised his eyebrows at Eve's attempt to thicken her Texas accent. "You just made that up."

She showed him her tablet. "It's right here. He put in the tip last Saturday night. It passed from the locals to us."

He reached for the door handle. "Which means the locals might be friendly for a change."

Eve chuckled. "Or lookin' to dump crazy Tuck Hatcher in our laps. You gotta learn to read the lay of the land, Dalton. This is Texas, remember? The local police are never cooperative, just out to save themselves some paperwork."

Noah snorted. "Aren't we all?"

The small town, four hours northwest of Austin, looked even worse once he climbed from his car. The dust covering everything from garbage cans to the sidewalks seemed like something out of a horror movie, but it was the smell that baffled him. It was a combination of something acidic with the stench of dead flesh. No matter where Noah turned, he couldn't escape it.

"Jesus, what is that?"

Eve pinched her nose. "Reminds me of my stint at the body farm in Knoxville. You never forget that smell."

A heavily twanged voice asked, "Can I he'p ya folks?"

Noah turned to face the front of the gas station and encountered an older man with saggy jeans and a thick mop of gray hair. He was hunched over but appraising them with his sharp blue eyes.

"Ah," Noah tried to ignore the god-awful smell, "yes, we're looking for a Mr. Tuck Hatcher."

The man removed a greasy rag from his back pocket and wiped his dirty hands. "What ya need 'im for?"

Eve tucked her tablet under her arm. "I'm Special Agent Taggart, and this is Special Agent Dalton. We're from the FBI Violent Crimes Division. The local police notified us about Mr. Hatcher's tip last Saturday."

The man returned his rag to the back pocket of his jeans. "That weren't no tip. It was a fact. Saw that funny stuff with my own eyes."

Eve nodded. "So you're Mr. Hatcher."

Tuck spat out a wad of brown goo on the ground. "You can call me Tuck. Everyone does."

Noah closed his eyes, overwhelmed by the horrible stench and Tuck's disgusting tobacco chewing habit. "What's that smell?"

Tuck inhaled deeply, clearly acclimated to the stench. "Pig farm. Bo Atwell's place. It's about a quarter mile from here." He turned back to Noah. "You only pick it up on this side of town."

Noah cringed. "Any chance this pig farm is close to the Lazy S Motel?"

Tuck spat out another wad of chew. "Nah. 'At's at the other end of town."

Noah didn't know if he should be thankful or terrified. What awaited them on the other side of town?

"Mr. Hatcher. We'd like to go over what you saw last Saturday night." Eve moved closer to Tuck, avoiding the spit piles he'd left on the ground.

"Come on." He waved a hand. "I'll show ya."

Tuck took off around the side of the station into an alleyway filled with everything from old, rusted car parts to boxes and metal gas cans.

Noah went first, wanting to protect his partner in case anything or anyone jumped them. The crunch of broken glass momentarily distracted him from the peeling red paint and cracked boards along the station's wall. The farther they walked toward the rear of the building, the more overpowering Bo's wretched pig farm stench became.

Tuck stopped at a gravel lot along the rear. A few cars, some with their hoods up, sat there. A chain-link fence surrounded the lot, with a few dead brown bushes dotting the outline of the property.

Tuck pointed at the fence. "They was there. Two vans parked with their backs facin' each other. I was comin' out the garage 'cause I thought I heard voices. When I stood in the doorway that leads to the lot, I saw 'em. Women. They was bein' led from one van to the other. At least five or six of 'em, walking single file-like. It was a handoff. You know, like they do when traffickin' people. There was two other figures dressed in black. Couldn't see 'em much, but I'm pretty sure they was armed."

Noah checked the distance to the fence. Adding the length and the fact that this occurred at night, he remained skeptical Tuck saw anything.

"How do you know they were armed?"

"The women." Tuck shook his head. "They weren't puttin' up a fight. Women fight back when you make 'em do somethin' they don't wanna do. I should know. Had three wives, fought like she-devils when I challenged 'em. Only way to make a woman not fight back is to stick a gun in 'er face."

Eve typed some notes. "How can you be sure they were women? It was dark and could have been hard to see much."

Tuck's craggy, wet laugh gave the impression he'd spent years smoking too many cigarettes. "I know a woman when I see one. Don't need no spotlight to make out their..." He scratched his head. "Not sure if they was old or young. Didn't get that good a look, but they was women. I'll swear to that in court."

And a defense attorney will chew you up and spit you out.

Noah examined the backside of the building, running his gaze along the rear garage doors. "You got any cameras back here?"

Tuck spat out another dark glob of chew. "Nah. Just trash cans an' cigarette butts."

Eve raised an eyebrow at Noah. "Might be why they chose the place. No surveillance."

Noah rested his hands on his belt, intrigued. Tuck seemed genuine, but he wasn't sure. Sincerity made him doubt people more. Liars were easier to spot.

"What did you do after seeing this exchange?"

Tuck stared at him, his mouth slightly ajar. "I called my boss. I asked Donald what we should do. It's his place, after all. I can't go makin' no reports about a crime without him knowin'."

Eve lifted the right side of her mouth in a smug grin. "Seems only fair."

Noah ignored her comment and concentrated on his line of questioning. "What did your boss tell you to do? Report it?"

"Heeeell no," Tuck hollered in a true east Texan twang. "The man didn't want no police crawlin' all over the garage.

He told me to forget about it. Said people mind their own business in these here parts." Tuck shook his head, appearing glum. "But that's not the kind of people I know. And he never saw what I did. Couldn't stop thinkin' about those poor women all night. So the next mornin', I called the police."

Eve lowered her tablet and met Tuck's gaze. "Thank you for doing that. There's a lot of women and young girls who go missing in this state every year. Our only hope of finding any of them is people like you."

The blush on Tuck's cheeks surprised Noah. He hadn't thought Tuck's hardened old soul capable of showing emotion. That was one thing that never ceased to amaze him about people. They never turned out to be quite what he imagined.

"The sergeant at the police station said the same thing," Tuck admitted, his reddish color fading. "He told me I was a hero. I ain't no hero. I just hope you guys can help find them women."

Noah took a step closer to the man. "That's why we're here. We take reports like yours very seriously." He glanced at the ground and moved some of the gravel around with the toe of his loafer. "I don't understand why your boss was so reluctant to report anything. Whether you saw men with guns was immaterial. Women were in trouble. That's pretty clear."

Tuck rubbed the back of his neck, appearing antsy. "You'd have to ask Donald yourself about that." He snickered. "I sure know one thing. He'll shit a brick when he sees you two comin'."

Tuck's wheezy laugh followed him into the garage as he left Noah and Eve outside in the gravel lot.

Eager to keep from being overheard by anyone inside the building, Noah scooted closer to his partner.

"You thinking what I am?"

Eve hugged her tablet to her chest, hiding her emotions behind a mask of stone. "That the owner was involved. Sure looks suspicious."

Noah faced the fence, getting another look at the scene. "He provides a location for an exchange, keeps his mouth shut, and collects a few bucks. Tidy operation."

Eve squinted at the field of high, strawy grass behind the fence. "He just never counted on his employee witnessing the whole thing. We need to meet with Donald Long. Pick his brain and run a background check."

Noah studied the back of the rundown gas station, understanding why the owner would take a bribe for being quiet. The business wasn't exactly booming. And from what he'd seen of Helton so far, he wondered if there weren't more men like Donald Long in town.

"Find out how to contact him. Sweet-talk Tuck." He waggled his eyebrows at Eve. "He likes you."

Her deadpan expression told Noah about his partner's thoughts on that subject. "All right, but you owe me. The next time we've got to deal with hookers high on meth or strippers with body lice, they're all yours."

Noah wrinkled his nose. "I'll be sure to stop by the drugstore on my way back to Austin."

Eve whipped her long blond ponytail behind her. "You're gonna be the death of me."

She headed toward the open bay doors of the garage, leaving Noah alone in the lot.

He'd feared getting used to a new partner when arriving at the Austin FBI, but things had worked out. The trust needed to cement a partnership was there, even if they were still working out some of the kinks in their relationship.

Pokey still had doubts about her, though, but that bamboo plant was cagey on a good day.

Noah took advantage of the break to retrieve his phone

from his jacket pocket. The rank smell from the pig farm wasn't as bad as before, but it was still turning his stomach. Wondering what Winter would make of the noxious situation, he sent her a quick text.

Arrived at the location. Will call when I settle into our motel. Hope you're missing me as much as I'm missing you.

He reread the text twice before sending it. He reveled in his feelings for her. He was like a lovesick schoolboy. His chest already ached at the thought of not having his wife in his arms tonight. Noah couldn't picture a life without her laugh, smile, or wicked sense of humor. She'd become a part of him.

But you can't keep her safe when you're so far away.

Noah clenched his fists, cross with the self-recriminations. Winter had been a crack agent. She could take care of herself.

He hoped.

8

The bright afternoon light filtering through Winter's office windows let her know the day had gotten away from her. The hours spent at her desk, running checks on Frederick Schumaker and Julia Eversmeyer, had given her new insights into the case. It also offered her a way to sneak into Schumaker's mansion without setting off alarms.

Winter stumbled on a solar power company website that Julia had worked a fundraiser for during their marriage. Pictures of the event were among the few on the internet that showed the couple together. Schumaker was even quoted by the local papers about how solar energy was "dear to his heart."

She printed off a few pages from the website, including a questionnaire for potential customers. Since many elite families in Austin had endorsed the solar company, someone as progressive as Freddie Schumaker might take the bait. Either way, it was time for Winter to try on her new role as a P.I., and that meant building her cover as fully as possible. Without the advantage her federal badge once offered, it was up to ingenuity to get her foot in the door.

She slapped the printed pages onto a clipboard, then headed for the bedroom, where she changed into a crisp blue business suit.

To look professional, she kept her makeup light, winding her black hair into a bun atop her head. The finishing touch was a pair of faux glasses she'd found packed away with some old Halloween costumes. When Noah had opened the box, hoping to unearth their coffee grinder, they'd both groaned.

Looks like it was actually a good find.

Winter stood in front of the mirror, admiring her outfit with a critical eye. It wasn't something she'd wear to a day at the Bureau, but if it gave her some short-lived credibility as a solicitor for the Texas-based solar power company, it would do.

It wasn't her best plan, but Winter needed access to Schumaker's home and a quick chat with a few employees to establish what kind of man Frederick Schumaker was. From there, she could better determine how to handle the rest of the investigation.

Winter didn't doubt her client completely, but Julia's tainted opinion of her ex-husband, even with the disturbing drawing from Gabriella, wasn't enough to make him guilty of anything. For that, Winter needed proof.

She climbed behind the wheel of her Honda Pilot and, after placing her gun in the glove compartment, typed the address Julia had given her on the GPS. The half-hour drive to the Schumaker mansion would give her time to plan her approach. She liked to prepare for all contingencies. That was what they'd taught her at Quantico, and federal badge or not, old habits died hard.

She smiled as she maneuvered down the quiet street out of her subdivision. She and Noah lived among doctors, pharmacists, lawyers, and quite a few teachers and professors. As far as Winter knew, she was the only private investigator.

And what if I'd stayed with the Bureau?

The notion came and went now and then, especially when she had too much time on her hands, and those dark memories would return. But Winter knew she'd made the right decision for herself and her husband. A fresh start in Texas was what they both needed. Staying in Virginia would never have allowed them to move on.

And the badge she'd once been so proud of had turned into a noose around her neck.

Now I can do what I want.

The wide streets surrounded by manicured parks and subdivisions packed with modest homes soon changed to a landscape of lavishly decorated gardens set before a myriad of multimillion-dollar homes that were jaw dropping beautiful.

White Greek Revival homes with elegant, fluted columns and lazy balconies stood next to castle-inspired fortresses and green, ivy-covered residences styled like French Chateaus. In the driveways, high-end cars gleamed under the late afternoon sun.

Winter felt small as she drove past black iron gates with swirls and elaborate initials woven into the metal. The wealthy parents of her first client, Mahoney Fitzgerald, hadn't been intimidating. But somehow, the neighborhood around Frederick Schumaker's mansion left her on edge.

Maybe that's because you're not a welcome guest but an interloper gathering information. Just act like you belong.

She slowed the SUV as the most audacious pair of arched gates on the street appeared. A small white guardhouse sat beside them with two bullet cameras pointing at the entrance. A road led past the gates, but Freddie Schumaker's mansion remained hidden from view.

The initials *F* and *S* woven into the black metal piqued Winter's interest. It seemed Schumaker wanted to stay sequestered and protected from the rest of the world. But if he feared recrimination or violence, why not extend the same security to his children? The lack of security offered to Julia when she had custody of the children indicated Schumaker preferred to keep only his affairs protected and private. Did that mean he had something to hide?

Winter put on a glowing smile as she drove up to the gate and rolled down her window. The muscle-bound guard stepping out from his small box tipped his head as he inspected the Pilot. The Glock 19 strapped to his hip was popular with various military agencies and law enforcement, making her wonder what he did before taking on this gig.

The guard lowered his reflective sunglasses. "Can I help you?"

She gave him her best smile, hoping to get the guard to listen to her pitch. "Hi, my name is Erica Mills, and I'm with Austin Solar. I met Mr. Schumaker at a fundraiser for our company a while back, and he told me how interested he was in getting solar panels for his home, so I wanted to stop by and see—"

"Do you have an appointment with Mr. Schumaker?"

She bit her lower lip, remembering how much Noah liked it. "Ah, no, but I—"

"I can't let you in without an appointment." The guard took a step back. "Why don't you run along." His tone made his words more statement than suggestion.

Winter pressed her lips together, wishing she still had a badge to flash in the cocky asshole's face. "Look, I know I don't have an appointment, and I know you're just doing your job, but I'm trying to hit my quota, or I'll lose my monthly bonus, and…" She put a hint of pleading desperation in her voice. "I don't need to speak to Mr. Schumaker. Anyone inside the house willing to listen to my pitch is fine. All I need is a name and a time I met with anybody for a lead to a sale, and I get to keep working for this company. Can you give a girl a break? Ten minutes. That's all. You can come and arrest me if I'm not back in time."

She held her breath, hoping the sob story might appeal to him.

He rested his hand on the door of her SUV. "I don't arrest people."

Winter looked over his taut physique, checking out how his blue uniform hugged his broad chest and shoulders. "Now, that's a shame. 'Cause I bet you're great with a pair of handcuffs." She added a sly smile, hoping the cheesy line got her point across.

The times men had said the same thing to her at Quantico, they ended up with a fat lip. But Winter guessed a man getting hit with the same line would fall for it, hook, line, and sinker.

Shaking his head, the guard backed away from the SUV. "You got fifteen minutes, and then I'll come in after you."

She widened her smile. "Is that a promise?"

He shook his head and slapped a button on the side of the guard station. "Get out of here before I do get my handcuffs."

A heaviness lifted from Winter's chest when the buzzer blared and the massive gates swung open. She was in. She maneuvered down a narrow, winding road lined with crepe myrtle trees and thick, evergreen yaupon holly shrubs.

Above the trees, the façade of Freddie Schumaker's home took shape. A three-story French provincial structure made of wood and dark red brick, it had long, arched windows symmetrically placed, with dormer windows along the slate-covered roof and copper accents glinting in the afternoon sun.

A massive copper lantern hung above a central rounded portico that protected two carved wooden doors with thick copper handles. The gardens, filled with tropical plants from bird-of-paradise to bromeliad, were some of the most vibrant she'd ever seen.

Winter grabbed her clipboard and left her SUV in the circular driveway. She climbed a set of stone steps with recessed lights set into the masonry, staring in amazement at the tall windows catching the sunlight.

She stopped at the massive doors, noting the geometrical patterns carved into the wood. She was about to press the doorbell when a sharp pain erupted in her temple.

Not now!

The pain only lasted a second or two before disappearing without progressing into one of her notorious headaches. She touched her upper lip. No nosebleed either.

Small blessings.

Headaches were the aftereffect of emergency brain surgery for a blow to the head when she was thirteen, an unwanted gift from the notorious serial killer Douglas Kilroy. Along with an unwanted psychic ability, often in the form of a bright red light around objects that should be of interest, she also had visions—images that led her to information that helped solve a case.

What was her "gift" trying to tell her now?

As she examined the question, one of the oversized doors opened, and a voluptuous woman wearing a bright pink sweater and black leggings appeared, tucking a lock of long blond hair back into her ponytail. "What do you want?"

Winter was initially startled by the woman's abrupt tone before realizing she was leaning against the doorbell. She immediately straightened. "So sorry. Felt a little faint there for a moment. Didn't realize I was creating such a racket."

The woman softened the tiniest bit. "How can I help you?"

Winter tapped her clipboard, keeping her sickly-sweet

smile in place. "Hi, I'm Erica Mills, and I work for Austin Solar. Mr. Schumaker and I met at a fundraiser for—"

"He's not here." The woman took a step backward, clearly ready to shut the door. "I'm the nanny. The butler usually answers the door, but I have no idea where he is."

Not ready to give up, Winter smiled even brighter, adding a note of desperation to her expression. "What's your name?"

The woman took a moment to inspect Winter from top to toe, and a deep crease popped on her brow. "Ah, Belinda Merril. Why?"

Winter removed any hint of emotion from her voice. In her experience, anyone stressed or in a hurry would calm down when approached with an even tone. "Well, Ms. Merril, I would love an opportunity to talk to you about what our company offers. Adding solar to this home could save hundreds a month on the electric bill."

Belinda rested her shoulder against the door. "I wish I could help you, but I don't have the authority to decide what power company Mr. Schumaker chooses. I just take care of his kids."

Winter took a step closer, emboldened. "Is there anyone else here who could make such a decision? An assistant or manager of the estate?"

Belinda pressed her overfilled lips together. Winter thought she would've frowned if her Botox had allowed it. "No. There's no one. Why don't you give me some brochures and a card, and I can leave them for Mr. Schumaker? He'll eventually get it. Maybe."

The lack of progress called for a change in tactics. Winter ran her fingertips over the exquisitely carved door. "I bet with a house like this, he's a busy man."

Belinda inched back from the doors, allowing Winter a peek inside the grand entryway. She sighed as she glanced back at the winding, walnut staircase. "Beautiful, isn't it?"

Winter followed her gaze and paused when she spotted the newel carved in the shape of a Greek goddess. Her hourglass figure, discreetly covered with delicate folds of linen, was an exceptional work of art. Cathedral ceilings with decorative plaster ornamentations of roses on long vines led to a central medallion of a stylized rose bouquet.

Life-sized paintings of heavily corseted women dressed in Regency attire stared back from walls lined with white silk and gold-gilded wallpaper.

The home reminded Winter of a museum. The trucking business was more lucrative than she thought.

"It's stunning," she whispered, wanting to appeal to Belinda's sense of pride.

Belinda smiled, taking the bait, and allowed Winter a better peek at the grand foyer.

"Yes, I'm lucky to work here." Her boastful smile slipped. "Even though Mr. Schumaker is a *very* busy man, as is his household. But he's also one of the kindest people I know."

Praise from any employee was expected, even if it wasn't true. God only knew that no one Winter worked with at the Bureau would be quick to tout the benefits of the long hours, insufferable caseload, and sometimes negligible pay.

A child's cough carried from upstairs and drifted along the entryway. Winter froze at the unexpected disturbance, anxious about their audience.

Belinda glanced up the stairs and back at Winter. "I really must go now. The little one has a fever, and the two others will be home from school soon."

Winter didn't want to push her luck by meeting the kids. Children had endless questions and would be sure to mention her visit to Schumaker. And she didn't want to explain herself if she ever met them with Julia. That could compromise her investigation.

"Thank you for your time. I hope the little one is better soon."

Still clutching her clipboard, Winter returned to her SUV while checking for any gardeners or groundskeepers she could interview. Despite the enormous grounds, she spotted no one.

Dammit.

The drive back to the entrance gate deflated her sense of accomplishment. There were no other workers in sight, leaving her with only the nanny's insights into Julia's ex-husband.

Even the bulky guard ignored her when she drove through the black gates, not even lifting his hand when she gave him a cheerful wave.

It would seem Winter's first foray into Frederick Schu-maker's world had been a bust.

9

The tinkle of silverware inside the dimly lit Roses Are Red restaurant played in the background as Harper Glynn caressed the Tiffany diamond necklace she'd just been given. Rich men were her go-to because their little tokens of affection helped pay the bills. The gift from her newest client was why she'd taken on this last-minute Monday night gig.

It'd been worth her change of plans.

The handsome man across the table was better than her average John. With thick blond hair—not a touch of gray—and cunning brown eyes, he kept her intrigued. His muscular arms and broad shoulders weren't half bad either. Still, it was his money she liked best.

She reached for his hand, bypassing her glittering white dinner plate and crystal flute filled with champagne. "It's beautiful. You shouldn't have."

He leaned back in his chair, away from her touch. This one wasn't much of an affection fiend like her other clients. She didn't take it personally.

His gaze lingered on the low cut of her dress. "Just something to entice you. There's more where this came from." His deep smoky voice was far from seductive. To him, this was clearly nothing more than a transaction.

Harper wanted to laugh. It was nothing but a transaction to her too.

She just couldn't show it.

If his bank account held up, she'd keep coming back, but he needed to believe it was because she was enamored with him. In truth, she was fixated on what he could give her.

Fancy dinners in exclusive restaurants—the type that probably cost more than most people's rent—were addictive. The presents. The wooing. This was the life she dreamed of when she left her parents behind in Dallas and set out on her own.

"Well, I love it." She beamed, keeping up the act. He didn't need to know the necklace would end up at a jeweler getting appraised for resale in the morning.

She took a small sip of her champagne, quelling her desire to gulp back the glass. Though she desired the buzz alcohol gave her, she didn't want to look juvenile. She'd been grateful the waitstaff hadn't wanted to check her ID. At twenty, she had a very good fake one, so she wasn't worried about that. She just didn't want her date to be reminded of her youth...one way or the other.

Some wanted her to be much younger.

Taking another fortifying sip, she decided intoxication would help brace her nerves for when her client would later expect payment in full for the necklace. Once home, she could down more wine to erase the constant sickness that haunted her after such a night.

Stop it. Be in the here and now.

Her mental chiding reminded her to focus. Before she could allow the man to whisk her into his bed, Harper needed to size up his appetite. She was good at feeling out the ones who liked it rough or the men who just wanted someone to listen.

This date wasn't like any of those.

Something else glistened in his eyes, but she couldn't figure out exactly what that mysterious element was. It made her wary.

An avalanche of anxiety hit Harper like a brick. It wasn't unusual to feel this way, especially with new clients. She chalked up the sensation to a lack of alcohol.

She took another long drink.

"If you'll excuse me for a moment." She picked up her silver clutch and pushed back her chair. "I'm going to powder my nose."

A true gentleman, her escort got to his feet and assisted her. She liked that. Most of her clients didn't treat her like a lady. Maybe this one would be different. Maybe her nerves were jumping for other reasons.

Old black-and-white photos in the hallway on the way to the ladies' room created a lump in her throat. The pictures included families dressed in early twentieth-century clothing, enjoying the beach or sitting at picnic benches. The smiling faces jarred her bitter heart. A family was something she would never have.

Especially now.

Harper's parents had intended for her to marry and breed a house full of children, insisting that college wasn't necessary for a girl and, therefore, a waste of money. So she'd set out to prove them wrong by paying her way through school. She'd done okay for a while, but tuition and rent left her in dire straits. Desperate for income, she'd stumbled across a Backpage-type ad that offered *Limitless opportunity for beautiful women with high standards and elegant taste.*

Harper reached the restroom door, remembering the first few gigs she'd taken. Her skin crawled at the memory of strange men's hands fondling her breasts. It kept her up some nights, but the money had been a godsend. One night's work paid for a third of what she owed her school. After two more gigs, she'd paid off that year's tuition.

I should have stopped then.

She shoved open the door, the burn of anger replacing shame. The money had been a powerful drug, and the attention, praise, and presents took over her life. She'd felt beautiful and in control. Something her parents never made her feel.

At the sink, Harper stopped and stared at her reflection. She examined the necklace, mesmerized by its sparkle in the fluorescent lights.

Harper wished the jewelry had emotional value, but no matter the allure, she would never see the glittering diamonds as anything other than rent money. It wasn't a gift from a boyfriend or someone she had feelings for. It was payment for the promise of sex.

It made her a prostitute.

For the past two years, she'd lived what everyone imagined was a glamorous life. Dining in fancy restaurants, receiving gifts, and enjoying a gorgeous apartment paid for by one of her regulars. But no one saw the sweaty nights rolling around in beds with older, out-of-shape men who secretly disgusted her.

Instead of focusing on their skin and bodily fluids, she only pictured the hundred-dollar bills she'd receive at the end of their escapades. And once alone in her apartment, she'd scrub the remnants of her date from her skin until the vodka kicked in.

Her dreams of getting a college degree had become a distant memory, and the rush she used to get from the dinners and presents from wealthy, powerful men had faded long ago. Harper didn't know when it had gone from a hobby to a job, but she'd become dependent on making men want her so she could enjoy the life to which she'd become accustomed.

She studied her reflection, mindful of any hint of wrinkles around her eyes. She'd heard the stories and seen the older call girls working the streets, vowing that would never happen to her. How long did she have before her clientele forgot her and started chasing younger women?

The rustle of movement startled Harper. She set her purse on the sink and rummaged for her lipstick. Through her peripheral vision, she glanced at someone in the corner of the bathroom.

Harper carefully touched up her red lips, liking how the color made her blue eyes pop. She dropped the small tube into her purse and did a quick toss of her long brown hair.

She didn't see the woman appear next to her and jumped when the din of rushing water filled the bathroom.

"You're so pretty."

Harper had become numb to such words, having heard them so many times from men anxious to get her into their bed. She smiled, touched to receive such praise from another woman.

"I'm flattered, but I don't think I'm anything special."

The admirer shook her head, her long hair cascading around her shoulders. "You're young and beautiful. The world is yours for the taking. It's an exciting time to be alive, isn't it?"

Harper eyed her companion, trying to gauge the young woman's age. With artfully applied makeup and expensive clothes, she could have been anywhere from sixteen to thirty. One thing the young woman seemed to have that Harper didn't was hope. Harper was a machine, good for only one thing. She didn't experience true excitement or joy or happiness anymore. That made her feel dead inside.

"Just don't let anyone tell you who you are or what you should be," Harper warned the stranger. "Fight for what you want. If you do, the world will remain yours for the taking. It's when others get inside your head that things go wrong."

The young woman's innocent eyes ate at Harper. She had no excuse for offering advice to anyone.

I'm an idiot.

She snapped up her bag and hurried from the bathroom, unable to look at the young woman she could've been if she hadn't answered that ad.

Once inside the dimly lit dining room, Harper walked back to her table.

Her new client sipped the last dregs of his champagne and stood when he saw her. But he didn't hold out her chair, showing the gentlemanly concern as he'd done before. Instead, he eased closer and gently held her wrist.

"Why don't we get out of here?" His warm breath tickled her cheek. "I've got some fun activities planned for us."

Harper caressed the diamonds around her neck as if gathering strength from their presence.

She placed her hand on his lapel, giving him a teasing view of her cleavage. "Nothing would excite me more than being alone with you."

A grin lit up his face, letting Harper know she'd said what he wanted to hear. Just like every other John she'd met.

His predictable reaction saddened her. For once, she wanted a man to say he wanted to get to know her before ripping off her clothes. But that wasn't the business she was in. Her job was to please men and ensure they kept returning for more. It was the one thing Harper Glynn was good at, no matter how disgusted it made her feel.

10

At my desk, tablet in hand, I listened to the groans and heavy breathing of sex. The slut made all the usual *ohs* and *ahs* one would expect to hear from a hooker wanting to please her client. It disgusted me how predictable these women were. The men too.

Harper Glynn knew nothing about the bug I'd planted in her purse while we shared the restaurant bathroom earlier that night. She'd been too into applying her lipstick and fawning over herself in the mirror. The whore should have paid closer attention to her surroundings.

When I realized I wouldn't be able to acquire my package from under her sugar daddy's nose—security cameras pissed me off—I went to plan B and dropped the small metal listening device to track her. At least with the bug, I could keep tabs on her whereabouts to ensure she was part of my next transfer tomorrow.

My fingers tingled at the idea of watching her dulled blue eyes close as I stood over her. She would find out who was in control. She would witness my power and discover how easily I could destroy her empty, insignificant life.

I tapped a pen against my desktop in time with the rhythmic thumping coming through my speakers. My anger rose with every gasp, with every moan, and with every single slap of skin on skin.

It took a tremendous toll on my patience to stay in control. Letting go of my anger was not acceptable. I couldn't let the world see the real me. They would try to stop me. I had to play the game until I had what I wanted. Until they experienced what I'd survived, no one would understand. I was alone.

I gritted my teeth as the disgusting pig said tender words to Harper. Each time he told the little slut that she was beautiful or commented on how good she felt, my stomach twisted into a thousand fiery knots. A loud slap resonated through my speakers, and my hatred for the man flared anew. It was all about his needs and desires, and he didn't care what happened to any woman as long as he enjoyed it.

And Harper allowed him to use her. Just like all the others. How much lower could she sink? Did she know she could never return from this? Never better herself after selling her body to the highest bidder. She'd become tainted goods, only useful for one thing. Like all the rest of her kind, she was trash, waiting to be disposed of by someone like me.

My hate for the leggy brunette churned into a bottomless pit of white fire. For all the glam and sophistication she'd attempted to put on at the restaurant, Harper proved no better than a hooker on any street corner. Nice clothes and shiny jewelry didn't make her superior. She still had to spread her legs in the end.

The diamond necklaces, the posh apartment, and the lines of married men wanting to take her out and pay her for sex sickened me. It was a disgrace to all the wives and mothers who did the right thing and ended up with cheating assholes, chasing the prettiest girl they could find. It was the same old story.

Nice girls finished last.

Not anymore.

With the crescendo of their sexual escapades charging me, I scrolled through the information I'd gathered on Harper Glynn. My surveillance included pictures of her apartment in the high-rise building next to a picturesque lake. The sports car she drove, the trips to the organic grocery, and the laps she ran around the jogging path outside her building. She received no visitors other than her clients. Pity.

It had been so easy to swipe her keys from her purse, press them into a mold, and return the ring before she knew they were gone on her last date at the very same restaurant. Idiot.

I also knew about her stint at the University of Texas. A little internet search and some basic hacking got me a peek at her records. I could even narrow down the month she'd started her life as a sex worker. Her school tuition bill had gone from past due to being paid in full. It was a shame, because she had so much potential, carrying a 4.0 GPA until she dropped out of her business classes. She'd given up on her brains and settled for what she could sell between her legs.

Disgusting.

Harper cried out. Faking her pleasure, no doubt. Women like that never enjoyed sex. It was business, and her groans of ecstasy were for the men's ears only. Their fragile egos needed the boost so they could strut around like roosters and feel good about themselves. How could anyone buy her loud cries? The little faker. Harper deserved everything I had planned for her.

They all did.

Itching to begin Harper's lessons in degradation, I reached for my phone. The erotic exchange filling my speakers made my hands shake.

Enjoy it while you can, slut.

After three rings, Ken answered. I tapped my foot, impatience getting the better of me. I didn't like to be kept waiting.

"Why are you calling me?" He sounded aggravated.

The impertinent bastard.

I tossed my pen onto my desk, ready to get to business. "Where do we stand? I have another to send down the pipeline."

"Are you c-crazy?" His hoarse voice cracked.

Ken was never all in with my endeavors and pressed his reservations at every opportunity. It took a lot of persuasion to get him to go along with my ideas initially. It seemed like he still needed an incentive to maintain our operations.

I turned off the speaker, wanting to concentrate on keeping the lowlife I depended on dancing to my tune.

"What's wrong?" I kept a lid on my irritation. No point in letting the dumbass know my true feelings. Emotions were a weapon when wielded by the wrong person. I had firsthand experience with that.

"The police are combing one of the drop-off points." He paused, seeming almost afraid to continue. "They know there's a ring. Someone reported seeing a transaction. We have to stop until things die down. For my safety and yours."

I eased back in my chair, weighing my options. I had contingencies in place, and quite a few people would go down long before me if things ended up in police hands. But I was quickly learning that the people I'd been dealing with were mostly idiots—drug dealers and foreigners who barely spoke English. What I was doing wasn't rocket science, but it required a certain audacity.

I sat upright again, confidence in my position surging. "My safety is never a concern. You and I know that."

Tilting my tablet up, I checked the notes I made. Timelines and details about the next package I planned to acquire. *Leave nothing to chance.*

I smoothed out a crease in my pants, hating when I appeared unkempt. "I've got two more. Get me drop points. I couldn't give a fuck about the police. They don't have anything and are just sniffing around. Besides, the locals are incompetent."

"What if they discovered some evidence?" The lilt of Ken's voice rose. "And what if it's not just the locals anymore? We can't risk getting the government involved."

One thing law enforcement was good for was dragging their feet. I'd done enough research to know the local police and even the Feds needed a lot of evidence before making a move. We could move the operation to another site, and the trail of evidence would turn cold.

I glimpsed the window above my desk. The twinkling stars above put on a pretty show, but tonight I wished for black clouds and lightning. The chaos would match my mood. "Worry more about what will happen if the team finds out you've been talking to the cops."

His silence made me smile. *Some people are just too easy.*

"I would never do that."

"So says you." When he didn't argue, I went on. "Get the money secured for the two I'm sending, and a location where to deliver the goods."

"You're a real bitch, you know that?"

I liked his spunk. It was the first time he came across like a real man since picking up the phone.

Digging my thumbnail into the wooden surface of my desk, I pictured what I would do to my reluctant associate one day. "Careful, my friend. If my packages aren't sold for top dollar, I might just hire someone to remove your package."

I didn't need to spell out that I was talking about the one hanging between his legs.

Annoyed with his excuses, I disconnected the call and set the phone aside. I turned up the volume on my tablet.

The crack of a hard slap wasn't a surprise.

Dear little Harper whimpered. "No, don't do that," she cried out. "No bruises. I told you I don't like it that rough."

"You'll take everything I give you," he growled. "Until I've gotten what I paid for."

Harper's high-pitched scream sent goose bumps running along my arms, and I covered my ears as my own memories assaulted me.

I had to remind myself that Harper deserved all of this, and more.

11

Settled on her comfy new couch, Winter listened to Noah's gravelly tone and the little cracks when he raised his voice ever so slightly. He regaled her with the amenities of the motel the Bureau had booked him in the small town where he'd ended up. His commentary on the squeaky bed springs, an ice machine dry as a desert, and the single, yellowed hand towel in his bathroom left tears of laughter in her eyes.

"I think Eve got the better room." Despite knowing his dismay was genuine, just hearing his voice warmed her. "She got three pillows as opposed to my one."

Winter's grip tightened on the phone as she thought ahead to a second night without her husband by her side. She believed moving to the smaller Bureau office in Austin would keep Noah at home more, but there were no guarantees as an agent. The work could call him away at any hour of any day. She hated to think how many more lonely nights she would spend staring at the ceiling above her bed without his warm, muscular body by her side.

Thank God for my work.

"Did I tell you about the diner they have here?" His laugh made her smile. "I don't think they've changed the menu since the eighties."

"I miss you." She pictured his handsome face. "It's not the same without you."

His sigh sank to the depth of her being. "I'll let you know as soon as I'm comin' home."

"Be careful," she whispered.

"Always. Love you."

With that, he hung up, and her house became unbearably quiet. The unpacked boxes scattered around the living room waited for her attention, but she ignored the pang of guilt and turned away. Not now. She wasn't in the mood.

She glanced at the sticky notes strewn across the coffee table. She'd scribbled down everything she'd gathered on the case, splitting her research into two piles. One dealt with Schumaker, and the other with Julia. The last thing Winter wanted was to make this into a *he said, she said* case, but until she had something solid, that was what it was amounting to.

Freddie Schumaker's pile of notes made him out to be what he appeared. Successful, wealthy, recently divorced, and sharing custody with his ex-wife. What social media she could find remained limited to a Facebook profile where friends and well-wishers shared posts. She'd found a few pictures of his children. Smiling faces didn't hint at trouble, even though Julia insisted her daughter's drawing proved otherwise.

The employee angle Winter hoped to use to her advantage today had petered out at Schumaker's estate. Although Belinda wasn't his only employee, Winter had to proceed carefully. If she approached the wrong employee or ran into the children, she'd lose the advantage, and the investigation would be in Schumaker's line of fire. She'd have to get creative, find a different route to get the much-needed information.

Despite Julia's worries, no one was untraceable. After years of work as a federal agent, Winter had plenty of options for surveillance. She still had a few tricks up her sleeve. Much better ones than the stunt she'd used today.

Even if every person Schumaker dealt with had nothing but good to say about him, his actions would tell the truth. Criminals got caught in the end because they kept making the same mistakes. Time would tell if Schumaker was such an individual.

Winter released a loud yawn. Her mind was fraught with schemes to crack Schumaker's well-guarded life, but she needed to go to bed. Her brain never worked right when fatigued.

She rose from the couch and stretched her back. A knock on her front door put her immediately on guard.

What the hell? It's close to midnight.

Picturing her gun upstairs next to her bed, she debated if she should make a run for it. The practical nature that served her well as an agent kicked in. She was home in a peaceful neighborhood. Justin was in his maximum-security cell, where she'd left him.

Winter tiptoed toward the door, avoiding the noisy spots on the old hardwood floors, and checked the peephole while holding her breath. She made a mental note to cover the peephole in the future. She didn't like that the person on the other side could see her shadow move in if they were looking for it.

Freddie Schumaker stood under her porch light, grinning.

Son of a bitch!

He appeared fresh from a party in a blue suit and yellow tie. The slight wave in his blond hair, his firmly pressed lips, and the muscles quivering in his square jaw sent a tingle through her.

Fear? She wasn't sure.

Should she answer the door? Get her gun? Or stand there and do nothing? Obviously, he knew about her. Why else would he be outside her home so late at night?

"I know you're in there." Schumaker's deep voice came from the other side of the door, sparked with an anger that belied his smile. "I'm guessing you're watching me through your peephole. I know you're alone, Mrs. Winter Black-Dalton, and that your husband's out of town." A few seconds of silence passed. "I have plenty of eyes in Austin. And I have the money to hire better P.I.s than my wife."

Though her mind hurled every curse she could think of, Winter stayed quiet. Silence could often be the most powerful weapon.

"Your grandfather and grandmother live nearby, don't they? And you've become quite close with your neighbors, the Ogilvies, and their basset hounds, since moving here from Richmond. January eighth was the big moving day, correct?"

Winter clenched her fist, wishing she could punch the wall, but she would give herself away. She hated that type of manipulation. Schumaker had arrived on her doorstep ready to intimidate her, but he didn't know Winter. Her determination to delve deeper into his life had just turned from a job into a vendetta.

"Did you ever stop to consider my security cameras?" Schumaker's voice grew colder. "Those are the most important eyes I have. I never fail to scan the footage made on the property each day, especially not after my youngest told me of the weird woman who stopped by."

She kept her eye on him through the peephole, the hairs on the back of her neck rising.

"How you got past my guard intrigued me." He wiped his eye, looking relaxed, as if he knew Winter would never confront him. "Random women touting solar power aren't supposed to get through. You didn't leave a brochure or a card. I knew you weren't who you pretended to be."

All of Julia's warnings circled Winter's head. She swallowed hard, biting her tongue. If Schumaker was a man with depraved habits, there was no telling what he was capable of. But was he dangerous? She didn't have enough information to ascertain that, but the way his grin expanded told her Freddie Schumaker was not the keen businessman and gentle employer he showed the rest of the world.

She was all too familiar with the masks people wore. Dealing with psychopaths and criminals had given her a hefty disregard for judging a book by its cover. Schumaker had the same audaciousness as others she had put behind bars, but there was something else oozing from his tall, toned figure...

He was cunning, like a predator waiting to disarm its prey.

"Facial recognition is a wonderful technological tool," he said, keeping that confident lilt in his voice. "It led me straight to your business, which happens to be in your home. How sad. You can't impress big clients without an official office. You should think about leasing some space in town."

Schumaker leaned in, putting his eye up close to the peephole. His nearness was jolting, but Winter didn't move. This man feared no one.

Neither did she.

"Stop investigating me. If you were even a halfway decent investigator, you'd already know Julia ruined her life, not me. She has no right poking into my business or my life. Neither do you. If you set foot on my property again, the police will be notified, and I will press charges. Find another client,

Mrs. Black-Dalton. My ex-wife will only cause you as much misery as she did me." Schumaker backed away from the door and adjusted his tie. "Good night."

He descended her porch steps and casually strolled down her walkway. He climbed into a sleek black BMW waiting by the curb and drove away.

Winter lowered her head and rested it against the front door. "Day one, and you've already blown your cover just like your client begged you not to do. Great job, Detective."

Her shoulders heavy and her mind racing, she switched off the living room lights and climbed the stairs to bed.

How she wished Noah had been home. She would have confronted the asshole with backup. Instead, she'd hid behind her door, feeling foolish. But what choice did she have?

Winter learned long ago never to face any threat without a loaded gun. But this man wasn't a criminal or psychopath, and this wasn't a matter of life or death. This was about pride, and Winter planned to put a big dent in Schumaker's, if it was the last thing she did as an investigator.

She opened the drawer of her bedside table and removed the small safe. A quick tap of the code unlocked it, revealing her Smith & Wesson .380.

Yeah, I'm sleeping with my gun until Noah comes home.

12

W inter stood outside the white door with a holiday wreath still hanging above the knocker. She adjusted the sleeve of her sweater with her free hand. The other clutched the yellow plastic container Gramma Beth had loaded with leftovers from last Sunday's dinner.

She didn't need to return the containers immediately, but since Schumaker's late-night visit, she'd been on edge. She wanted another opinion and a shoulder on which to ease her burdens. With Noah out of town and on assignment, her grandmother was the next best advisor she had.

The door opened to reveal Gramma Beth wearing another one of her 1950s-style house dresses. Despite the early hour, she wore lipstick in a soft shade of pink, her wavy silver hair was brushed to perfection, and she smelled of crisp, floral notes. Her perfume, no doubt.

"Goodness, Winter." Gramma Beth looked as confused as she was glad to see her granddaughter. "What are you doing here at this hour? Shouldn't you be working on a case?"

Winter stepped inside. The aroma of coffee momentarily distracted her from the reason for the visit.

"I wanted to return these to you." She handed Gramma Beth the container.

Beth shut the door with her hip. "Bull. I know you better than that, dear. Something's bothering you. When you're stewing, you always have those lines between your eyebrows."

Winter put her hand to the faint wrinkles in her forehead that were giving her away, wishing her grandmother didn't know her so well.

Gramma Beth narrowed her gaze and Winter's shoulders relaxed, then she nodded toward the open kitchen. "Come on. We'll sit and have some coffee, and you can tell me what's bothering you."

She didn't argue, even though she felt foolish for being made so quickly, but it was a comfort not having to hem and haw. Having people who knew her so well made things easier. They understood and gave advice earnestly and without manipulation. She'd learned that in the Bureau. Some agents she never knew how to trust, but with others there was an instantaneous rapport.

Autumn Trent's face came to mind, and Winter felt a little more of the tension ease out of her. She was a true exception. She needed to call Autumn soon. In fact, she probably should have called her friend instead of bothering her grandmother.

As if she could read her mind—and she probably could—Gramma Beth waved at her to sit. A round table with chairs covered in cushions touting butterflies in a field beckoned in the breakfast nook. Winter settled in as her grandmother filled two mugs with coffee.

"Now, what's going on in that pretty head of yours?" Beth set a mug of steaming coffee in front of Winter. "I 'spect this is about more than missing your husband."

Winter wrapped her hands around the mug, relishing the warmth on her stiff hands. "I do miss him. We spoke last night, and I hated hanging up. The house seems so empty without him."

"And?" Beth took a chair next to her, eyebrows raised.

Winter questioned if she should relay the entirety of Schumaker's visit. She didn't want to cause unnecessary worry.

Beth placed her hand over Winter's wrist. "You can talk to me. I know I'm a poor substitute for Noah, but you need to talk about whatever's on your mind. I can tell."

Winter placed her hand over her grandmother's. "There's no comparison. You're both there for me, always. Don't ever say you're a substitute. You're not. It's just that…"

Beth lifted her mug to her lips. "I know, sweetie. He's not here, but I am, so spill the beans."

"I got a visit from someone yesterday." Winter's hand tightened around the mug. "My current client's ex-husband showed up on my doorstep. This woman, my client, fears her ex might be up to no good."

Beth's gaze sharpened in concern. "I'll bet. But why did he come to your house? How did he know where you lived?" Her grandmother's voice rose, hinting at her concern.

Winter shrugged, not wanting to get into how Schumaker was armed with facial recognition technology. "All I know is that he wasn't happy about me working with his ex-wife and wanted to let me know."

"Not sure I like the sound of that." Gramma Beth grunted. "Ex-husbands of clients shouldn't be dropping by your house unannounced."

Winter nodded. "Yeah. That's what I wanted to talk to you about. The incident gave me an idea. What do…" She paused, almost choking on the words as she remembered Schumaker saying them last night. Beth's hand squeezed tighter, and Winter found her voice again. "What do you think about me getting an office? Somewhere in the city. I could lease a space."

Winter waited, examining every line in her grandmother's face, searching for a hint of her feelings on the matter.

A smile spread across her grandmother's lips, and the morning sunlight from the windows glimmered in her eyes. "That's a wise idea."

Anxiety about her approval eased, and Winter relaxed a little in her chair. "I never planned to work from my house forever. I didn't move to Texas only to have my casework literally show up on my doorstep. After the run-in last night, I figured it might be best to keep my private life separate from my career."

Flashes of the skinned rat that had shown up in her driveway during the Mahoney Fitzgerald case was another example of removing her work life from her private life, but Gramma Beth didn't need to know about that nasty incident.

"About damn time you figured that out." Grampa Jack limped into the room on legs that appeared to be as stiff as the Tin Man's. "I listened at the door as you two hens clucked about Winter's business. Never mix business with your personal life, sweetheart. It always ends up bad."

Beth stood and went to her husband's side. Her frown deepened as she watched him almost robotically reach for the coffeepot. "You're hurting today, aren't you?"

He waved her off. "Just my morning aches. I'll take a pill, and it'll improve in a little while."

Winter hated seeing her grandpa in pain, but that was lupus. There were good days and bad days, and her grandfather made the best of it. Seeing the man who raised her since the death of her parents entering a decline pulled at Winter's heart. She wished she could wipe away his suffering, so he could be the Grampa Jack she used to know. At least he was stable for now.

Winter took in the loving way her grandmother filled a coffee mug for her grandfather and went to the cabinet over the sink for his pills. Her tender kiss on his brow as she dropped a pink pill into his hand brought a tear to her eye.

That was marriage…loving and staying with someone through the worst times and celebrating the best. She looked forward to years with Noah, surviving all the ups and downs.

Not everyone was so lucky. She remembered Julia, and how her marriage hadn't survived the bad times. Whose fault was that? Did Schumaker leave the relationship before or after Julia's affair? And did it really matter who was to blame?

"You should get yourself a guard dog too," Grampa Jack said after taking his pill. "You need a partner to cover your back. Nothing better than a big ole dog to scare the crap out of pesky clients or their exes."

Winter could imagine Noah's face when he found a large German shepherd sharing their bed. "I'd settle for a home security system. We're too busy for a dog."

"You can add that when you get your new office." Beth returned to the table and eased into her chair. "Nothing wrong with added security, especially with everything you and Noah have been through."

Jack set his coffee mug on the counter. "No, hold on a minute." He rushed from the room, seeming livelier than when he'd shuffled in.

Winter leaned out of her chair to track his progress into the living room but lost him behind the wall. Seconds later, she heard him give a triumphant "Ha!" and he came hobbling back into the room, holding the morning newspaper.

"We'll find you a place today, I bet." He joined Beth and Winter at the table, accepting his wife's help to get seated, and opened the newspaper. Winter didn't like how heavy his breathing had become after the short walk, but she did enjoy the new brightness in his eyes.

Winter lifted her mug to allow the paper to take up the table, while her grandmother glowered at Jack.

"Can we have our coffee first?" Beth complained.

Jack finished spreading the paper out. Beth all but snatched her coffee up, but it didn't faze him. "Why wait?" He grinned at Winter. "Fortune favors the bold."

Beth put on an indignant scowl, adding to the lines around her mouth. "She's renting an office, Jack, not crossing the Rubicon."

Winter snickered at her grandparents' bickering, but she agreed with Grampa Jack. Waiting would only give more clients an opportunity to invade her personal life, and the next one to do so might be more like Margaret von Gork than Freddie Schumaker, or worse. She needed an office in town. Her home should be a place of safety and privacy, and she wasn't going to spend the rest of her life spooning with her gun whenever Noah was away.

Her grandfather combed through the *Space Available* ads. It wasn't long before Beth stood over his shoulder, pointing out the best ones.

The pair warmed Winter's insides at their interest in her business, but she didn't have the heart to tell them she had an easier way to find a rental space. She retrieved her phone from her pocket and, with a single search, found far more listings than the paper offered.

When she held up a location, complete with pictures, price, lease terms, and a map to the site, Beth and Jack looked like deer caught in headlights.

"What about this one?" Winter asked, amused by their vapid stares.

"Can I go with you to check it out?" Beth took a sip,

setting her mug down on top of the newspaper. "We can furniture shop for the new place while we're at it."

Jack shook his head, then slid the paper out from under the cup, folding it up. "Leave it to you to turn a business venture into a shopping spree."

Beth nudged her husband with an elbow. "The child needs to make her office look nice for clients. You'd fill the place with boxes and lawn chairs for people to sit on."

Jack pointed an accusing finger at Winter. "She's the one living out of boxes, not me."

Winter cleared her throat, eager to head off the topic of her slow unpacking process. "The twenty-eight, nearly twenty-nine-year-old child would love to have you come along, Gramma Beth." She let her smile tell her grandmother she held no hard feelings over being called a 'child.' "Another set of eyes is just the thing I need to find the perfect spot for Black Investigations."

Beth squared her shoulders and raised an eyebrow at her husband. "See?"

Jack stuck the folded newspaper under his arm. "Just don't pick the most expensive location. The kid...I mean the *lady's* got to eat."

"I know that, Jack." Her grandmother followed him out of the kitchen. "I'm not an idiot."

Winter took advantage of the break to place a few calls to agents representing the top three places her internet search had pulled up.

She listened to her grandparents in the living room, still needling each other, but mixing praise between the sharper banter. It made her chuckle. She and Noah did the same thing when they got on each other's nerves. Somehow, blending the sweet words with the sour made everything more palatable.

Winter tuned out her grandparents as they talked about

her welfare, and she concentrated on the agents who gave her information on the places available for rent.

In less than ten minutes, she'd set up three appointments for later that morning. The timing couldn't have suited her better. She could find a place in downtown Austin, sign the lease, and get started on her new office before Noah returned from his assignment.

He'll probably wish we'd gotten the dog instead.

Winter went to get another cup of coffee, both to clear the remaining fog from her brain and to celebrate her decision to open an office. Her phone rang as she reached for the coffeepot.

Julia Eversmeyer's name flashed on the screen.

She checked on her grandparents. They were still in the living room, discussing what furniture she should buy.

Taking advantage of their distraction, Winter slipped out the kitchen door to the covered patio outside. The cool air didn't bother her much, thanks to a warm belly of coffee.

"Julia, is everything all—?"

"He came to see you?" Julia practically screamed into the phone. "I told you we had to keep the investigation from him, but you walk up to his front door and begin snooping around without thinking. I thought you were a professional."

Winter immediately grew defensive but forced the irritation from her tone. "I was trying to get an assessment of him other than what I got off the internet. I did have a word with the nanny, who spoke highly of Mr. Schumaker before your daughter interrupted us."

"Yeah, he told me Gabriella gave you away." Julia's voice calmed a few octaves. "Freddie left me a very long voicemail. He threatened me if I didn't leave him alone."

"I'm sorry." Winter stared at the clear sky, wishing for clouds to match her mood. "I let you down, and that was not my intention."

She waited, hoping she hadn't blown her case.

"I don't blame you. I blame him." Julia returned to the same skittish woman she'd met at the café. "Everyone who works for him thinks he's wonderful. The employees all speak highly of him, but they weren't married to him. He isn't a perfect man. That picture my daughter drew proves it."

Winter had entertained doubts about the case until Schumaker showed up on her doorstep. He came across as controlling...the type of man who would get his way no matter what. That was the only explanation for threatening her and following that up with threats against his ex as well. She could only imagine what he'd said to Julia in his voicemail. Winter had gotten a firsthand glimpse of what Julia had endured during her marriage.

"Can I meet with you this afternoon?" Julia asked. "Gabriella has a dental appointment at one o'clock, so I get to pick her up from school early. I want you to meet her, and maybe you can get additional information. The things she won't share with me."

The idea intrigued Winter. She'd been itching to go to the source—the artist of the picture that had set Julia off. If she could speak to the little girl, she might better understand Schumaker's home life. She thought about the man on her doorstep and his frigid voice. "What about your ex-husband? I think it's safe to say he'll find out."

Julia's strained laughter was unexpected, making Winter question the real toll this investigation might take on the woman's fragile state of mind.

"Let him find out," Julia spat, with all the venom of a cobra. "He'll be pissed, but what does it matter? The damage is done. He knows I've hired you, and maybe he might watch his step."

Winter doubted it. Schumaker didn't strike her as a man

about to back down because of a little heat. "He might take you back to court for some concocted reason. Are you ready to deal with that?"

"I know." Julia's voice deflated, her anger waning. "The best shot I have now is getting something on his ass to use in court to take my kids away from him. Whatever you need to do, do it."

Winter was proud of the woman for standing up to her ex. There would be a battle ahead, of that there was no doubt, but that Julia remained prepared to meet the repercussions head-on made Winter admire her a little more.

In the past, the courts often labeled women who fought against tyrannical husbands as bad mothers or troubled bitches, but times were changing. All Winter had to do was get something on Schumaker, and Julia's problems would abate. Reason enough to dig harder into the asshole's life.

Winter opened her calendar app. "What time do you want to meet?"

She watched through the windows as Gramma Beth returned to the kitchen and picked up her coffee mug from the breakfast table. She met Winter's eyes through the window over the sink as she washed out the cup.

"There's a shop downtown that Gabriella loves called iBake Cupcakes," Julia told her. "Let's meet there around two thirty. My daughter might be more willing to talk if I bribe her with sweets. I can get you the address—"

"I'll find it. Don't worry. I'll meet you there."

"Thank you…really." Julia sounded on the verge of tears.

"You're welcome."

She walked back through the patio door as her grand-mother refilled her coffee.

"I just saw you wash that."

"I was just being nosey, dear. Better view from the window."

Winter chuckled.

"I have so many ideas." Beth seemed at least ten years younger as she planned. "We can head to the city, shop, grab a bite to eat, and get you set up in an office."

The way her grandmother bubbled with excitement, as she went on about what she would wear and the places they could shop, chased away last night's stress and filled Winter with the warm fuzzies.

This is why we moved here.

The huge smile on her grandmother's face had been worth the bother of the unpacked boxes crowding Winter's living room. She wanted to leave the horror of her past behind, and she prayed that she never encountered such evil again. Maybe a new office would be the first step to ensuring she and Noah had a real refuge from the dangers of their jobs.

And if Freddie Schumaker threatens me there, he'll have to do it in public view.

13

Harper placed her hand over her face to cut the glaring noonday sun filtering through her bedroom curtains. The combination of Xanax and Ambien she'd popped the night before made her groggy. She took the medication to forget about her date, but the memories of his treatment remained. The evening left her more unsettled than usual, and with bruises to show for it.

She rolled over, berating herself for agreeing to his request for rough sex. What did it matter? She'd known worse. One obsessed accountant had urged her to quit the profession, and when Harper refused, he'd beat her beyond anything that qualified as "rough sex." Her lifestyle had its downsides, but the money and perks were great. So why had it grown tiresome?

At twenty, she was young enough to start over. She'd saved enough to return to college and could choose a new path. She was smart enough to figure out a new plan. It would be worth it.

The diamond necklace glistening on her nightstand caught her eye. She rolled over, retrieved the brilliant stones, and stared at her latest gift. Precious gems used to give her such a high. She was usually on top of the world after receiving such a valuable gift. It made her feel special, but now the necklace held no allure. It might as well be gravel.

A cough came from the corner of the room.

Harper bolted upright, letting out a startled shout. She scanned the room and found the intruder sitting on the red velvet stool of her antique vanity set. Harper locked eyes with the woman, and a glimmer of recognition settled over her. It was the young woman from the restaurant bathroom. The one she'd spoken to, telling her to live the life she wanted.

"How did you get in here?" Harper hated how her voice shook, but she couldn't have steadied it for the world. "Or past the doorman? All visitors are supposed to be approved."

The intruder casually checked her nails. "You put an awful lot of faith in a guy making minimum wage."

Harper wasn't about to put up with the young upstart coming into her apartment and starting shit. She would have a sharp word with the building super, but first, she'd let the snot-nosed trespasser have it. "I demand to know how you got into my apartment. If you don't tell me, I'll call the police."

"I don't have to tell you anything." The young woman leveled her haughty gaze across the room. "See? Aren't you glad I took your advice about not letting people tell me what to do?"

Her snicker was slight, but it struck Harper as deadly. There was something off about the woman.

The fear the stranger's intrusion generated quickly morphed into anger. She'd deal with this person the way she dealt with her obsessed clients.

This is the last thing I need right now.

Harper tossed aside her bedsheets, no longer affected by

the drugs in her system. "You need to go." She used the same tone her mother used to take with her.

The intruder flipped her long hair around her shoulder, showing an air of defiance. "Do I?"

Her cold, hard stare sent goose bumps along Harper's arms. It was as if she were dead inside. Harper expected that of someone like her, beaten down by the business, but this young woman didn't appear to be anything like that.

Like her.

The more Harper thought about their meeting in the ladies' restroom the night before, the greater her unease. Had that been planned? "Why are you here? What do you want?" She thought of the true crime shows she'd binged and remembered the importance of connecting with criminals. "What's your name?"

The sun glistened on the diamond necklace. Harper noticed how the young woman's eyes veered toward the expensive gift. "Barbie."

Her mind filled with reasons for the intruder's presence. "Are you after my jewelry, B-Barbie? Is that why you broke in? Take it and go."

Barbie shook her head. "I'm not interested in any of that. I'm here for you."

Harper's stomach clenched as her fear escalated. "Me? Why?"

Barbie stood from the stool and pulled a wickedly sharp knife from a sheath at her waist. "Get dressed. You're coming with me."

Harper's throat closed so tightly that she almost couldn't respond. Keeping her gaze on the blade, she managed to whisper, "No."

Reaching out, Harper picked up the first object to hand. A book. Better than nothing. With a throw that would've made her middle school softball coach proud, she hurled the novel at the intruder.

Either she'd lost her aim, or her target had the reflexes of a cat. The book crashed into the wall instead.

Harper's rebellion had only pissed Barbie off. "You bitch." Knife at the ready, she stalked forward, her eyes small, angry slits. Harper backpedaled as far as she could but was stopped by the nightstand.

Barbie lunged, shoving her over and onto the mattress. A second later, the knife was at Harper's throat. She didn't dare swallow, let alone say a word.

This is how I die.

"Do you want me to slit your throat?" Barbie pressed all her weight down on Harper's chest. "Blink once if your answer is no."

Harper blinked once.

Instead of letting up the pressure, the knife sank down a little deeper. Warmth ran down the side of Harper's neck. Just when she thought Barbie was going to slit her throat anyway, the pressure let up, and the woman climbed off her chest.

With a cry of relief and horror, Harper placed her fingers on the wound, and sure enough, they came away red. It wasn't gushing, but the sight of her own blood made her head swim.

With a smug smile, Barbie held up a cell phone so that Harper could see the screen. "Think that was bad? You've not seen bad." She wiped the bloody knife off on Harper's sheets. "Cause any more trouble, and I'll call my associate. He's parked right outside your parents' home in Dallas. You remember them? The family you walked out on so you could chase your dreams of college?" Her laugh was low, almost deadly. "But you didn't end up a college graduate, did you?"

The impertinence in her voice, the way she cocked her

head, silently judging, brought a bitter taste to Harper's mouth. "I—"

"If you refuse to go with me because you couldn't give a damn about your parents, I understand." Barbie lowered her phone. "But what about your little brothers? Do you want to be responsible for their deaths? Accidents happen."

Her cruel grin was slow, and Harper's stomach turned. "What are you saying? You can't be serious. Why would you...?" She struggled to think of something else to say, some way to stand up to this Barbie from Hell, but fear kept her silent.

"Your brothers are so handsome." Barbie's voice sounded playful, almost childlike. "It would be a shame for them never to finish high school. Imagine all the things they'd miss out on. Prom. Graduation." She leaned over the foot of the bed. "Are you sure you won't come with me?"

Harper's heart pounded. Her mouth went dry. She'd received threats before, but none that involved her family. She'd kept them safe. No one should have known they existed, but this bitch did.

The sick stalker put her fingers, shaped like a gun, to her head. "Mama will go first, since she's home alone." She simulated a gun firing. "Boom. My associate will wait for your little brothers to come home from school. Boom. Boom. Two for one."

Her delighted laugh drained the oxygen from Harper's head. "No."

"The *pièce de résistance* will be when Daddy gets home. I'll make sure my second aims high, to see all the blood and brains everywhere. Boom, boom, boom. We'll make his death nice and messy right after we tell him that his little girl spreads her legs for a living."

Harper held her fist to her heart and closed her eyes. *Not my brothers.*

Adrenaline had her wide awake now, but it was upstaged by fear so great she thought she might pass out. She questioned whether she could take the waiflike prowler and wrestle her out of the apartment, or at least get away. Was a gun hidden beneath the heavy coat her tormentor wore? Could she risk it?

Whatever happened to her, Harper couldn't live with herself if her little brothers got hurt or even discovered what she'd been doing all these years away from home.

Harper said nothing as she climbed from the bed, knowing she had no choice but to comply. She could live with the shame of her family knowing, she decided, even resign herself to never hearing from them again, but she could not live with the guilt of causing their deaths.

Barbie grinned and pointed at some clothes laid out at the end of the bed. "Hurry up and put these things on." She opened another drawer and pulled out a scarf. "This too."

Harper inspected the jeans and casual shirt, angry with herself for taking all the drugs last night. She should have heard someone in her bedroom going through her dresser drawers.

"You have sixty seconds to change, or I make a call, and your family dies."

The icy way the woman spoke made Harper shake. She'd been with men who had threatened and hit her, but she'd never been so scared.

"After you've changed, we'll calmly proceed down the back stairs to the service alley at the side of the building. I have transportation waiting for us."

The reality that Harper might never see her apartment again escalated her trembling. She knew the odds of surviving if she willingly left with the woman were practically zero. There had to be another way. Harper needed to buy time while she thought of a way out of her dangerous situation.

She shook her head. "No. I won't go."

Harper braced herself, waiting for a flurry of shouting or a knife to the gut, but nothing happened.

Barbie lifted her phone and pressed a number on the screen.

Seconds felt like hours as the muffled ringing carried around the bedroom. Someone picked up.

"Send the proof," she said into the phone. "Looks like it's plan B after all."

"Roger that," a gruff voice replied.

Harper wasn't a fool. She'd made plenty of fake calls getting out of dates with unsuitable men by calling others in her trade. She would need more than a deep voice on the other end of a phone line to change her mind.

A video appeared on the phone screen. Barbie flipped the phone around, allowing Harper to get a good look. She sucked in a breath, frozen in terror when she saw a masked individual sitting in a vehicle outside her parents' modest ranch-style home.

The scream that rose from Harper's throat radiated all her fear and misery. "No! Please, don't hurt them. They're innocent."

Barbie pointed at the bedroom door. "Are you ready to cooperate now? If so, I'll put plan B on hold."

Harper swallowed back tears as she reached for the clothes on the bed. "Let my brothers live, and I'll do whatever you want."

This was her end. Harper always believed it would be because of a psychotic date or an obsessed regular. Never something like this.

Not that it really mattered. Did she even deserve to take up the planet's oxygen supply?

As Harper dressed, the numbness creeping along her arms and legs traveled to the black hole where her heart used to be. She didn't want to give the sick individual pulling her strings any more power over her emotions. Better to not feel anything, she reasoned.

"Good girl," a malicious voice whispered in her ear. "And you were wrong, you know. When others get inside your head, it's not a bad thing. It means everything is going according to plan."

14

Winter parked outside iBake Cupcakes just minutes before her appointment with Julia. The drive back to Gramma Beth's place in the Destiny Bluff subdivision took longer than expected, but Winter had a good idea which of the three office spaces she liked the best.

Beth had been a tremendous help, even suggesting a style of furniture that would add a homey feel to her office. Spending an entire morning window-shopping with her grandmother had been just what she needed to forget the gloom left by Freddie Schumaker.

Once inside, the aroma of sweet confections made her mouth water. The glass display case was filled with an array of colorful cupcakes decorated to resemble anything from unicorns to superheroes. The white tiled floor hosted black iron tables while a coffee refill station stood adjacent to the panoramic windows overlooking the street.

She spotted Julia sitting at a corner table away from the afternoon sun creeping through the store windows. The little girl seated with her was the most adorable child Winter had ever seen.

She wore a blue school sweater with an eagle emblem on the chest and already had a few smears of blue icing across her lips. With long blond hair pulled into a ponytail, big blue eyes, and a missing front tooth, she was cuter than in the pictures Winter had seen online.

Winter arrived at the table and smiled down at the precious little girl. "Well, hello there."

Julia's smile wobbled a bit before she hugged the child to her side. "Gabriella, this is Mommy's friend. The one I told you we were here to meet."

Winter stuck out her hand, but Gabriella had other plans. She jumped from her chair and stepped toward Winter, hugging her legs.

The simple, sweet act melted Winter's heart.

Gabriella gazed up into her face, the icing on the corners of her mouth adding to her cute factor. "Hello, there. I'm Gabriella. What's your name?"

Winter knelt, getting on the child's level. Her years in the field taught her to never approach a child from a position of authority if you wanted them to talk. They'd clam up.

"I'm Winter. So very glad to meet you."

Her smile seemed bright, and Gabriella had none of the dark signs Winter had witnessed in other abused or neglected children. Her eyes, having accessed Winter's face, gobbled up the activity in the bakery and eventually made their way back to the display case, as if sizing up her next cupcake.

The activity didn't raise any red flags. Children hiding secrets kept their heads down and rarely looked strangers in the eye.

"Do you know what an elephant is?" Gabriella asked in a high, breathy voice.

Winter nodded. "Yes, I do. I've even seen one up close."

Gabriella's eyes widened. "Really?"

Winter took her hand and guided the child back to her chair. This hardly seemed like the same young girl who'd drawn the unsettling picture of the *nakid notty girls*.

"Did they smell bad?" Gabriella giggled. "My teacher said they stink."

Winter settled in a chair next to the little girl. "Yes, but they were so magnificent that I didn't notice too much."

"I didn't watch the teacher's movie on elephants today because Mommy came and got me." Her attention fell to the half-eaten cupcake on her white plate. "All my friends were jealous because I got out of school early."

Crumbs dotted the table like confetti. Winter brushed away the ones within reach and wrinkled her nose. "Really? They were jealous that you were going to the dentist?"

Gabriella giggled as she poked her finger into the treat's cakey middle. "No, once I told them that, they all felt sorry for me. Nobody likes the dentist. I don't like the dentist, either, especially when they use the icky toothpaste at the end that feels like sand. I like when they give me prizes, though. One time I got rainbow slime, and today, he gave me some cat stickers and an eraser shaped like a kitty's head. Do you want to see it?"

Winter stared in wonder as the girl started digging through the top pocket of her uniform. *Does she ever stop to take a breath?*

"Your eraser and stickers are in your backpack, sweetie," Julia said in a gentle voice. "We left it in the car. Remember?"

Gabriella's face fell, and she picked up the fork next to her plate. "I didn't have any cavities. My brother had *two* cavities the last time he went to the dentist. I bet he'll be proud of me."

Julia retrieved a paper napkin and dipped it in the glass of water next to Gabriella's plate. "Let's clean you up. You've got blue icing everywhere."

The child giggled as her mother dabbed the napkin on her mouth and cheeks, tapping her nose with it at the end. Gabriella's squeals of laughter made Winter smile.

Julia's love for her daughter poured from the woman in every word she spoke and move she made. And Gabriella appeared perfectly at ease with her mother. Winter noted nothing dark or untoward. No scared faces, wary eyes, or the slightest hint of distrust. The air between them remained calm. It was just a mother and daughter meeting a friend for an afternoon snack.

It reminded Winter of the times she and Special Agent Autumn Trent had met while on the job. A special agent in the Richmond Behavioral Analysis Unit, Autumn was a forensic psychologist who specialized in profiling serial killers. Her insights had helped on so many cases, but the friendship Winter had forged with the cool, outgoing woman had been her touchstone. The way they laughed together and shared inside jokes about the characters working with them at the Bureau…she missed her dear friend desperately.

Most of all, she longed to talk about their freaky paranormal gifts and commiserate over the downside of such abilities. Autumn had also suffered head trauma as a child and woken with a profound ability to read the emotions and feelings of others through touch. She had helped Winter during her darkest days, and the miles between them had pained her immensely over the last few weeks.

A nudge on Winter's arm brought her back from the past.

"Are you okay?" Gabriella's small brow wrinkled. "You got on a sad face."

Winter didn't realize she'd drifted away and chastised herself for being so easily distracted.

Get it together. Do the job.

Touched, Winter smiled at the little girl. "I'm fine. I was thinking of someone I love and miss very much."

Gabriella picked up her fork, inspecting the prongs. "I feel the same way when I'm with Daddy and miss my mommy. And I always miss Daddy when I'm with Mommy. It's not fair."

Winter pounced on the opportunity to bring up Schumaker. "What's your favorite thing to do with your mommy and daddy? Do you have special things you do with each of them?"

Gabriella held her fork like a trident and banged it on her plate. "Mommy takes me to the movies, and we get huge buckets of popcorn."

Julia took the fork from her. "Extra butter, right?"

"Right." Gabriella licked her lips. "Daddy always takes me to the candy store. He lets me pick out whatever I want. Belinda gets mad sometimes because she says I have to eat healthy stuff, but that makes Daddy laugh."

Gabriella covered her mouth and giggled again. The innocent, lighthearted laugh warmed Winter, reminding her that there was still good in the world, no matter how much evil she'd witnessed.

"But we don't get to do that much." Gabriella's pout was adorable. "My daddy is always very, very busy."

Winter kept her smile in place, wanting to keep the child talking. "What keeps him busy?"

Gabriella cocked her head, as if lost in her thoughts. "Daddy stays busy at work and even after work. He doesn't like to be by himself." She cupped her hand against her mouth and leaned over to Winter. "I think he might be scared of the dark," she whispered.

Winter noted Julia's narrowed gaze. She lowered her head to address Gabriella. "Why would you think that?"

Gabriella swung her legs beneath her chair, her feet not yet touching the floor. "I sometimes go down to the kitchen for a glass of water after bedtime. I can see the lights on in the pool house windows. Daddy is always doing things in there. And he's never alone. He's got girls with him."

Winter kept eye contact with the little girl, hoping to get her to concentrate on the questions she wanted to ask. "Gabriella, do you know what things your daddy is doing when you see him after bedtime?"

Gabriella shrugged. "He's playing games."

Nakid notty games?

Winter sat back in her chair and glanced at Julia. Games could mean anything to a young child. Board or card games represented fun. It was hard to tell.

Winter wondered how to ask a five-year-old about her use of the word *nakid*. She needed information on the girls Gabriella had seen in the pool house, what happened there late at night, and if the girls in question were underage. Those questions raced through her head as a start. But she had to be careful how she asked them. She couldn't lead the child in any way.

A childlike song jangled from somewhere, interrupting Winter's train of thought.

Gabriella reached into the depths of her pink purse and pulled out a pink phone, silencing the ringtone with a thumb swipe as she squealed, "Daddy's calling."

Julia stiffened and shot a panicked glare at Winter, as if she might be able to magically make the call drop.

The little girl had already started talking without taking a breath. "The dentist said I had no cavities, Daddy. That's better than Gilbert. And guess what, Daddy. Mommy took me to get cupcakes at my favorite place. I ate a fish one. And I met a friend of Mommy's. She's nice and told me she's seen elephants. Real ones. Can you believe it? Her name is Winter."

Fiery knots formed in Winter's stomach. She hadn't expected the child to blurt out every detail about their meeting. Someone warned her once that kids were like tape recorders, remembering everything said to them. She'd never experienced that before. Still, she'd never been around many happy-go-lucky children like Gabriella.

Gabriella held out the phone to Winter. "Daddy says he wants to talk to Mommy's friend."

Julia muttered the exact word that popped into Winter's head. "Shit."

15

Noah sat at a desk in the back office of Helton Gas, running the footage from the security camera in front of the building one more time. He strained to get a good look at the two black vans arriving within five minutes of each other, but the bad lighting and video quality didn't leave him much to go on.

He'd uncovered that they stole the license plates off cars out of Louisiana and Mississippi. One over three years ago, while the other was reported almost five years ago. They had probably switched them out again since the Saturday night drop, making any statewide BOLO pointless.

What worried Noah more was the length of time since the plates had been reported stolen. It meant this operation might have been carrying on for a few years. He wished he had more to go on, but the lack of cameras in the rear of the station kept him from confirming Tuck Hatcher's testimony about the women.

Most of the local businesses in the small town lacked the surveillance equipment he needed to track the direction the vans took. He only had a few glimpses from different store security systems. One van showed up in a parking lot camera going through another small town west of Helton. The trail went cold after that.

Noah rolled his shoulders, trying not to allow his frustration to get the better of him. His last shot would be getting something out of the station's owner, Donald Long. He needed Long's take on what had occurred in his business's back lot and his reason for discouraging Tuck Hatcher from reporting it.

He stood, worked the kinks out of his back, and waited for Eve to return to the office with the station owner. He prepared himself for the tough questions he would ask, and for the pushback Donald Long was sure to give him.

The man's background check was clean. Not even a local speeding ticket. That alone gave Noah pause. It meant the businessman was either on excellent terms with the local police, or he drove like a little old man going to Sunday church.

A knock on the door let Noah know Eve had returned with their person of interest. He faced the tiny office entrance, and the moment he saw the thick man with the balding head of brown hair and beady brown eyes, Noah didn't need to possess Winter's special abilities to know Donald had something to hide.

Tattoo sleeves of women in come-hither poses covered his forearms with more peeking out of his shirt collar. He wore cowboy boots and jeans, but the gold watch on his wrist didn't exactly seem like something a gas station owner in the middle of nowhere would own.

"Mr. Long." Noah offered a nonthreatening smile. "Thank you for coming to talk to us this afternoon."

Long moved with an apprehensive stride into the room,

keeping his wary gaze on Noah. When he spotted the security monitors frozen on a black van, his posture changed, and he became as stiff as a board.

Noah pulled out the desk chair and motioned for Donald to take a seat. "I have some questions about the night Tuck Hatcher witnessed those vans in the back of your gas station."

Donald settled into the chair with a stony countenance. "Yeah. What of it?"

Eve shut the door. Donald flinched at the lock clicking into place.

Noah leaned against the desk, striking a casual pose, wanting to put the station owner at ease. "I'm curious why you would want to tell anyone who witnessed such a suspicious event to keep quiet? Aren't you a concerned citizen?"

"Don't give me that horseshit," Donald grumbled. "I've lived in rural Texas long enough to know that gettin' involved in anybody's business is dangerous. I don't need my station burned down because Tuck glimpsed somethin' he didn't understand."

Now Noah's attention sharpened, though he maintained his casual pose. Nothing about what the man had just said sounded right.

Folks in rural Texas were a close-knit group who took care of each other and helped each other out. Besides, burning down a building in any part of west Texas was a risk most residents wouldn't take. The constant wind could jump the fire to nearby buildings or grass, burning the entire town to the ground.

So why is he lying?

"Why would someone burn down your station if Tuck reported the incident?"

Donald fidgeted and folded his thick arms over his chest.

"I had a friend a few years back stick his nose in somethin' he shouldn't. Charlie saw a couple fighting outside his bar and thought the man was gettin' too physical. He called the cops. They took the guy in. His girlfriend refused to press charges, and the guy was let go. Two days later, Charlie's bar burned to the ground in the middle of the night."

Noah didn't believe him. "But what Tuck saw hardly sounds like a domestic dispute. Women were in danger. Doesn't that bother you?"

Donald's dark brows came together, hinting at his irritation. "Whatever it was, it sure as hell wasn't none of my business. It could have been a bachelorette party van. Maybe one broke down, and another came to get 'em. What difference does it make? I don't know what went on here that night, and I don't wanna know. I just keep my mouth shut and run my business."

Noah's inner alarms went off. *Yep, he's hiding something.*

Getting to know your accused was the first point of action whenever doing an interrogation. Hitting with the harder questions came during the second and third meetings. He'd learned to let a perp sweat a little. Soon enough, they'd get scared, make a mistake, then they would sing.

"I need you to stay in town until we clear this up." Noah pushed off the desk. "We may want you to come back later."

Donald got to his feet and puffed out his broad chest. "Why? I didn't do nothin'."

"Far too many people have gone missing in this state, and what we discover here may help find them, so until then…" Noah pointed at the floor, "you stay put."

Donald shook his head, letting out a long hiss between gritted teeth. "I think you're wastin' your time. Tuck misinterpreted things, is all. The man's always messin' up around here."

Eve stepped forward, challenging him with her gaze. "Why not fire him?"

Donald gave her an intimidating once-over. "There ain't no one else to replace him."

A tense moment passed between Eve and the gas station owner.

Noah waited it out, knowing that observation of a suspect during questioning was just as important as what they said.

Eve gestured to Donald's wrist. "Nice watch. Looks expensive."

Donald eyed the timepiece and grinned. "It's a knockoff, but nice try."

He gave Noah one last angry glower and hurried out of the office.

After Eve shut the door behind him, Noah rubbed the back of his neck, convinced the stiffness came from his lousy bed at the cheap motel.

"You buy any of that?" Eve whistled through her teeth. "I think he's as suspicious as a two-headed snake."

Noah glanced at the closed door. "Donald Long barely makes enough in gas sales to cover the mortgage on this place, so yeah, he's as sneaky as a snake with a motive to increase his income. The good news is, we're on to him. And just like when snakes shed their skin and leave a trail, this slithery bastard has left breadcrumbs out there for us to find."

Eve wrinkled her brow. "What are you getting at?"

Noah glanced back at the monitor frozen on the black van. "If Helton Gas is some exchange point in the trafficking ring, it's possible that other gas stations are as well. We might have found a route we can track."

Eve's throaty chuckle carried across the small room. She

rubbed her hands together, a playful gleam in her eyes. "I guess we're gonna be doin' us some snake huntin'."

Noah didn't share in her enthusiasm. Expanding the case meant more time away from Winter. He wondered what type of snake she'd be keeping company with this week.

Just don't let it be the deadly kind.

16

Winter's heart thumped heavy in her chest as she stared at the pink phone in Gabriella's tiny hand. Knowing that the man who'd stood on her doorstep threatening her was on the line didn't fill her with an aching desire to resume their hostile discussion in front of Schumaker's daughter and ex. She needed to protect the mother and daughter, not set them up for more problems with the suspicious man.

Winter reached for the phone, but Julia snatched it from Gabriella. She stepped away from the table to deal with her ex-husband out of earshot of their daughter.

"Why didn't Mommy let you talk to my daddy?"

She gazed into the little girl's blue eyes, already regretting the lies she would tell her. "Well, your mommy and daddy have things to talk about that are more important than me."

"Like what?" Gabriella asked while keeping an eye on her mother.

Winter clocked Julia's position a few feet away from the table. She had her back turned to them, but the way her hand waved wildly about made it appear that the conversation wasn't going well.

"You." Winter kept her voice even and pleasant. "Mommies and daddies are always talking about their kids. They worry so much about you and your brother and sister."

"They must worry a lot." Gabriella tilted her head as her gaze remained glued to her mother. "Mommy's mad. Why is Mommy mad? Is it about Daddy again?"

Try as she might, Winter couldn't think of any way to explain to the child that her mother's animated gestures and raised tone were nothing to worry about. Julia's performance even drew a few curious glances.

When she turned around, Julia had tears in her eyes as she hissed, "I can spend time with whomever I please. Stop telling me what to do."

Winter faced Gabriella and picked up her plate with the half-eaten cupcake to distract her from her mother. "You want to try another one? A pink rabbit this time? Or maybe a green one with a dragon on top?"

The ruse worked, and Gabriella turned to her, grinning at the prospect of more sweets.

Winter stayed tuned to the conversation, but Julia had lowered her voice, making the rest of the call hard to hear.

"Can I really have another cupcake?" Gabriella asked, excitement brimming in her eyes. "Mommy told me I was only allowed one. That's why I took the blue fish one. Blue is my favorite color. But I like pink too. What's your favorite color?"

Winter strained to listen, but all she could detect was something about courts and another hearing before Julia told Schumaker to go to hell.

She grinned at the little girl, trying not to show any concern. "I guess my favorite color is blue too."

"Wow!" Gabriella's eyes widened. "I knew I liked you. Only nice people like blue."

Julia rocked back her head and let out a silent scream that would have shattered glass had the woman let it loose. By the time she returned to the table, though, her beautiful smile was firmly in place.

Winter could appreciate Julia's attempt to spare her daughter from seeing her heartache, but she felt the child picked up on more than her mother gave her credit for. "Everything okay?"

Julia returned the phone to her daughter and worked her purse free from behind the chair. "We have to go."

Gabriella grabbed the phone and frowned. "What about my second cupcake? Winter said I could have another one."

Julia's lips spread into a thin line. "Not now, honey. We'll come back another day, and you can have two, maybe even three. But right now, we have to go home."

Winter went to Julia's side, growing anxious. "Are you going to be all right?"

Julia slipped the strap of her purse over her shoulder while she waited for her daughter to put her phone in her purse. "This is Freddie's week, and I was only allowed to see Gabriella because of her appointment. It only happened because Belinda had a doctor's appointment at the same time. I want to get Gabriella back to the house before he arrives home from work. It will make things worse if he sees me. I don't want my children witnessing any more screaming matches."

Winter had never intended to cause Julia any problems with Schumaker. The children didn't need to be the rope in their parents' tug of war, especially not the youngest of them. Still, she saw Gabriella's quivering bottom lip as she listened to her mother's every word, and Winter felt lower than dirt.

"Call me later," Julia insisted as she took Gabriella's hand.

Winter didn't get to say goodbye to the little girl before Julia rushed them out the door. The child's pout and tear-filled eyes remained imprinted on her mind.

Poor kid.

Frustration with the case and the children caught in the crossfire festered in Winter's chest. She hated seeing any child suffer, and she guessed the Schumaker children would witness more ugliness between their parents before things got better.

She returned to her chair and stared at Gabriella's uneaten cupcake, reviewing everything the littlest Schumaker had told her.

Schumaker was up to something in his pool house. After his children—and probably most of his help—had gone to bed, he entertained women. It didn't appear to be more complicated than that. Whether he had a drug habit or an underage girl habit, Winter couldn't decide. She needed more facts to determine if Freddie Schumaker was a lonely, horny divorcé or a sleazy sexual predator. She needed to see what was going on for herself.

If Gabriella had caught her father's late-night activities, the man wasn't hiding them as well as he thought. There might be a way for Winter to get a peek into the pool house when Schumaker was there.

With a plan brewing, Winter opened the map app on her phone and punched in the address to his mansion. The estate perimeter had a defined boundary of fences and gates, but the surrounding land appeared pristine.

On her phone, she could make out an uncleared field with a few trees located close to the back of Schumaker's property. Perfect. She could bypass Schumaker's security by gaining access to his property through the unclaimed land.

With a little patience and some good binoculars, she could set up an old-fashioned stakeout and unravel the mystery of what Schumaker did in his pool house after his kids went to bed. Winter might even ID a few of the girls if she was lucky.

It had been a long damn time since Winter'd had to climb a tree. She just hoped she remembered how.

17

Harper groaned, and the horrible, dull throbbing in her head grew worse as she attempted to open her eyes. Everything was blurry, and an icy wave of panic raced through her.

Why can't I see?

Her vision slowly cleared, and she could make out the cement floor beneath her. The cold closed in, wrapping around her bones. She shivered to get warm, but it did little good. That was when she noticed she couldn't move her arms.

She tried to sit up but failed. Cool metal kissed her wrists. Handcuffs. Had to be. It wasn't the first time she'd been in cuffs, but that was usually in bed while a man leered down at her. That was supposed to be fun... play...kink.

Was she being played with now? A joke taken a little too far?

She attempted to move her legs, but they remained pinned in place. Her head felt like it weighed a hundred pounds, taking all her energy to lift.

That was when she locked eyes with the woman across the small, dank room.

Handcuffed and with her ankles bound with duct tape, the woman appeared lifeless. But her eyes were open.

"I'm Bridget." The woman barely squeaked out the words.

A fresh surge of adrenaline shot through Harper, giving her the strength to fight her restraints. "Where am I?"

"It's no use." Bridget closed her eyes. "You won't get free. What's your name?"

Harper fought a few seconds more, not stopping until she was sweating, and her body began to ache. Heaving in a deep breath, she rested her shoulders against the hard floor. "Harper. How long have I been here?"

"Nice to meet you, Harper." Bridget groaned as she rolled to the side. "I don't know. I woke up, and there you were. Just like magic."

By the frailty in her voice, Harper could tell that Bridget was in terrible shape. The dim bulb hanging from the center of the room showed her disheveled hair, pale skin, and the dark circles rimming her eyes. Bridget was like a ghost.

"How long have you been in here?"

Bridget stared off into space as if trying to count the days. "Less than a week, I think. I'm not sure. I lose track of time without any sunlight for reference."

Harper's stomach heaved at the thought of spending more than another hour in the god-awful place. "Do you have any idea where we are?"

Bridget laughed, though the sound was edged with fear. "Hell, or at least, that's what I call it. It doesn't matter. I doubt we'll ever leave here alive."

A bitter taste climbed Harper's throat, adding to the panic coursing through her veins. "How can you say that? We must fight. We have to…to try and survive."

Bridget turned away, raising her face to the ceiling. "You

can't fight her. She's the worst part of all. The crazy bitch always stands over me, screaming that I don't matter anymore. You know, I'm beginning to believe her. If I mattered, I wouldn't be here."

Harper struggled to make sense of what Bridget had told her. She guessed that the crazy woman was the same one who had abducted her from the apartment. If Harper couldn't use her body to fight, at least she still had her mind. She needed to focus and figure out what to do.

"Tell me about her. What does she look like?"

Bridget's labored breathing was the only noise in the room. She turned, and the shadow of despair distorting her features sent a new burst of fear through Harper.

"I think she's the same woman who brought me here. I get the impression she's preparing to do something with us. To us. I'm not sure what."

Harper grabbed at a glimmer of hope. If they could stay one step ahead and give their minds something to focus on, they might have a chance.

Bridget's long, low moan echoed across the damp space. "This only happened to me because I was trying to be a good person. Something I haven't been for a long time. I stopped to help that crazy bitch." Her voice rose, showing she still had some life in her. "I thought it was the right thing to do. That *she* was a good person, that I could be a good person. I've done horrible things. I sometimes think I don't deserve to get out of here." Her sobs, drifting between the two bound women, made the room seem even colder.

Harper grew alarmed, wondering if Bridget's mind had wasted away like her body.

"You *are* a good person." Harper softened her tone to offer encouragement. "You will continue to be a good person. We're getting out of here. To do that, we have to work together. Now, think."

She might have dropped out of college, but Harper remembered reading in a psychology textbook that talking to a person, giving them exercises to work their mind, helped settle their anxiety. It could also bring some delirious moments of clarity. She desperately needed to keep Bridget grounded. Spending time with an unhinged, delusional cellmate would only add to her downfall.

"I know how I got here." Harper kept her gaze on Bridget. "I woke up to find a strange woman in my apartment. She threatened my family and said if I didn't cooperate, she'd kill them. What choice did I have? The moment I stepped out of my apartment building, I was shoved into a van and stabbed in the neck with a needle. The last thing I remember is falling on the blanket on the floor of the van. What's the last thing you remember before waking up in here?"

Bridget's fleeting smile evaporated as she returned her interest to the ceiling. "I remember the day my daddy blew his brains out. The blood, the mess he left behind. Then the peace of knowing he was gone, and I was safe. That was a great day." She snickered.

That made Harper wonder at her mental state.

"The son of a bitch deserved worse, though. It should have been slower and more painful. I would've liked to have watched that. Payback for all the years of pain he caused me. Why do you think he did it?"

Harper's throat tightened. Having a coherent conversation with Bridget might not be possible. Any plans to get away were all up to her.

She worked her way off her sore shoulder, no longer interested in talking. She wondered if Bridget was right, and they would never get out. Their only solace would be to escape into their happy memories before facing the end. And so far, Bridget wasn't pulling that off either.

The thought of dying in here terrified Harper more than

anything. Giving up wasn't in her nature. She wouldn't go down without a fight. And she planned on taking the bitch who put her in this dark room with her.

Harper swallowed back her tears when she realized the only person sharing her torment was no longer coherent. Worse than the thought of her isolation in the horrid room was the unimaginable fact that she might never get out of this prison alive.

18

The road ahead was dark, with only the occasional flare of a streetlight to guide my way. I gripped the wheel, searching for the turnoff leading to the rendezvous point. Getting rid of my packages would be the highlight of my evening. I had taken out the trash.

That's what they were to me. Women with no future who sold themselves to the highest bidder. They got what they deserved. I was only the instrument of their fate.

I glanced at my partner in the passenger seat. Ken sat slumped against the door, playing some game on his phone.

His careless attitude infuriated me. "Put that away and pay attention."

He scowled like a child told to put away a toy.

Keep it up. One day, I'll cut that impertinence out of you. I glanced at his crotch. *Or off you.*

The dirt road heading off the highway appeared, and I took a sharp right. I almost lost the back end of the van.

I grinned as Ken banged his head against the window from my reckless driving. If I couldn't kill him, I'd torture him within a breath of his sanity.

"Jesus." He rubbed his head. "Take it easy, will ya? You'll damage the goods."

Like he cared about "the goods." If left to my partner's discretion, none of the women I'd targeted would ever turn a profit for either of us. The fool would have raped them and left them for dead on the side of the road.

Men and their lust.

It ruled their heads and was why so many made mistakes. I was better than him, better than all men. Every dick owner I'd ever known had tried to push me past the brink of despair, but I wouldn't let them. In spite of them, I'd planned every detail, had contingencies, and remained dogged in my determination to cover my tracks. My idiot partner couldn't tie his shoelaces on most days.

Loose rocks from the gravel road clanked along the undercarriage as I headed toward a faint light.

I stayed diligent, checking my mirrors once again to make sure no one followed. The police, who were always breathing down our necks, necessitated rotating exchange spots, but I refused to let down my guard.

I'd never do that again.

An outline of a structure appeared. It turned into a tall building in the middle of a cleared field and was our designated drop-off point. It resembled more of a shed than a building, with a metal roof and fluted metal along the sides. The storage site was owned by a garage I frequented in the past and once housed auto parts.

I parked in front of a pair of wide doors and gazed up at the lamp above the entrance. Moths fluttered around the yellow bulb, sending dancing shadows along the ground.

I scoured the surrounding grounds and grumbled. "Where the hell are they?"

Irritated, I pulled out my phone and hit my contact's number.

It took him two rings to pick up, adding to my frustration. "You there?" he demanded in his hoarse voice.

"Where's your guy?" I tightened my grip on my phone, wishing it was his throat. "There's no one here."

"Hang on." The rustling of papers filtered through the phone's speaker. "These people don't miss a pickup."

His flippant attitude rubbed me the wrong way. He wasn't the one out here risking his neck. I was. "Your friends better not miss my payment either."

"They won't? The money will be transferred as soon as the package is secured." My contact hesitated and cleared his throat. "It's probably best if you stay in the van during the exchange. Let your partner handle it."

My fury simmered. "Why would I do that? This is *my* deal. You need to mind your business and let me handle things. You're just the setup guy. I'm the brains behind this operation. Don't ever forget that."

At that, he grunted. His mounting insolence would have to be dealt with soon.

"Don't push me." I deepened my voice. "You don't want to know what I can do to you."

His heavy sigh didn't soothe my anger. "All I'm saying is, it isn't safe. These men take what they please, and you have all the qualities they're looking for in a package. Let your partner—"

I hung up the phone before he could finish. *Asshole.*

Ken shrugged. "He has a point."

Headlights appeared in my rearview mirror. "Shut up and open the back of the van."

I climbed out, disgusted with the incompetents who assisted me. *The world is filled with imbeciles and whores.*

Another nondescript black van pulled alongside me as my partner opened the rear doors. I peeked inside, eager for a check of my cargo.

Harper and Bridget were both still drugged and unconscious. Harper's eyes rolled back, and her head lolled as I
grabbed her hair. Perfect.

Because of law enforcement's current interest in our
affairs, my associates requested the packages remained
senseless. It made transport a little more difficult, but the
added security was necessary. It seemed walking women
moving from one van to the next had aroused suspicion at
one of the drop-off points. That was not something any of us
wanted.

Dressed in all black, two burly men with arms thicker
than tree trunks exited the other van. My associates liked to
use ex-military for these runs, but the bulky men seemed
excessive for transporting sedated cargo.

One of the thugs moved toward me, his eyes darting into
the back of the van. "She alive? I was told she put up a fight."

The comment floored me. "Do you think I'd be stupid
enough to risk losing money? She's breathing. See for
yourself."

I stood back so he could inspect the merchandise. The
rear end of the van dipped as he stepped inside to get a closer
look.

When the thick henchman slung Harper over his shoulder, I couldn't help but smile. My smile grew even bigger
when the second dude carried Bridget off.

Bye bye, bitches.

The shipment had passed inspection, and the transfer was
underway. It was another successful drop that removed more
trash from the streets.

Today was a good day.

My partner slammed the doors shut and got back in
the van.

One of the hired muscle heads walked toward me,
carrying his phone.

He was less than a foot away when he held it up. The screen's bright light created a halo around me, and I worried that the glow would arouse unwanted suspicion.

But I had to know…

The transfer number on the screen flashed *sent*. Seconds later, my phone pinged, informing me that the transaction was complete, and my bank account was fifty thousand dollars richer.

Not bad for one night's haul.

One of the delivery guys sized me up. I knew that wry, hungry grin. I'd seen it on other men's faces ever since my figure became attractive to them. It was what happened when they let their dicks do the thinking. God, how predictable the opposite sex was.

He licked his lips. "You're pretty cute. You could fetch a good price where we're going."

I put my phone back in my jacket pocket, the same one that held my compact-carry Beretta. My fingers curled around the gun's handle. I eased it out of my jacket, determined to kill anyone who tried to turn me into the trash I hauled.

"I'm not one of the packages. I'm the supplier."

He inched closer, getting right in my face. His breath stank of beer. "We don't need more suppliers. We need more product. Good stuff customers will pay extra for."

With my finger on the trigger, the muzzle was against his temple in a flash. I knew it was a risk, but I had to show him who was in control. "I'm not interested." I stared into his cold eyes, showing no fear. "Are we done here?"

His hearty chuckle pissed me off. He stepped back, still laughing. "Sure, little girl. We're done here. For now."

My partner tugged on my arm. He'd gotten back out of the van when my gun came out. "We need to go."

I wanted to yell at the incompetent fool for telling me

what to do. I was in charge, but arguing in front of the associates was a bad move. No need to seem weak, especially since they now considered me potential fodder for their horny clients. I needed to maintain my edge.

Fuming, I headed back to the van. How dare those small-brained Neanderthals think I was in the same category as the lowlifes I transported? I wasn't trailer trash hooked on meth or a stripper dancing for drinks. I was a queen, and any man who crossed me would live to regret it.

I started the van, keeping a wary eye on the other vehicle in my side mirror. I slowly drove away, picturing our next meeting with that dick-for-brains and his cohorts. I'd have to keep my gun in my hand for all future transactions. It was the only way to guarantee my safety.

And if they so much as look at me, I'll blow them away.

19

After leaving the main road, the terrain in the field was not as rough as Winter had anticipated. The barren land gave the back of Schumaker's property a great deal of privacy and made for the perfect hiding place. Winter parked her SUV behind a line of trees, watching the moonrise for a moment before hopping out.

Ever since he showed up on her doorstep, she'd had an axe to grind with Freddie Schumaker. No one intimidated Winter, and she'd tangled with a lot worse than caustic businessmen like him. She was determined to find out the type of activities he tried to hide in his pool house, and that her plan lacked foresight didn't bother her.

She left her SUV behind and slung a backpack over her shoulder, ready to hike the short distance to the edge of the Schumaker property. The weight of her pack, the high grass, and the still surroundings reminded Winter of her training days at the FBI Academy. The sprints and long runs through open terrain while in full tactical gear were necessary to graduate. She'd loved the challenge then. Now she liked the solitude.

Ever since her brother kidnapped her nearly a year ago, Winter preferred her own company or that of her closest friends and family. Crowds, parties, and noise were like poison now. She knew she was different, something she hated to admit, but her history with two serial killers, as well as the visions one of the madmen left her with, cut her off from being categorized as normal ever again. Her circle of friends who could ever understand such a history remained small, and she preferred to keep it that way.

She crossed into a dense covering of brush dotted with a few trees, tucked up against the east side of the Schumaker estate. The high-powered binoculars in her pack made it so she didn't have to get too close to the property, but she did need a high vantage point to scope out the pool house.

Winter didn't take long to find a sturdy live oak with limbs bent low to the ground. It had a dense coverage of leaves, perfect camouflage, and she could easily shimmy down the thick trunk to get away if discovered.

She adjusted her pack and started up, taking her time to find her footing in the dark. Winter was a kid again, climbing trees and playing spy games with her neighborhood friends in Harrisonburg, Virginia. Luckily, she wasn't the same puny ten-year-old girl. She'd maintained her peak physical condition with running and rigorous workouts, making her ascent to the top a piece of cake.

However, finding a comfortable position to perform a stakeout was harder. She grimaced as a twig poked her butt. She slapped another out of the way. A rough patch of bark scraped her arm.

Just please don't let anything crawl on me. Ugh!

It took some maneuvering, but she found a good spot that gave her a full view of the side and rear of the mansion. The lights were on inside, and shadows moved back and forth in front of the large windows. Someone was home.

A spacious backyard had flickering brass lanterns show-casing the manicured gardens, crepe myrtle trees, and an array of lush, green ferns. Assorted benches and outdoor chaise lounges surrounded a kidney-shaped pool. At the far end, behind the pool, was a red-brick cabana with open French doors and white curtains billowing in the gentle breeze. The babble of the rock waterfall carried to Winter's spot. A hot tub closer to her vantage point showed no signs of life.

Winter sat back, taking in the idyllic locale and thinking of her husband.

He would love this.

Climbing trees to spy on suspects was right up his alley. She could picture him sitting back, listening to his country music—verbal valium to Winter—and chewing on beef jerky.

Barely two days apart, and she missed Noah like crazy. His case had kept him busy, giving them little time to talk. Winter wondered if she might catch him before his head hit the pillow. Her heart ached to hear her husband's voice, so she wrestled her phone from her pack, willing to take whatever minutes he could spare.

"Hello, beautiful." His deep drawl was heaven to her ears.

Winter peered around the dark land surrounding her. "What are you up to?"

Noah's chuckle warmed her bones. His laugh always chased away her worries. "I'm lying on my crappy motel bed, listening to my stomach gurgle after I ate what I think was a fish sandwich at the local diner."

She checked the back of the house with her binoculars again. "How's your case going?" His heavy sigh told her what she needed to know. "That bad, huh?"

"I spent the day with Eve, combing the area these traf-fickers work and branched out to other possible drop-off spots. But we didn't come up with a thing. We could be hitting the wrong places, or the people we're talking to are lying. I have a feeling quite a few people work for these guys, which only makes it harder to find evidence. They clean up after themselves very well."

The discouragement in his voice made her want to drive the four hours to his motel and wrap her arms around him. She decided to lighten his mood.

"Wanna guess where I am?"

"Um…unpacking boxes in our living room?" He sounded too hopeful.

Maybe telling him she was on a stakeout wasn't such a good idea. *Well…in for a penny and all that.*

"No, not yet. I'm sitting in a tree, doing surveillance on my client's ex. I didn't bring a cushion, so I have a branch poking me in the butt."

He chuckled. "Well, that's a new one. Why the tree?"

"It was the only way I could see into the ex's back garden." She peered down at the hot tub. "You should check out this setup. The house belongs in Beverly Hills, not Barton Creek."

"Just don't fall out of that tree." His tone turned sexy. "We have some catching up to do when I come home."

She could almost feel him beside her, brushing her cheek with kisses. "I sure hope so."

The lights along the first floor of the Schumaker house switched off. Winter perked up. "I've got to go. I think my subject is about to make a move."

Noah yawned. At least he wasn't too concerned about her whereabouts. "Be careful. I'll call you tomorrow. Love you, darlin'."

She smiled. "Love you too."

Winter tucked her phone away and checked the house with the binoculars again. The activity had moved upstairs. She hoped that meant bedtime for the children was about to begin.

She kept checking the time on her phone. One by one, the upstairs lights snuffed out, leaving the house in darkness. Her skin prickled with anticipation. It was almost eleven. Schumaker's nighttime activities should be about to start.

The flash of headlights at the entrance to the estate piqued her curiosity. The slam of car doors from the garage entrance and muffled voices drifted to her tree.

She waited, holding her breath out of habit. It wasn't long before there was activity in the garden. Shadowy figures moved out from the overhang along the rear of the house. The sound of women giggling trickled through the air. Soon, three figures walked next to the lanterns in the gardens on their way to the pool house.

A tall man had his arms around two slender women in colorful dresses. Winter exchanged the binoculars for a camera, twisting the lens until she could make out Schumaker's angular features.

Click.

His smile appeared charming, but to Winter, it came across as fake. The way he gripped the butts of the women showed his true intentions for the evening.

Click.

Winter repositioned herself as he led the two women into the pool house.

Cursing her vantage point, Winter wished she could have seen the women's faces better and gotten a feel for their ages. If she could identify one and run a check, she might get enough to slap Schumaker with corrupting a minor and statutory rape charges. It wasn't much, but it would help Julia's case.

Within seconds, the pool house lights turned on, giving Winter enough illumination to see inside the small building. Laughter carried across the back garden to her tree.

A loud pop caught her attention, and she spotted Schumaker pouring glasses of champagne for his guests. She concentrated on the women, noting their faces. They appeared to be women and not underage girls. At least this time.

Click.

After a few toasts and some glasses of champagne, the partiers loosened their inhibitions and began exploring each other. Schumaker initiated, kissing his partners' necks while his guests worked off his jacket and unbuttoned his shirt.

Click.

Winter continued taking pictures while Schumaker twirled the women around until they showed him their backs. Wearing a broad grin, he unzipped their dresses simultaneously, looking pleased with his agility. The women showed no apprehension as their frocks dropped to the ground. They stepped away, wearing only their lacy bras and panties.

The activities were about to become heated, but instead of sex, Schumaker pointed at a large, covered table in the center of the pool house.

When Schumaker snatched the cloth away, Winter almost laughed. As she figured, it was a pool table with the cues resting in a crisscross on the green felt. Schumaker handed each of the puzzled women a cue stick.

"The sticks?" Winter whispered to no one as she pictured Gabriella's drawing.

The little girl had captured what she'd seen. They weren't knives or swords or needles. They were cue sticks. That was what Gabriella saw. The *nakid notty girls* playing pool with Schumaker.

Schumaker racked the balls, and Winter could almost hear the smack of the cue ball hitting its targets. When he sank the first one in the corner pocket, he pointed his cue at one of the women. She removed her bra but made no move to cover her bare breasts. She lifted her glass of champagne, toasted Schumaker, and laughed.

Somehow, the intimidating man on Winter's doorstep didn't jive with the college bad boy she watched entertaining call girls with strip pool.

Schumaker sank another ball and required a racier article of lingerie. The laughter became nauseating.

This is what Gabriella witnessed.

Winter had been right. Simple surveillance was all she needed to solve this case. There wasn't much she could do about the bitterness between Julia and Schumaker, but she could walk away knowing the mother of three had nothing more to worry about than a horny but juvenile ex who enjoyed some PG-rated kink.

Winter was thinking about packing up, desperate to climb down from her tree. Her butt hurt, and she just wanted to go to bed. She couldn't, of course. She needed to see this through to capture any and all evidence on film.

Headlights suddenly flashed before a large outbuilding to the side of Schumaker's bazillion-car garage. Winter repositioned herself, interested in the new arrivals. She strained to glimpse the road to the mansion but wasn't sure a car had come from the security gate. She would have seen the lights before now.

An uneasy hitch caught her chest when she directed her binoculars to a black van sitting in front of the white building. The headlights flashed again.

Is that a signal?

Lights off, the van pulled into the outbuilding. Winter waited for the driver to emerge, but she didn't see anyone leaving.

Is that an employee with a delivery?

"Kind of late for that," she muttered while keeping her gaze focused on the outbuilding.

She waited for any activity, her camera ready.

And waited.

And waited.

No one left the van that she could see, and naked pool didn't evolve into group sex.

Interesting. Or not so interesting.

She waited two more hours, not leaving until all the lights inside the pool house went out and all was quiet. Seemed like the girls were spending the night. Time to go home.

After Winter packed up her gear, she headed down the tree. The late-night arrival remained a mystery, but as far as Winter was concerned, she'd hadn't witnessed anything nefarious.

Tomorrow morning, she'd contact Julia and put her mind at ease. Schumaker might be an asshole, but from what she'd been able to see that night, he wasn't the depraved character his former wife believed him to be.

20

W inter sat at her desk in her cozy home office, coffee mug in hand, and studied the flashing message light on her office phone. She had three messages waiting from potential clients and was almost ready to settle on which downtown location she liked best. She might make it as a private investigator after all.

But before she could take on another client, she needed to finish up with her current one.

After the night's activities, Winter had recharged her batteries by sleeping in. She dialed Julia's number, enjoying the morning sun shining through her home office window. She was glad to have slept so well, despite Noah's absence from her bed. Or maybe it was the satisfying conclusion of her case with Julia that enlivened her. Either way, optimism for a new day flowed through her.

"What did you find out?" Julia sounded as nervous as the first day Winter laid eyes on her.

There was no point in beating around the bush. "I got a look at what's happening in your ex-husband's pool house, and I think I know what Gabriella's drawing is about."

"That son of a bitch," Julia shouted. "He's hurting women, isn't he?"

Winter peered into her coffee, wishing for another fortifying sip. "Well, I'm not sure about the hurting part, but he is entertaining ladies back there."

"Hookers? He's bringing hookers into my children's home, and what?" Julia's rapid-fire breathing burst through the speaker. "He's having orgies. That's it, isn't it?"

Winter kept her voice steady. "All I could see was Freddie playing strip pool with a couple of women. They did that for several hours and then the lights went out and I wasn't able to see anything else. I don't know if they're call girls, but I feel certain they're not underage. What's going on appears to be between consenting adults."

A few tense seconds passed before Julia blew out a long breath. "That's a relief, but it still doesn't make me feel better. After what happened this morning, I'm damn near frantic. Something isn't right at the house."

The office phone on Winter's desk rang twice. She waited as the call rolled over to voicemail before she spoke. "What happened?"

"My son called this morning saying he felt sick and wanted to come and stay with me. Of course, I had to clear it with Freddie first. But when I spoke to him, our call ended abruptly. I heard Gilbert shouting in the background. Something about Freddie taking away his phone. He sounded upset."

The hairs on Winter's arms rose. "When was this?"

"About half an hour ago. I've been trying to get ahold of someone at the house, but no one's picking up. Not the kids' cell phones, or even the house phone the staff answers. I was about to go over there myself when you called."

"You can't just go over and demand to be let in. You don't need that trouble with Schumaker." Winter tapped the rim of her mug. "I can call the police and demand a wellness check. I have a friend at the local station who owes me a favor. His name is Darnell Davenport."

"I need to go with you," Julia argued.

The office phone on Winter's desk rang again. She ignored it. "No, I'll go." The blinking message light distracted her. "Schumaker can't do anything to me, not when I'm with a police officer. You stay put."

She checked the number of voicemails waiting for her. How could she have six messages already?

"You have to call as soon as you know something." Julia's voice had a panicked edge to it. "I'm going crazy with worry."

"As soon as I know, you will. It'll be all right. Stay calm." Winter hung up, not sharing Julia's concern.

She'd seen enough cell towers go down from storms, blown transformers, or human error. She remained convinced the Schumaker household appeared cut off at the owner's demand, not in trouble.

The flashing message light deflated Winter's optimistic mood. She didn't need a new office. She needed an assistant. Unfortunately, finding the time to find an assistant was a task for an assistant.

She sat back in her chair, eyeing the boxes piled in her living room. *Maybe I can get an assistant to unpack for me too?*

Winter put her office situation on the back burner and dialed Detective Davenport's number. Of all the people she could call when in a tight spot, he was one of the few she trusted.

He answered on the first ring, which, from what little she'd learned about him so far, was so Darnell. As a driven perfectionist, he was skeptical of everyone he met, but once you earned his confidence, he appeared to be intensely loyal.

"So how's Austin's newest P.I.?" Darnell asked in a deep, throaty voice. His friendliness could be disarming, and though she'd only met the detective once, she'd like him immediately.

"In need of a favor."

There was a moment of silence before he groaned. "Should I be worried?"

"Not worried. Not yet, anyway." She crossed her fingers that she was trusting the right person. "I've got a client. Freddie Schumaker's ex."

"You do like to swim in the deep end of the pool. He's big money."

"I know, but it seems his ex can't get ahold of anyone at the house. The phones are all dead. Her kids are there, staying with their father. It was a contentious divorce, and I don't want my client going over unannounced."

"I remember the Schumaker divorce. There was a sex tape, I believe."

Unbelievable.

Is the sex tape all anyone remembers?

"She's a panicked mother, terrified for her kids, and I just want to put her mind at ease and do—"

"A welfare check," Darnell cut in.

Winter sighed. "Yeah. Can you help me?"

In the background, ringing phones and the buzz of conversation drifted through her speaker. It reminded her of her Bureau office. The VCD was never as busy as a police department, but it had the same tempo.

"I have some free time later this morning. I don't want you at the station, so I'll pick you up from your house at eleven, and I'll drive us there. But let me do the talking. Agreed?"

Winter wanted to balk at the instructions, but knew she had no choice. She wasn't a federal agent anymore. She was an investigator who had to bend to the will of local law enforcement.

"Thank you, Darnell. If I can ever repay the favor, let me know."

He chuckled. "How are you going to help me?"

Winter grinned, glad to get a rise out of him. "I'm surprised at you, Detective Davenport. I can do certain things for you that officers can't. And you can do the same for me. Ours can be a mutually beneficial relationship."

Darnell laughed, louder than before, and hung up.

Winter wasn't put off. She knew to get ahead in her business, she needed to develop a good rapport with the police. One day, Darnell would need her help. And she'd be there, ready to return the favor, no matter how disagreeable.

If asked to dig a grave, Winter wouldn't hesitate. She'd just grab a shovel and get to work.

21

S trips of sunlight landed on Harper's face, waking her from a restless sleep. She batted at the intrusion and opened her eyes, her head still foggy. Muscles trembling, she sat up and peered around. Perched on a cracked and rotted wood floor, Harper discovered she and Bridget had been moved from the cell made of cinder blocks to a crumbling room with peeling paint on the walls and a reek of urine.

They weren't alone in the room. Others were there—whether sleeping or drugged, she couldn't tell. They were all women. Pretty, young, bruised, and emaciated, left sprawled on the floor, as if they'd been tossed in like ragdolls. They wore anything from sweats to leggings to fancy dresses. A wave of nausea overtook Harper as she counted twelve women who didn't look older than twenty. And there were three girls…

They're just children.

One of the youngest couldn't have been more than ten. Harper's heart ached as she took in her school uniform. The pricey private school was outside of Austin. That meant the women were local, like her.

The pieces quickly fell into place. She clenched her fist, pushing back against whatever drug had infiltrated her system.

Think. Find a way out.

A moan to her right had her searching a tangle of legs and arms. Bridget, the pretty brunette who'd shared her cell during the past few days, struggled to raise her head.

Harper helped her into a sitting position, patting her cheeks to rouse her. Which was when she realized she was no longer bound. Neither was anyone else. She wasn't sure if that was a good or bad thing.

It was good because she had more freedom of movement. But she wouldn't have this freedom if her captors weren't sure she couldn't escape.

Focus on one thing at a time.

"Wake up, Bridget."

The other woman wiped her eyes. "Where are we?"

Harper let her go. "My guess? Next stop on whatever pipeline we're on."

Bridget blinked, as if trying to rouse herself. "Pipeline? What are you talking about?" Her mouth slipped open when she spotted the youngest captive. "She's just a little girl."

Harper wiped the sweat from her brow. "And worth more to sex traffickers. Everything makes sense now. We've been sold. I've heard trafficking is big in the area."

She closed her eyes, overcome by a wave of nausea. Harper remembered her brutal capture and how the woman who took her tempted her with a drink of water, only to drive a needle into her neck. "What do you last remember?"

Bridget shook her head. "We were in that room, and the woman came back. She shot us up with something, and then we passed out."

Harper's last vision had been of the cruel bitch injecting a weak Bridget with a syringe. The poor woman had been too frail to fight back.

"So why are we awake and the others still asleep?" Harper asked, thinking out loud.

Bridget rubbed her temples. "Maybe we're meant to be awake to see what happens to us. It's payback for the bad I've done."

Harper examined her companion, remembering the strange things she'd talked about in the dark. She wanted to shake the woman's shoulder and snap her out of her delusions. Instead, she kept her voice soft and encouraging.

"Bridget, you need to stay with me. We didn't cause what's happening here. We're the victims. We've been packed into this room like cattle, waiting for…I don't know what, but I need you to focus."

Bridget's bloodshot eyes checked her over. "What do you want to do?"

"Escape," Harper whispered.

Bridget's low chuckle was like a storm siren in the quiet room. "I think we're way past that point. Whoever set this up isn't going to let us walk away."

Harper's muscles trembled, and she hoped it was the drugs wearing off. "Won't be easy, but it's worth a try. I know one thing. I'd rather fight my way out and risk dying than going wherever they plan to take us. I won't end up handcuffed to a bed while a parade of men rape me until I don't even know my name."

Bridget's droopy eyelids popped open. This was the most lucid Harper had seen her companion since first meeting her in their dark hell.

"Yeah, I don't want that either." Bridget sucked in a breath and raised her head. "Let's fight back."

Harper had never been so happy to see someone come to

life. It was as if she wasn't alone anymore. Bridget's drifting in and out of clarity over the past few days had frustrated her immensely. Now, she had an ally, a cohort, a friend.

She fixed her gaze on the door across the room. "Someone's going to come through there. It's the only way in or out. They won't be expecting a fight." She scanned the other sleeping women around her. "We're supposed to be drugged like the rest. That sadist who held us hostage must have screwed up the dose somehow."

"So what do you want to do?" Bridget asked.

Harper climbed to her feet. She wobbled, praying she had the strength to carry out her plan. She reached for Bridget and helped her from the floor.

"I'll wait at the door. You'll hide behind it." She kept her arm around Bridget's waist, holding her up. "I'll charge whoever enters, hopefully knocking them off their feet. You make a break for it and run out the door. I'll be right behind you. Promise."

Bridget stumbled backward, trembling. "What if there's more of them waiting outside? What if we run straight to our deaths?"

Harper held her shoulders, squeezing hard, desperate for her words to get through. "I understand if you don't want to chance it. I don't blame you, but if we stay, *they will kill us.* Maybe not for days, months, or even years, but when we're no longer profitable, when the men who have raped and tortured us no longer want us, they will end us. I'd rather die trying to escape than let those bastards break me."

Bridget hesitated, appearing to weigh her options. Still shaking, she placed her hand over Harper's and blew out a breath. "Okay, I'm with you. No matter what."

They held hands and made their way across the floor, careful not to step on anyone.

Harper showed Bridget where to wait and took her position just outside the door, clenching her fists, ready to throttle the first person she saw.

Time ticked by. Minutes, an hour, she wasn't sure. The light shining through the slivers in the wall moved slowly across the floor.

Harper struggled against bouts of fatigue and dizziness. Bridget remained propped against the wall, paler than a ghost.

"You still with me?"

Bridget gave her a thumbs-up as footsteps sounded outside the door.

Harper's heartbeat pounded in her ears as the rattle of the lock carried into the room. She tensed, summoning every ounce of energy she had.

The moment the door swung open, Harper charged.

She couldn't tell if it was a man or woman, as she was blinded by the morning light, but she lowered her shoulder and hit them right in the gut like a defensive lineman going after a quarterback. Her victim fell backward, landing on their ass with an angry grunt followed by a shriek of pain. She'd injured them.

Harper jumped to her feet as the fresh, cool air, free of urine and fear, injected her system with a shot of adrenaline. She looked down as the person, a skinny young guy, held his gut and choked as he tried to catch enough air. She stepped over him and turned to look for Bridget.

"Run!" Harper screamed, just as Bridget tore through the doorway.

Harper spotted a line of trees that hopefully led to woods where they could hide. A football field away. A few sheds stood in front of the trees, but she didn't see any other people. Well, not yet, anyway.

In any case, she took off running when her feet touched the ground. The fresh air she sucked in continued to clear her head, and the thrill of freedom spurred her on. Harper wanted to cry out when she looked up at the sun peeking out from behind a gray cloud. It seemed like an eternity since she'd been outside.

The icy grip of fear replaced her momentary exuberance when shouting erupted behind her.

She picked up her pace.

Bridget kept up with her, kicking her heels in a steady run.

Harper's heart hammered, her lungs burned, and her legs ached. She wanted to collapse after just a few yards, but the terror of returning to that disgusting room kept her going.

They were almost to the trees when a gunshot rang out.

Harper stumbled, terrified by the loud bang. She ached to glance behind her and count how many were on their tail, but it would only slow her down.

Just keep running.

When she reached the cover of the sheds, Harper paused and searched for Bridget. She wasn't there.

She hurried on to the safety of the trees, stopping inside the shady sanctuary to check on the whereabouts of her friend. She found Bridget leaning against one shed a few feet away, holding her side. Blood oozed around her hand and dripped down her leg.

Terror tightened Harper's throat. "Bridget!" She made a move toward her, but Bridget raised her hand.

"No. Go. Run."

Harper watched as the young woman then did something truly heroic…she smiled.

"I'll be right behind you. Promise."

Harper didn't want to leave her, but with the thick stream

of blood coming from Bridget's side, she couldn't run, and Harper couldn't carry her. She had to get help. For Bridget and all the girls. She hurried deeper into the woods. She had to survive. She had to tell the world about the others that were left behind.

She had to.

22

Noah sat behind the wheel of his car, tired of the layer of dust covering his suit, the taste of grit in his teeth, and the constant stuffiness in his nose. Roy Rogers sang a song about tumbleweeds tumbling down windswept streets. Here, he was witnessing that actually happening. Every town he and Eve had visited west of Helton was the same. Small streets, dust coming off the surrounding dry land, and tumbleweeds out the ass.

"If I see one more of those damn balls on the side of the road, I'm gonna shoot it."

Eve chuckled as she held onto her paper cup of dark roast. "Wait until you start seeing things comin' out of them tumbleweeds." She sipped her coffee, eyeing the two-lane highway ahead. "I once drove two days straight across the state doin' interviews. When I got back to Austin, I was convinced aliens existed and tumbleweeds were where they hid out."

Noah checked the side of the road. "Two days, and I'm about to lose it. All this driving makes me miss the green of Austin."

Eve glanced out her window. "I don't know. There's somethin' awfully pretty about the dry land out here. Sure makes for beautiful sunsets."

For his part, Noah preferred watching sunsets with his wife and tended to ignore them while working. "How many more of these small towns do you want to hit today?"

Eve set her coffee in the console holder. "I'm worried the trail might have gone cold on those vans. We keep heading west, and everyone we talk to hasn't noticed a thing. We need another plan of action."

"Don't give up yet. We haven't even made our second stop of the day. Maybe the next gas station will give us something."

"I sure hope so." Eve reached around to their grab bag of food for the trip. She removed a paper napkin and wiped her hands. "If I have to set foot in another slimy convenience store and buy one more six-pack of coke and day-old hotdog, I might shoot *you*."

Noah cracked a grin, grateful for Eve's snarky sense of humor. Thank goodness she kept him entertained on the long drives between the list of gas stations they were inspecting.

Eve pulled up the map on her cell phone. "The next one, Crockett Rocket Gas and Go, is just ahead."

"Crockett Rocket?" Noah made a face. "Did you just make that up?"

Eve picked up her coffee. "Not even if I was drunk."

A sign appeared touting the clean bathrooms and well-stocked snack store of Crockett Rocket Gas and Go. They even had a logo of a squirrel wearing a red vest with a white rocket ship on it.

Now I've seen everything.

The rundown station, which resembled an old red barn, appeared not long after the sign. The station had only one old-fashioned pump and several rusted and broken-down junkyard cars in front. The only thing Noah was confident they would get from the dilapidated structure was tetanus.

He parked in front, peering into the grimy window. "Are you sure this place is even open?"

Eve put her phone in her jacket pocket. "It's open. The lights are on."

Noah rechecked the building's façade. "How can you see any lights through those windows?"

Eve opened her door while Noah turned off the engine, still peering through the windshield. He moved the front of his jacket aside as he stood from the vehicle to show off the badge clipped to his belt. It saved time if everyone knew who he was before asking questions.

Or pulling guns.

His partner entered the small store, setting off the bell above the glass door. Noah hurried to catch up, grimacing against the stiff cold breeze. The temperature was colder here than in Austin.

Inside, the heated air smelled of stale coffee and motor oil. He couldn't decide which was worse.

The convenience portion of the station consisted of two aisles. One for chips, the other for candy. A glass cooler stood at the rear, offering beer and soft drinks.

Behind the register were two doors that opened onto a full-service garage. An old Ford pickup sat on the rack, minus its four tires.

Eve stood at the register, her attention fixed on the redheaded man-child with acne and a cigarette he didn't appear old enough to smoke tucked behind his ear. His glassy, bloodshot eyes stared at Eve, and his unsteady sway, along with the t-shirt proclaiming, *Stay High Get By*, intrigued Noah.

"You cops?" the attendant asked.

Eve glanced at Noah and did the official introduction.

"We're checking gas stations along the highway between here and Helton." Noah removed a grainy photo from his coat pocket and set it on the counter in front of the clerk. "You ever see black vans like this stopping here? Maybe with women on board. Scared women who look out of place."

The young man ignored the photo and pointed at Noah and Eve, grinning. "You two seem out of place, man."

Eve rested her elbow on the register counter. "What's your name?"

He checked out the gun her posture exposed. His head bobbled. "Kip."

Noah glanced over Kip's shoulder to the garage. "Is the owner here?"

Kip scratched a pimply arm before quickly folding both across his midsection. "No, man. It's only me. The owner never comes in no more."

Noah nodded toward the garage. "Who works on the cars?"

Kip wiped his nose on his sleeve. "Damn if I know."

The attendant couldn't stop fidgeting behind the counter. Eve kept her gaze locked on him. Neither she nor Noah spoke, letting their silence intimidate their intended target. This proven interrogation method worked particularly well on the guilty and the high.

It didn't take Kip long to crack. "You gonna buy somethin' or what?"

The edginess in his voice wasn't lost on Noah, and he couldn't figure out if the guy was coming down or still up in the clouds.

Eve leaned across the counter. "We're not buying anything, Kip. We're waiting for you to tell us what you know."

Kip dropped his gaze and picked at a scab on his hand. "I don't know nothin'."

With his panicked voice rising to a crescendo, Noah knew he wasn't telling the truth. He didn't need to be a body language expert to work out that much.

"I've heard the same thing from guys with a lot more backbone than you, son. Why don't you come clean. We're not here to bust you for using."

As much as Noah wished he could arrest the kid and get him into a rehab program, he knew the chances of that succeeding were a million to one. Kip had all the tells of a hardcore user.

In that instant, Kip's hands erupted with shakes and jitters. He tried to hide it by putting his arms behind him, but it was too late. Noah knew he'd started coming down from whatever he'd taken.

Only the hard drugs gave someone such an instant withdrawal. With heroin and meth being popular in this part of the state, Noah suspected Kip was much more of a hardcore user than he first imagined. "I think you do know something. You flinched when I showed you that picture."

Kip stuck out his chin, appearing indignant. "N… No, I didn't."

He hadn't flinched, but Noah wasn't about to tell him that. Neither, apparently, was Eve.

"I saw it too. Tell us what you know. Otherwise, we'll have to take you back to our headquarters and question you." Eve flashed a quick grin. "And we might have to keep you three, four—"

"Five, six days." Noah jumped in, guessing what Eve had planned. "You sure you can last that long without a fix?"

A junkie faced with being without his drug for a long time would go to great lengths to avoid withdrawal. Even snitch to two federal agents.

Kip's eyes bulged. "You can't take me anywhere without a warrant!"

Eve folded her arms, rocking her hips in a cocksure manner. "We don't need one when we suspect someone is lying to us. When lives are in danger, we have carte blanche."

The color in Kip's cheeks drained away. "What's cart...? Is that some kind of torture?"

Noah refrained from rolling his eyes. Sometimes, the criminals made it way too easy.

"We can't tell you that." Eve whipped her long ponytail around. "It's classified."

Noah had to bite his lower lip to keep from laughing. "Now, you want to change your statement about the van?"

Kip glanced at the photo on the counter. He placed his hands under his armpits to stop his shaking. "No. I mean, maybe. Hell, I don't know."

His quavering voice was good. He was close to cracking.

Noah put his index finger on the picture and pushed it closer. "Think, Kip. Think real hard."

Eve flourished a set of handcuffs she'd retrieved from her jacket. "Should I cuff him now?"

Kip backed away from the counter, holding up his hands. "All right. All right, already. I'll tell you what I know, just don't take me in, man. This job is all I got, and if I lose it, I won't get another in this stinking town. Everyone knows me and won't hire me, because..." He didn't need to finish the sentence.

Eve tossed the cuffs on the counter for purely dramatic effect, Noah guessed. She scrunched her lips together. "So talk."

Kip wrung his hands, taking one last glance around the empty store.

Paranoia—gotta love the side effects of drug use. Sometimes, it made Noah's job so much easier.

"I've seen them vans before. Black ones. They roll through here at odd times."

Noah leaned on the counter, his appetite whetted. "What's in the vans?"

Kip ran his hands through his red mop, appearing ready to tear his hair out by the roots. "Women. The young and pretty kind."

"Trafficking?" Noah's stomach clenched at the possibility.

Kip nodded. "There's a ring in these parts. I'm not involved, and neither is the station. Mr. Henry flat-out told those guys to take a flying leap, but a lot of other businesses are involved. The money's good. Real good, and when you're desperate…" He shrugged his bony shoulders. "Anyways, I know where they keep them girls. There's a house nearby, sort of a holding place. Everyone in town knows about it."

A mixture of anger and relief rolled through Noah. How could people be so apathetic? At least he had something solid to go on. "Where?"

"I'll draw you a map." Kip searched under the counter for paper.

Eve nodded at Noah. "I'll get in touch with the local police. We'll need them to assist." She stepped out of the shop.

Noah glared as daydreams of throttling the young man for not speaking up sooner danced through his mind. "Why have you never said anything before?"

Kip placed a scrap of paper from the register's receipt roll on the counter. He clicked the pen several times before he spoke. "'Cause I didn't want to fuckin' die, man."

Noah restrained his fist from connecting with the man's jaw. "We can protect you. You could have spared dozens of women from a fate worse than death."

Kip lowered his head. "I know, but I guess that don't matter now. Those guys will find out I tipped the cops.

They'll come for me. And there ain't a damn thing you can do to save me."

23

Winter sat in the passenger seat of Detective Darnell Davenport's unmarked car, gritting her teeth. She wished that she hadn't agreed to let the detective pick her up from her home. She'd prefer to be driving herself, but what was done was done.

Ahead, the same muscle-bound guard she'd had a run-in with two days ago flagged the vehicle to a stop outside the Schumaker mansion's gate.

Well, if he recognizes me, I'll just power through.

Darnell rolled down his window and flashed his badge. "Detective Davenport here to do a wellness check. We've had a request from the mother of the children in the home."

Winter smiled as the beefy guard lowered his reflective sunglasses and checked the car's interior.

Though a hint of recognition flashed through his eyes, he motioned to the gate. "Go right ahead, Detective."

Winter missed her badge more than ever. That one little shiny piece of metal took away the roadblocks men like Schumaker's security guard put in front of her at every turn.

Darnell waited as the ornate, black, monogrammed gates opened. "He seemed friendly."

Winter snorted. "Yeah, try doing it without the badge. That requires talent. Trust me."

He tapped the accelerator. "I'm not even going to ask what you're talking about. I don't want to know."

He was right. He didn't.

They drove along the road, and when the three-story, custom-wood and dark-brick home appeared, Darnell gave a low whistle. "Damn. I've never seen anything like this. Even in Austin."

Winter glanced at the opulent home. "You mean you didn't grow up with a silver spoon in your mouth?"

"No way." He shook his head. "My mother was a school-teacher, and my father worked the railroad. I was the first to graduate college in my family."

"That sounds like a pretty good childhood. It's not the money that matters, but the love."

Winter often envied those who had known happiness growing up. She had large chunks of her childhood she longed to forget.

Darnell climbed the stone steps, and Winter stuck close to his side. She stopped beneath the massive copper lantern and reached for the doorbell to one side of the carved doors.

"You sure about this?" Darnell traced the geometrical designs carved into the wood. "A house like this probably has loads of security."

"Yep, Schumaker's got cameras everywhere. They've probably recorded us arriving, but that doesn't mean someone can't get inside. There are ways on the estate without setting off the security systems."

Darnell narrowed his eyes. "If you've been here before without permission, I don't want to know. So don't say another word. And let me handle this, before you incriminate yourself."

Winter opened her mouth to argue, but one of the large doors opened.

"Ah." Belinda Merril's smirk reeked of contempt as she glared at Winter. Her sweater was a lighter shade of pink today. "What are you selling this time?" Her gaze turned to Darnell. "And you brought a friend. How nice."

Darnell flashed his badge, his face like stone. "I'm Detective Davenport with the Austin PD. I'm here doing a wellness check on one Gilbert Schumaker. His mother, Julia Eversmeyer, notified the police that she hasn't been able to contact her son."

Belinda's swagger melted as she eyed the badge. "Gilbert's fine. He's upstairs sick, is all." The contempt in her gaze returned to Winter. "What's she? Your sidekick?"

Darnell pocketed his badge. "Ms. Black is here at the request of Ms. Eversmeyer. Now, I need to see Gilbert."

Winter almost wished she could return to her old job and experience the rush the badge gave her.

Belinda backed away from the door and waved them inside. Her bare feet didn't make a sound on the marble floor. "Mr. Schumaker is at work, but I can take you to Gilbert. He's in his room. In bed."

They stepped inside the massive grand entryway, and Winter kept her attention on Darnell. He soaked in the decorative plaster ornamentation of roses in the cathedral ceiling and the ornate benches made of thick mahogany with burgundy velvet cushions.

His eyebrows rose as he inspected the newel carved to resemble a Greek goddess. "Quite a place," he muttered as they crossed the white marble floor to the walnut staircase.

"I'll be glad to reassure you that Gilbert is in no danger." Belinda started up the wide staircase. The black leggings showed her curvy bottom off perfectly. "I understand Julia's concern for her son, but he's well cared for. It's natural for a child to want their mother when they're ill. Gilbert is sixteen but still a child in so many ways."

Winter's patience smoldered as she followed the nanny. "Then why did his father take away his phone?"

Belinda stopped at the second-floor landing, her smile intact. "I'm sure Mr. Schumaker had his reasons."

She led them down a hallway decorated with the same white silk and gold-gilded wallpaper seen on the first floor. Doors made of thick, dark wood lined the hall.

Belinda stopped at the second one on the right. "He's in here." She knocked before entering. "Gil, it's Belinda. Your mother has sent people to see you." She turned the brass doorknob and walked into the room.

The home's grandeur disappeared, and an adolescent boy's hormones took over the space. Walls covered with pictures of fast cars and women wearing barely-there bikinis greeted them.

A dresser with a few open drawers had clothes strewn on top of it, while a desk by the window displayed the latest in gaming computer equipment. A partially opened closet showed a floor covered with athletic shoes and boots. And in the center of the room, Gil hid under a royal-blue comforter on a raised platform bed. Beside that, a violin sat on a metal stand.

The tossed clothes and gaming devices Winter understood. The violin took her a moment to digest.

Someone rustled beneath the covers of the bed. A blond, brown-eyed young man with Schumaker's sharp features and Julia's mouth sat up and stared at his visitors.

"Belinda?" Gilbert blinked his red-rimmed eyes. "What's going on?"

Darnell stepped forward before Belinda could speak.

"Forgive the intrusion, Gilbert, but your mother sent us to check up on you. I'm Detective Davenport, and this is Winter Black, a friend of your mother's."

Gilbert's eyes widened, and Winter instantly regretted barging into the home. "I'm sorry. Your mother was worried when she couldn't get ahold of you after you told her you were sick. She said something about hearing your father threaten to take away your phone before you were cut off."

Gilbert sat up, revealing blue pajamas with his initials swirled onto the top pocket.

Personalized pajamas? On a teenager? Now I've seen it all.

"Ah," Gilbert's gaze darted to Belinda, "my dad was being an ass. I wanted to go to my mom's, and he got mad. Anything about her lately sets him off. I figured it was the divorce. He's been a dick since…I mean, he's been upset since then."

The young man's red face concerned Winter. He had fair skin, and the reddish hue made him appear feverish.

"You're sure you're okay?" Winter stepped closer to get a better look.

Gilbert ran his hand through his hair. "It's just a bug. Probably what my little sister had a couple of days ago."

The red in his cheeks darkened.

Winter turned back to Belinda, wondering if she saw the same thing. Either he was an expert blusher, or Winter's ability was giving her a sign. Something about Gilbert was off. He was keeping a secret from everyone.

Neither Belinda nor Darnell seemed too interested in Gilbert's changing color, which only confirmed Winter's belief that her gift had picked up on the boy's inner turmoil.

Darnell checked his watch. "Thank you for your time, Gilbert. Now that we know everything's okay, we'll leave you to recover." He turned to Winter with a *we need to get out of here* glower.

Winter wasn't in a hurry to leave just yet. "What did Gabriella have? I mean, if she recovered quickly, then there's a good chance you will too. Or has Grace been sick too?"

Gilbert shot a wary gaze at Belinda, his forehead turning the same color as his cheeks. "Uh…" He coughed into his hand.

Belinda went to the bed, and placed her hand on Gilbert's forehead, caressing him in a motherly fashion. She seemed to dote on the boy.

Winter wondered if she'd noticed the same discoloration. Belinda's affection struck her as rather much for a nanny. Or maybe that was Winter's skepticism coloring her thinking? After all, what did she know about raising kids?

"He needs his rest." Belinda curtly motioned to the open bedroom door. "I can show you out."

Winter didn't want to leave the boy, but she couldn't think of a reason to stay. She followed Belinda and Darnell out of the bedroom and waited in the hall as the nanny shut the door. The click of the lock set off a flurry of horrible fears.

Was the eldest Schumaker child being poisoned? Abused? What could have caused that odd color on his face? Had Gilbert seen something far worse than Gabriella had witnessed in the pool house?

The questions kept surfacing.

Winter scanned the upstairs hall for signs of something amiss in the household, but there were no pieces of over-turned or broken furniture or bottles of anything cluttering trays. Maybe she'd worked too many cases with abused children and psychopaths. Had she let her imagination get the better of her?

Belinda reached the first floor and walked straight to the front doors. Her abrupt manner raised even more suspicions, and Winter couldn't help but wonder if the nanny knew more than she'd admitted.

Shown out of the home without even a goodbye, the slam of the massive, wooden door pissed Winter off.

"Well, that was a waste of time." Darnell removed his keys from his pocket. "The kid's fine."

"Is he?" Winter wasn't convinced. "Did you see his face? He was so red. That's not normal."

Darnell stopped halfway and glanced at her. "Like I would know what's normal for a sick boy." He chuckled. "Find another angle, Black. You got nothing on Schumaker or his child-rearing abilities."

Winter grumbled under her breath, wanting to challenge her friend. He was right, though. There was nothing to suspect Schumaker was criminally negligent with his kids.

So why was there a nagging sensation in her gut?

Unsettled as ever, Winter no longer believed her case with Julia Eversmeyer was over. She had a feeling it had only just begun.

24

The clock on the wall moved at the speed of a turtle on Xanax. I couldn't wait to leave my desk. Mundane tasks bored me. Besides, I'd become preoccupied with my newest obsession.

Cleaning up the world.

The doodle of a woman bound and gagged on my tablet did nothing to keep me awake. I drew my package, wanting to remember her pain, memorialize it. If I had to live with what he'd put me through, then I'd make sure everyone else he touched did too.

When my phone vibrated in my backpack, I perked up. Anything to get away from my desk.

I snuck the phone from the side pocket, making sure no one saw. I was overly cautious about my business. Nosy people were a liability. I never liked loose ends.

A text stared back at me. *We need to talk ASAP.*

I stifled a scream. My damned partner had sent the message. What did the pesky little asshole want now?

Gathering my things, I slid from my desk and stole away to

the rear exit. No one even noticed. If stopped, I could use every woman's excuse for needing a speedy escape to the bathroom. Everyone hated talking about periods, men especially.

In the hall, I checked for any others lingering about. The last thing I needed was anyone following or interrogating me.

The white walls with decorations touting the different community clubs made me nauseous. Social activities weren't my thing. Well, that wasn't entirely true. I had extra-curricular pursuits that I enjoyed immensely. Making others suffer gave me a rush.

I knew what that made me. I looked it up online once. But I didn't *kill* for pleasure. I merely removed people from the general population. I saw it more as ridding the world of undesirables. In the end, I was doing society a favor. One day, people would thank me.

I made it to the bathroom and diligently checked every stall. Once I knew I was alone, I went to the sink, set down my pack, and called the idiot back.

One ring, two rings, three rings…

"Where the hell are you?"

Ken's panicked voice struck me as odd. He seemed fine earlier.

I scoured the bathroom, more than a little concerned. "It's two o'clock on a weekday. Where else would I be? Why are you calling me?"

"You've got to listen to me."

I ignored his scratchy, high-pitched voice and checked my lipstick in the mirror. Perfect as usual. "I've got a phone pressed to my ear, don't I?"

"The police were here today." He lowered his voice. "I think they might know about our packages."

I turned away from the mirror, an icy chill surrounding

me. "What are you talking about? There's no way they can trace anything back to us."

"We need to stop this, or at least lie low until things calm down."

I checked my nails, picturing them clawing out his beady little eyes. "No way."

Heavy breathing came through the speakers. "I'm not going to prison over this."

I snickered at his fear. I'd always suspected he'd turn yellow when things got dicey. "I told you when we started this you'd flake on me one day. I just never believed it would be so soon. Whatever."

"So you'll let me go?"

He came across as way too hopeful. I hated when he got cocky.

"Hell no. We are *not* stopping deliveries. Takes more than me to run this operation, so you're in it until I say we're done."

Seconds ticked by as tension seeped into the call.

"And the police? What are *you* going to do about that?" There was a hint of challenge in his tone.

I stayed quiet, letting him stew. He couldn't stand silence. People like him filled their lives with noise, probably because they feared thinking. People like me knew how to strike terror into the hearts of most by saying nothing at all.

"Are you there?" Exasperation saturated his words.

I grinned. He was so easy. Keeping him on edge, scared and paranoid, was fun. Besides, he was mine for however long I needed him, which wasn't long. My partner had outlived his usefulness.

"The police will always be sniffing around, hoping to catch the right scent." I turned back to the mirror, bored again. "They're dogs. Dumb, trained pack animals who can't form an intelligent, unique thought. Get used to them nipping at our heels, because our business is far from over."

"I was afraid you'd say that."

He would go along, I could tell. The only good thing about my partner was his predictability. Sort of like a cow, he'd happily graze until it was time for the slaughter.

"I'll be bugging a new package tonight, so get things ready for transport." Loud voices arose outside the bathroom. "Oh, and no more talk of quitting. We're both in too deep to walk away."

I hung up, tired of his excuses. I'd known Ken and my contact were cowards before I'd started this little venture, but their continual whining was ruining everything. And they'd introduced something else into the equation.

Fear.

Try as I might, I couldn't shake the worry that Ken might be right. Our days in the business were numbered. Sooner or later, the police would close in.

Well, then, I'll make sure to leave a trail of evidence leading them in someone else's direction.

25

Noah stood, gun ready as he waited behind a rusty metal shed next to a line of trees. A patch of woods was behind him, and the sweat running down his back chilled him in the stiff breeze. The white clapboard house stood in the distance, more a large building than a home. The rundown structure had a heavy chain and lock across the front door, making it suspect as the holding facility used by the traffickers. Or at least, that was what they hoped after following Kip's directions to the property.

SWAT officers in full tactical gear spread out on the open clearing in front of the sad building. They hunkered down behind abandoned cars, other smaller sheds, and one large trash pile. To the casual eye, the unkempt property—crowded with weeds and piles of dead leaves—appeared abandoned, but the fresh tire tracks and colorful dresses and women's shoes found in a refuse pile told another story.

The SWAT commander held up a hand and waved, signaling his team to move toward the suspected prison. Noah waited with Eve behind their shed, far from the raised structure. He might not have liked being away from the action—no former Marine would—but he had Eve to consider. Besides, breaching and clearing was SWAT's job. To take out the criminals and rescue as many victims as they could.

Noah studied the building and monitored the SWAT officers' approach, wishing the sky was dark for extra cover. They'd discussed a night raid but didn't want to wait hours for the sun to set.

His finger tensed on the trigger guard, and he breathed in and out, a steady rhythm that matched his focus as the men and women in black tactical gear jogged toward their target.

Two team members leading the charge held shields and metal battering rams to break through the house door. As the breach team closed in on the locked and chained entrance, gunfire erupted.

Noah never flinched as a hail of bullets rained down from one side of the property. With no rounds zipping by him, he knew he was safely out of the shooter's sights. Going into combat mode, he followed the racket to a metal outbuilding that overlooked the entrance to where the victims might be. He scanned the scene for any sign of the traffickers.

Shouts from the SWAT team echoed across the cleared field as they fanned out, taking cover.

The rapid fire of an assault rifle quickly overtook the pop of handguns. SWAT closed in on the outbuilding, hiding the attackers from view. Noah kept his gun aimed at the building, in case any shooters tried to make a run for it.

The *rat-a-tat* of shots died out. Noah hunched forward, attuned to every sound. The cries and shouts for help didn't come from the SWAT team but from the ones who'd set out to destroy them.

SWAT converged on the outbuilding. One or two more pops of gunfire carried over the land, then silence.

Noah edged out from the side of the shed where he and

Eve waited, anxious for the *all-clear*. The fighter in him wanted to join the tactical team, but his job was to arrest, not to take out the trash.

A deep voice boomed across the property. "Clear."

Noah lowered his weapon but kept it ready. He moved out from his spot with Eve by his side. They crept across the brown grass and tire tracks that cut into the dirt.

Once at the shed, he took note of how many bullet holes marked the metal walls, and the dozens of casings along the ground. If any of the traffickers were alive, he'd be shocked.

He went around the shed, watching as SWAT team members returned to the original objective—the largest building.

Noah took in the carnage behind the metal outbuilding. Four down, all carrying handguns, all dressed in jeans and t-shirts covered with bloodstains and dust. Three lay faceup, their eyes toward the blue sky. One had fallen into a clutch of yuccas. No one bothered to pull him out. The holes in his back were too many to count.

The only survivor was a kid. Peach fuzz on his chin and brown eyes wide with terror, he crouched, his hands behind his head, shaking. One officer kept a rifle pointed at his head while the other secured his wrists with metal cuffs. He didn't have a scratch on him. After the firestorm of bullets, Noah considered him lucky.

Eve nudged Noah's arm. "We should question him."

Noah wasn't interested in what he had to say until they'd completed their perimeter search. He wanted to find the victims. That was his priority.

"Later." He turned to the largest structure. "I want to watch them break through the door of that house and see if anyone's inside."

Eve went with him as they cut around the metal

outbuilding and walked ten feet to the front of the white clapboard structure.

Up close, the house was rickety as hell. The walls had holes big enough for Noah to stick his fingers through. Warped steps and a slanted roof had the entire thing looking ready to cave in. No electrical lines ran from the pole on the property to the building. The exposure to the cold alone might have killed anyone left inside such a prison.

A member of the tactical team held the battering ram in front of the door, while another snapped the lock with bolt cutters.

One man close to the entrance shouted, "SWAT, open up!"

Noah remembered the rhyme he'd learned at the Dallas PD for entering houses. Under normal circumstances, you had to give the perps time to respond to your intention to enter. Just not too much time. *"One, two, three, four, five, then you can go in live."*

These circumstances weren't normal, though. Plus, anyone inside was fully aware that cops were on the premises after the volley of shots fired just outside.

The crack of metal meeting wood cut through the air. The door splintered into several large pieces and bent inward, falling off its hinges. The lead man moved into the darkness beyond the door, closely followed by a teammate, her assault rifle raised and ready.

Noah longed to push closer and see inside, but tactical always went first. That was their job, to gain entry and clear the way. He dabbed the sweat from his brow. It might be chilly outside, but his skin was on fire.

Suddenly, the first officer into the building stuck his head out of the doorway. "Agent Dalton, Agent Taggart, you'd better get in here."

Noah reached the door, and the acrid smell of urine and

feces smacked him hard. When he crossed the threshold, it took a second for his eyes to adjust after the sunshine outside. The first thing he could make out was a human leg.

The limb belonged to a very young woman sprawled across the floor, her head resting on the lap of another very young woman, weaving from side to side as her head sank forward.

The entire room contained women or girls in various stages of dress. Some wore sweats or shorts or leggings, while others had on fragments of evening wear. All were tattered and filthy.

"There's fifteen of them, by my count." The first officer inside carefully stepped over two women sleeping at his feet. He shined his flashlight beam into a corner. "She doesn't look a day older than my daughter. Eight, maybe ten at the most."

The little girl's grime-covered face caught in the beam. She was deathly white. She didn't flinch while the bright light stayed on her.

That a child had become caught in the sick kidnappers' trap made Noah want to go outside and shoot the last survivor.

How could anyone do this to a child?

Noah saw other young women showing the same stupor. Someone had drugged them, probably to keep them quiet. That had to be why they hadn't heard any shouting coming from inside after the shootout.

Eve stood at his side, her blank face reflecting the numbness taking over his insides.

"It's all right. We've got them. They won't get sent farther down the line to God-knows-what hell would be awaiting them."

Noah closed his eyes, wondering how many more operations might be running. How many more women had they failed to save? "We need a doctor on site and ambulances to transport the sick. We have to find out what they were given and treat it."

A few of the women stirred. They stared blankly at Noah and the others in the room. He saw no fear, no terror in their eyes, which awakened a sickening burn in his belly. Maybe it was the drugs or the shock of what they'd been through. The screaming and trembling would come later and stay with them for a very long time.

"Mommy?" The little girl in the corner stirred. "Is my mommy here?"

Eve dashed to the child's side, maneuvering around the women still asleep on the floor. She crouched and swiped thick brown bangs from the child's eyes.

"Your mommy's not here, baby. But we can call her."

"Are we safe now?" Her weak voice carried across the room.

The team members who had filtered inside stopped and stared at her.

Noah could see the anger and sadness etched into the rough faces. He offered the youngest survivor a smile. "Yes, you're safe now, sweetheart. We're the good guys, and we'll make sure you get home. What's your name?"

"Luna." The child wiped her eyes, rousing a little more. "Did you find the others?"

Noah inched closer, his mouth dry. "What others?"

Luna pointed at the door. "There were two of them. They were brave and fought their way outside. I heard shots right after they ran, but I don't know if they made it. I want to know if they're okay."

An officer with a flashlight approached Noah. His grave face turned toward the open door. "I'll get my team to comb those woods. That's the only place they could have hidden. Everything else around here is open pasture."

Noah stroked the girl's hair. "Hear that? We're going to look for them now."

While Eve tended to the child, Noah returned to the entrance, taking in the women still passed out on the floor. He wished he could do more for them, but he wasn't a doctor.

Outside, he stopped and surveyed the clearing to the line of trees, wondering how two women, drugged and sickly, could have outrun their five captors. If dead, their bodies might remain buried on the grounds. He'd order a forensic team to the site. There could be other unlucky ones who hadn't survived.

Something brushed against Noah's hand, disturbing his thoughts of the protocol and procedure he needed to follow.

He glanced down. Luna wobbled on her feet with Eve behind her, helping her stand. She gazed out the door with him, the red evening light landing on her face, showing how frail she'd become. He questioned how she could have the strength to get off the floor, but he understood. Anyone would have crawled out rather than spend another moment inside that prison.

Luna raised her head, staring up with sunken brown eyes. "Can you find them? The ones who got away."

Her timid voice cut him to the core. He wished he could reassure her but knew the chances of that were slim.

Noah took the little girl's hand. "I'm sure gonna try, honey. We're all gonna try real hard."

26

Winter pressed her hand over her eyes as she waited for Julia to answer her phone. It didn't take long.

"Did you see him? Is he all right?"

The beleaguered mother of three sounded like she was at the end of her rope. Winter's heart went out to her. The woman's back and forth with her ex probably wouldn't stop after Winter walked away. Two headstrong people set on revenge—that never ended well for anyone, especially the children.

"He's fine. He was in bed, and he was indeed sick. He said his father was being an ass and took away his phone because he didn't want Gilbert to call you. There's nothing to worry about. Short of him being a little nervous around us, he's fine."

Winter cursed herself. She shouldn't have said that. Julia would find something to worry about in the statement.

"Nervous? About what?"

"I think seeing a police officer flustered him. That and his illness just made him nervous and flushed. He wasn't at his best. That's all."

"Thank you." Julia sighed, seeming appeased, and the calm returned to her voice. "Thank Detective Davenport for me as well."

Winter glanced over at the detective, who hadn't taken his hands off the wheel. "I will. He's going to drop me off at my new office. Signing the papers today."

"Congratulations." Julia sounded as if she actually meant it, filling Winter with hope that she'd be okay. "We should celebrate."

"That would be nice."

Julia ended the call, and she and Darnell rode in silence to downtown Austin. A part of her was glad for the quiet, but she knew it was because the detective was still more than a little pissed at her.

"Julia says thank you. And I owe you one."

He lowered his dark sunglasses and leveled his brown eyes on her. "I'm just glad the kid's okay. Broken families can get messy, especially when ungodly amounts of money are involved."

Winter wanted to argue that it wasn't money that made broken families messy. She should know, but she kept her experiences in such matters to herself.

"If I can ever return the favor, call. I'm sure you can find some way to make me pay you back."

His hands loosened on the steering wheel. "You got that right."

Twenty minutes later, Winter stood outside an unremarkable storefront. The large, grimy display windows and dark, gloomy interior didn't seem too inviting. A *For Rent* sign still sat in one window.

Darnell drove away. As she watched his red taillights disappear into traffic, Winter revisited her brief meeting with Gilbert. She wasn't convinced things were okay at the Schumaker home, but she had no way to convince the by-the-book detective of her special ability and how it made her doubt the teenager's sincerity.

Justice revolved around evidence, and until she had something concrete to prove Julia's children were in trouble, she had to keep her mouth shut.

Winter turned and faced the old storefront that had called to her when hunting for office space. A single-story corner space with two large, east-facing windows. It was perfect. Several smaller windows along the northern adjacent-facing wall were edged in white trim, creating a wide transom. The afternoon light trickled across the sidewalk but didn't creep inside the storefront. Perfect for when the heat of summer hit the city.

She hugged her leather messenger bag closer. Winter had taken one of those big adult steps, the kind she'd dreamed of as a kid. She'd started her own business, and now she would have a home for that business. One separate from her actual home.

Winter pictured Noah's face when she showed him the new location of Black Investigations. "He'll love it."

"You ready to sign?" The voice belonged to a leggy woman approaching up the sidewalk. She dangled a pair of keys from her long, manicured fingers.

Winter examined the woman's green jacket and matching pants. The way she swept her hair into a casual bun with a few strategically placed tendrils hanging around her face made Winter jealous.

Why can't my hair look like that?

"Emma." Winter extended her hand. "Right on time."

Emma Pole held up a briefcase. "When a client's ready to sign on the dotted line, I'm always on time." She handed the keys to Winter. "You do the honors. It's going to be your place, after all."

Winter grinned as she worked the lock. Her giddiness

escalated as she pushed the glass door open and stepped inside.

Dust and the lingering smell of shoe polish drifted by, but she didn't care. She had a new place to set down roots for her business.

"The old shoe store must have been in this spot for fifty years." Emma walked in behind her. "But times change, and we move on."

Winter waited as the agent strolled inside like she'd rented the place, not Winter. Emma tossed her briefcase onto a Formica countertop, where the store register once sat, and placed a hand on her hip.

"Let's get you signed and sealed."

Between the tax documents, the lease agreement, the city's paperwork, and the bank paperwork, Winter felt her hand would fall off from writing her signature. But an hour later, she was the new renter of the storefront property on 4th Street.

"You're all set." Emma shoved all the paperwork into her briefcase and zipped it closed. "I'll get copies to you of everything in about three days. The electricity and water have to be changed into your name, but you can handle that online. Doesn't take long. The last owner paid the bills through the end of the month, so you have time."

Winter couldn't stop grinning. "Thanks, Emma."

The real estate agent walked toward the window and removed the *For Rent* sign. She tucked it under her arm and opened the door. "Call if you have questions. Best of luck. Let me know how you get on."

Emma stepped outside. Winter stood in the weak pool of light before her display windows, keeping an eye on the agent as she strolled toward a silver Mercedes.

Business must be good.

Getting back on task, Winter bounced her phone in one

hand, her mind on fire with ideas. The walls and ceiling would need cleaning, and maybe some fresh paint. The carpeting definitely needed to be replaced.

Where to start?

She first had to develop a decorating theme, wanting to stick with neutral colors that didn't detract from her business. Since painting would have to wait, Winter decided that she'd tack up a few posters to highlight the local flavor of Austin. She'd dug around in a bargain bin at a nearby record store and found some for the Crawfish Festival, the Oyster Festival, and the famous SXSW. When she stumbled on one for the annual Squirrel Fest, celebrating the large furry-tailed rodents that seemed to be the real owners of the city, she had to buy that one too.

After deciding on where each poster would hang, she set to work, making the boring lists of everything she would need, from a copier to a coffee maker. As she scribbled and erased and rewrote, the monumental task of running an office settled into her chest like a too-big bite of a hamburger.

Yeah, I'm gonna need that assistant sooner than later.

She was deep into estimating how many reams of paper she might have to order monthly when the door opened behind her.

Winter spun around, automatically reaching for the holster she'd resumed carrying from her days in the Bureau. When she faced the intruder, she moved her hand away from her gun.

She wondered if that habit would ever go away.

As her gaze adjusted to the fading light, Julia came into focus.

She held up a bottle of champagne. "I thought we should celebrate your new establishment with a drink." She grinned at the large green bottle. "Or a few drinks."

Winter's mouth slipped open, amazed at the woman's investigatory skills. "How did you find me?"

Julia sauntered inside, her heels thumping against the thin carpet. "Emma Pole is an old friend. I ran into her, and she told me she'd just leased this place." Julia set the bottle on the counter. "Didn't take much for me to coax your name from her. So I thought I would come by and help you christen the place."

Winter chuckled. "That's something my husband would say."

Julia raised her eyebrows. "I just brought the champagne. I'll leave the rest to you and…what's your husband's name?"

"Noah." Winter wasn't comfortable sharing her personal details with a client but figured the woman would find out eventually.

Julia set her Fendi bag on the counter and pulled it open. "How long have you been married?"

Winter eased alongside the counter and set her phone down. "Just a couple months."

Julia procured two paper cups from her purse. "Ah, newlyweds. I wish you all the best. I might sound jaded but enjoy it while you can. Gets harder the longer you've been together. And with kids."

Winter picked up a cup, rolling it between her hands. "I appreciate you coming and the champagne, but why are you here?" She studied Julia's face. "This isn't about celebrating my new office, is it?"

Julia pushed her purse away. "I want to ask you about my son." She picked up the bottle. "I got the impression there was something you weren't telling me. Gilbert's many things, but nervous isn't one of them."

Winter was at an impasse. Her feelings about Gilbert—about the whole family—weren't based on facts but impressions. Psychic impressions. When she mentioned his sister's name, Gilbert's deepened color sent up red flags in Winter's head. The change in his aura meant something was wrong. But how could she communicate that to Julia without sounding crazy?

"What kind of relationship does Gilbert have with his older sister?"

Julia removed the foil from the top of the champagne. "Grace?" She lifted a shoulder. "Other than the usual sibling rivalry, they get along well enough. He looks up to her, always has. They're very different, though. Grace is a perfectionist. From her hair down to her shoes. She thinks she's the new Queen of England. Everything has to be in place, and she must look her best. Gilbert is…not type A, and it drives her mad. I learned to let go of Gilbert's wrinkled shirts and messy room long ago."

The pop of the cork was loud in the empty space. Winter's instincts urged her on, wanting to pry deeper into the Schumaker family dynamics.

"What about Grace and Gilbert's relationship with Freddie?" She waited as Julia filled her paper cup with the bubbly drink. "I saw the pictures he posted online. They appear happy, but that doesn't mean they are."

"Oh, Grace adores her father," Julia countered. "A daddy's girl through and through. Freddie spoils her rotten, and believe me, she uses that to her advantage."

Winter made a mental note to meet Grace one day. "Was there ever a time when Freddie's relationship with the kids seemed off?"

Julia set the bottle on the counter. "When I suspected he had a porn addiction, I noticed little things he did with the kids that bothered me. His short temper and how he badgered Grace about her appearance. He told her how to wear her hair and how much makeup to put on. Freddie didn't like her wearing revealing clothing or putting on lipstick. I kept telling him to leave her alone, but he didn't listen. His activities in the pool house explained what was going on. He wanted Grace to not be like the girls he took to bed every night."

It made sense. A highly sexual father would want his daughter to be demure, unlike the women he pursued. Or...it could mean something else entirely.

"Were there any other things you noticed about Freddie's relationship with Grace or the other children? Strange behaviors that never made sense before?"

Julia bit her lower lip, appearing pensive. She lifted her cup. "Belinda. I always suspected something was going on with her and Freddie. Not now, of course. Belinda is too old for his tastes, but in the beginning, when she first arrived, she was right up his alley." She took a deep swig of her drink.

Winter ran her finger along the edge of her cup. "I wondered when she raved about how great an employer Freddie was. She seemed too complimentary."

"Belinda has been with us for fourteen years. She's always worshiped Freddie."

"Why didn't you say anything to me before?"

Julia kept her eyes on the counter. "I felt foolish. The jealous wife questioning the pretty nanny. There are plenty of clichés to describe how I could've come across."

The way Belinda's face lit up when she spoke about working for Schumaker hadn't sat right with Winter. A woman passed over for a younger replacement might not feel so enthused about her former lover. It also didn't explain how she doted on Gilbert earlier that day. Was she holding on to the children to stay relevant in Schumaker's eyes?

"Have your children ever seemed distressed around Belinda or anyone else at the mansion?"

Julia shook her head. "No. Belinda may have slept with Freddie, but she does love the kids. Everyone who works at the house does. My ex thoroughly vets anyone who works around our children. They have friends among the staff. People they talk to. In some ways, those are the ones who got them through the tough months leading up to the divorce. Why do you ask?"

"That's probably it." Winter considered all the possibilities. "You were dragged over the coals of public opinion in the divorce. I'm sure your kids weren't immune to seeing what you went through. That would explain their suspicion of strangers and why they want to protect you, Freddie, and Belinda."

"You think they're protecting Freddie?"

Winter studied the elegantly dressed woman with perfectly coiffed hair and precisely applied makeup. "Of course they are. Children will protect their parents. Seeing a police detective in their home probably set off Gilbert's fear that you or his father were in danger. I just wanted to make sure there wasn't something else going on. Someone he feared in the house."

Julia picked up her purse. "No. They're safe behind Freddie's gates. I know that. The only person I want to protect them from is their father." She tapped the top of the champagne bottle. "Take that home and enjoy it. I'll talk to you later."

Julia walked out of the office, her head held high. Winter didn't try to stop her.

Winter stared out the windows, catching the last rays of the evening light, wondering about the red glow her ability had shined on Gilbert.

I might never figure this out. But I sure want to.

Her cell rang, and Darnell Davenport's name flashed on the screen.

"Sorry to call so soon, but I think I have something you want to hear." Impatience oozed from his voice.

Winter's grip tightened on the phone. "I'm listening."

"The owner of an escort service, a Vaeda Smith, has reported to Austin PD that one of her employees, a Harper Glynn, is missing. She believes something horrible has happened to the woman because she can't reach her. She's texted and called numerous times. She said that Harper is never more than two feet from her phone."

"Why's that odd?" Winter tapped her cup of champagne.

"Because she'd been on a date with a client the night before the text was sent."

Oh no. Winter had a bad feeling about this.

"Why tell me this?"

Darnell hesitated. "Because the night before Harper went missing, the owner had her booked on a date with one, wait for it, Frederick Schumaker."

Winter almost dropped her phone. "Are you sure?"

Darnell chuckled. "I'm sure. Seems there's more going on at that house than we ever imagined."

27

Noah surveyed the array of ambulances and teams of EMTs treating the women brought out from inside the dilapidated one-room house. Luna waited with a few of the younger women, wrapped in a blanket and sipping from a water bottle.

The young man arrested after the shoot-out sat in the back of one of several police cars on the property, his head down, avoiding eye contact with anyone. A survivor from the gunfight rested on a stretcher as an EMT tended his wounds. Noah itched to question both men, but he had another pressing matter to attend to.

"You ready?" Eve asked.

Noah had been ready to find the two missing women since learning of their escape. He just hoped they could locate them in time. He checked his gun and nodded. "How many are going with us?"

She glanced at the police officers waiting behind them. "Five of the local PD are joining us. A few of the SWAT guys asked to take part. They want to help find the women. A dog is on its way."

Noah faced the group. "We know two women escaped. A witness said they took off for the trees a few hours ago. There's nowhere else to hide except in these woods. Every other direction leads to open fields. We know the perps fired on them, but we have no signs of any fresh graves on site. Check the ground for blood stains or any trail we can follow. Hopefully, they're still alive."

He led the team to the edge of the property. He checked on Eve as he walked into the thicket of trees, cursing the thickets pulling at his clothes. The evening light disappeared quickly as the canopy of tree limbs covered them.

Switching on the flashlight he'd borrowed, Noah just hoped they found the two missing women before dark. Even one night alone in the cold woods, sick and possibly injured, could finish them.

"Fan out," he called to the others in his search party. "We don't have much time until dark. The more eyes we have checking every inch of these woods, the better."

Eve touched his elbow. "I'm sticking close to you."

Noah didn't argue. He preferred to keep her with him in case more of the sons of bitches who'd held the women were hiding amid the brush.

He stepped through tangles of twigs, drifts of dead leaves, and trash from the traffickers' camp. The crunching steps of those moving around him worried Noah. Those loud movements might scare the women or attract more unsavory characters their way before they were ready.

He reached out to move a low-hanging branch out of the way. Something wet touched his hand.

"Your jacket." Eve's voice became a whisper. "There's blood on it."

He spotted the brush of crimson on his jacket. There was more on his hand.

"One or both women were injured."

Eve moved ahead of him. "They might not have gotten too far." She stooped and examined a small pile of leaves. "There's a lot of blood here."

Ahead in the brush, a loud, "Over here!" reached Noah's and his partner's ears.

Noah picked up his pace, jogging as best as he could over the rough terrain. He spotted one of the SWAT guys kneeling on the ground.

Next to him was the body of a woman. Her dress had torn across the shoulders, with patches of blood covering most of her abdomen. Her brown hair, though matted with dead leaves, gleamed in the red light coming through the trees.

Noah stopped, shaking with despair that the poor woman had barely made it twenty feet from the entrance to the woods before collapsing.

"There's a lot of blood around here." The SWAT member examining her glanced at Noah. "She was shot in the side and bled out."

Noah said a silent prayer for the victim. He wished he could tell her how proud he was that she'd fought back. She battled in the face of danger, showing more courage than most. It was a shame he could never tell her that. He wanted her to know.

Eve clicked her walkie on. "I have a deceased Jane Doe about twenty feet from the beginning of the trees."

Noah searched the area around the body. He found a footprint in the soft dirt about a foot away. "The second escapee headed this way."

The SWAT officer checked the ground above Noah found the print. "Looks like she was alone too. No other signs of prints. The traffickers didn't follow her."

"Could mean she was shot too?" Eve secured her walkie to her belt. "She couldn't have gotten far if she was."

Noah scoured the darkening woods. "If you knew traffickers were after you, what would you do?"

Eve pulled back her shoulders. "Run until I couldn't run anymore."

"Exactly." Noah faced one of the police officers from the local town. "How far do these woods go?"

The slender man with the deputy badge removed his hat and ran his hand through his ruffled reddish hair. "Miles. Stops at Myers Creek. There's a cattle ranch on the other side."

Noah nodded to the officer. "Go back and send some men to the ranch. They can see if she made it through."

The deputy thrashed through the thick brush as he headed back toward the clearing.

"So what do we do?" Eve's question carried across the still terrain as the other search party members gathered around her.

Noah removed his flashlight from his pocket and shined it into the trees ahead. "We go on. We've got to find her. If she's still alive, we'll have a very damning witness to this entire operation."

And I'll be damned if I'm gonna lose one more victim.

28

R ylee Baxter sat at her dresser mirror, putting the finishing touches on her eyeliner, making her blue eyes pop. She'd tucked her shiny sable hair into a sophisticated French twist, hoping to impress her date that evening. A heavy hitter in Austin with a lot of cash and a big mansion. Just the kind of man she'd always wanted.

Her gaze drifted to her bedroom entrance as men fighting with loud grunts and cries of pain distracted her.

Jud and his stupid video games.

A weed-obsessed high school dropout with aspirations of being the next Tony Montana, her boyfriend wasn't much help when it came to paying the bills. At eighteen, Rylee did the best she could. When she made it as a Playboy Bunny, she'd kick his worthless ass out of the trailer she busted her butt to keep.

She turned back to her mirror, questioning why she stayed with a man who didn't care if she slept with other men. Jud had been charming at first and supported her career goals. He even took a few nude photos of her to help her practice for *Playboy*. After he'd moved into her trailer, the gentleman who opened all doors for her and paid all the dinner tabs vanished into the lump that had become attached to her couch.

She gathered her purse and coat before stopping in front of her mirror. Satisfied her curves beneath her tight dress would impress the hell out of her new client, Rylee walked out of her bedroom.

Jud didn't even look up from his video game.

"I'm on my way to shove my tits into another man's face," she shouted over the rapid-fire combat mission playing on the TV screen.

Jud cursed at the screen but never turned to her. "Pick me up some donuts on your way back. I'll have the munchies by then."

Rylee debated the satisfaction she'd get from driving the heel of her stiletto into his neck. Jail time and possibly losing her tiny home deterred her from fulfilling her fantasy.

She marched toward the door, hoping the rideshare she'd texted arrived on time. She couldn't be late for this gig.

Once she slammed her trailer door and stepped into the cool night, she shrugged on her coat, hoping it didn't wrinkle her dress. She walked to the main road through the trailer park, coming up with a new life plan that didn't involve Jud.

Rylee was big on making plans. She hadn't been born into money, but she had a beautiful face and a lot of ambition. She would achieve superstardom in a series of well-thought-out steps.

Step one was getting to know wealthy men who would help her get into *Playboy*. The escort business was the fastest way to accomplish that and pay the bills. Step two involved doing anything and everything to get ahead once she got a spread in their digital magazine and moved into the famous mansion. Girls got TV gigs and movie parts from just posing. Step three was stardom and all the perks it would bring.

The glare of approaching headlights brought her out of her daydreams. One factor she hadn't planned on was Jud. The perpetually high gamer—who cleaned out her fridge every night after smoking a mountain of weed—was a problem.

In the same way Dorothy Stratten's lowlife husband ruined her financially before ending her life, Jud would probably be Rylee's downfall too. Not directly, of course. He could barely lift a finger to criticize her, much less hold a gun on her. But his dealer or his loser friends were another story. She needed to dump his ass, and soon, before bad things started happening.

Rylee had spent days studying all the successful Playboy Bunnies, wanting to emulate their careers. She noticed that those who fell as quickly as they rose had husbands or clingy boyfriends.

Yeah, I'm not making that mistake.

She opened the back door to her ride, and a new sense of purpose ran through her bones. If she played her cards right and impressed tonight's new high-roller client, she might land herself a sweet apartment and leave Jud for good.

Rylee settled into the back seat as the rows of old, worn trailers whipped past her window. She spotted the lights of the tall buildings of downtown Austin. She wished she could wine and dine with the hip crowd who frequented the city every night, but that cost money. Besides, such activities were lost on Jud. He was always too loaded to do anything.

The lights from the thriving downtown dimmed, and green lawns and cozy homes soon replaced her view. She enjoyed a comfortable drive from the outskirts of the city to where the wealthy lived. She didn't concern herself with the cost of the transportation. Her generous *John* had included the rideshare fare with his fee. That was pure class, as far as Rylee was concerned.

Towering mansions, lit to show off their luxury, and lush gardens kept her nose glued to the window. When the car stopped at a guardhouse, she sat up.

Never been through one of these before.

The guard waved her car in. Rylee's stomach danced with butterflies as she waited for the main house to appear.

The towering dark red brick structure generated an astonished gasp. She'd never seen such a big house. Well, almost. Cinderella's Castle was the biggest. She was seven when she saw it with her mom and stepfather. She'd wanted a house like that ever since.

Rylee told the driver to follow the road to the garage along the side of the house. Her client had been insistent about avoiding the front entrance and using the side door leading to the pool house.

The driver paused long enough for her to get out and close the door before pulling away, leaving Rylee at the bottom of a few stone steps leading to a French door with a copper awning.

Before she climbed the steps, Rylee adjusted her dress over her naturally large breasts. She gripped her black clutch and smoothed out the creases in the green silk fabric. First impressions mattered.

She checked the door for a handle, but there was no sign of one. She was about to knock on the glass when a shadow moved behind the entrance.

A maid in a white uniform and blue apron opened the door, her hair pulled back into a tight bun. Thick makeup gave her an almost clown-like appearance, but underneath the heavy foundation, the woman's expression was stone cold. Rylee hadn't expected to run into the help. Her client had assured her they would be alone.

"Ah, I'm here to see—"

"Mr. Schumaker will be along soon." The maid moved away from the door, eyeing her clingy dress. Judgment oozed from the woman. "He's running behind this evening."

Rylee took a tentative step inside the rear entrance of the home.

The family room was built out of brick with one wall of windows to view the kidney-shaped pool and lush gardens dotted with flickering brass lanterns. That drew her attention as much as the bookshelf lined with puzzles did. Wooden ones, metal ones, jigsaw ones, some that had rope, some made of keys, some plastic cubes, and others 3D stars or all sorts of shapes.

"Gosh, does Mr. Schumaker like puzzles?"

The maid took her purse and helped her out of her coat without saying a word.

Rylee wasn't sure what to do. She was used to dealing with her clients, not their staff.

"Follow me." The maid walked toward a door beyond the windows, also made of glass.

Rylee struggled to keep up with the young woman, clicking her heels on the red pavers as they passed luscious beds of green ferns. They hurried past the pool, and she admired the water's shade of deep blue. Ahead was a red-brick cabana with open French doors. The lights were on inside, and a soothing jazz tune drifted out to the pool area.

The music, the gardens, and even the smell of chlorine from the pool all seemed like heaven. One day, she would have a house like this.

When I'm a star, this will be how I live.

The maid touched her arm. "Wait inside."

Rylee didn't appreciate the intrusion but did as she was told.

When she stepped inside the door, she glanced back at the maid still holding onto her coat and purse.

Something felt off. She couldn't put her finger on it, but Rylee could have sworn the woman had it out for her. Jealousy? Probably.

Still, Rylee didn't turn her back on the maid.

29

Winter bolted from her SUV and ran to the elevator of the pricey, high-rise apartment building, apprehension bubbling in her veins. When Darnell Davenport called her with what he'd found at Harper Glynn's apartment, she'd caught a rideshare to her house, jumped into her Pilot, and headed that way.

To be involved in an investigation again, even though she wasn't technically a law officer, gave Winter such a rush. She had Schumaker to thank. His relationship with Harper Glynn, along with what she'd discovered during her investigation, had unwittingly landed her in the center of a missing persons case.

She arrived on Harper's floor, cursing the slow elevator. She was through the gap before the doors fully opened.

Winter jogged down the hallway, thinking of Noah. What would he make of her late-night adventure?

He'd wish he were here with me.

She found Darnell standing outside apartment 4401. Nothing was out of the ordinary. No sign of forced entry and the upper-end hallway seemed normal.

"Glad you could make it." Darnell glanced at the phone in his hand. "I'm waiting for my search warrant. They're getting special permission to serve after hours."

Winter glanced at the door and then at Darnell. "On what grounds? I don't see anything suspicious."

Darnell crooked his finger and then kneeled on the floor. "Check the underside of the doorknob."

Winter followed his finger until she spotted the smears of blood. They weren't noticeable from far away. No one passing by would see it. Only a cop searching for evidence would identify the blood.

She got closer to the doorknob. "How did you get this address?"

"Vaeda Smith had it. She's worried about the girl and has been calling me every other hour. So I visited the apartment to see if the woman was here, maybe ignoring her employer. I found the blood and called it in."

His phone vibrated, and she wanted to jerk it from his hands. She wasn't sure if it was lack of sleep or the unresolved issues she had with Freddie Schumaker's case, but something didn't sit right with her. Too many questions and not enough answers always made her jumpy.

"We got it." Darnell read a text on his phone. "We've got permission to enter." He returned the phone to his jacket pocket. "But the damn manager who has all the keys is an hour away."

Winter glanced around. "You want to wait for backup?"

Darnell rolled up one sleeve of his jacket. "Why do you think I called you? You are my backup."

Without saying another word, he put his shoulder into the door, attempting to force it open. The wood creaked, but the door did not budge.

Winter held up her hand, stopping him from ramming into the door again. "I learned a little trick at the Academy."

She inspected the jamb to make sure it was wood instead of metal. It was.

She'd much rather pick the locks but didn't think showing that particular skill to the police detective would be a good idea.

Darnell stepped back. "The Academy, huh?"

Gauging the correct distance, Winter centered herself and kicked just left of the knob. Even with a deadbolt, the wood frame gave, and the door flew open, slamming against the inside wall of the apartment.

Darnell rushed in, gun in hand. Winter was right on his tail.

"Miss Glynn, this is the Austin Police." Darnell held his gun in front of him. "Please let us know if you're in here."

Silence. The emptiness of the apartment ratcheted up Winter's fear for the woman.

The short hallway from the front door opened to a spacious living room. Darnell stopped and flipped on the lights.

Winter appreciated the young woman's taste. Everything was upper end. Beige and taupe tones in the upholstered furniture and rug complemented the thick mahogany coffee table and entertainment center. Winter's little furniture shopping adventure with her Gramma Beth gave her an idea of what Harper had spent to decorate her apartment. What she saw amounted to much more than Winter could hope to spend on her house and office combined.

Nothing appeared toppled over. The books remained in the bookcase. The pictures on the wall were straight. There were no signs of someone fighting for their life. No blood splatter and no disarray.

Darnell turned to Winter. "It's clean. I'm guessing our missing person isn't here."

He ventured deeper into the apartment, passing the

kitchen. All the stainless appliances gleamed, the sink was empty, and the coffeepot had been turned off. Winter stayed with Darnell as he inched along a hallway.

Right after he pushed the first door on the right open and turned on the light, Darnell glanced over his shoulder at Winter. "We've got something."

She went around him to peek inside the door. Her fists clenched. They had a crime scene.

Darnell entered the room first. This was his case, after all.

Winter swept over every detail with a trained eye. A man's tie lay on the floor a few feet from the bedside table. The bed remained unmade with what appeared to be a splotch of dried blood on Harper's sheets. More blood was smeared at the foot of the bed.

Darnell handed Winter a pair of gloves. "Seems like Vaeda's concerns about her girl were correct."

"Not enough blood for her to have bled out, though. That's a good sign." Winter slipped on the gloves, eager to get inside the room. "You think Schumaker may have had something to do with this?"

"Let me get the crime scene techs in here and see if they can recover fingerprints or some type of DNA from the sheets first." He pulled out his phone. "I'll check out the rest of the apartment while I call this in."

Winter stepped into the bedroom, making sure not to disturb any of the evidence.

She stopped and carefully eased a closet door open with one gloved finger. The dresses hanging inside had designer labels and belonged to a very slender woman. The shoes on a rack to one side were high heels, except for a pair of running shoes and some black boots.

Winter knew the escort business paid well, especially for a girl with great looks and a good head on her shoulders.

Based on the contents of Harper's apartment and closet, she was a very successful escort.

The bathroom light flickered once or twice before coming on, but the scene in the bedroom hadn't spread to this location. A tray of cosmetics sat atop the clean white vanity. White towels hooked over silver holders had no blood and no signs of being used recently. Even the clear shower stall was dry, without a single water streak.

Winter hovered her finger along the edge of the Jacuzzi bathtub, breathing in the scent of the aromatic candles on the ledge along the back wall.

The room offered no clues to help solve Harper's disappearance. She was about to walk back into the bedroom when the partially closed door to the toilet spoke to her. She didn't know if it was the position of the door or the darkness inside that nagged at Winter, but something told her to check it out.

Once the light in the stall flipped on, the brilliant shine of something perched atop the toilet's tank gave her pause.

A man's watch. Platinum and diamonds.

Winter picked it up. When she flipped the watch over and checked the back, she froze.

Frederick D. Schumaker II. The engraving left no doubt as to the owner.

But how had it gotten there?

Holding the timepiece gingerly, she wondered why a man as powerful and intelligent as Schumaker would have left such blatantly incriminating evidence behind. But he wouldn't be the first person to overlook something important during the heat of a crime. Winter had seen such screwups before.

Walking out of the bedroom, Winter was eager to find out what Darnell thought of her find.

❄

WINTER PUSHED HER ACCELERATOR HARDER, passing the slower cars on the dark, empty road, rushing to keep up with Darnell's speeding cruiser. She still couldn't believe the detective had managed to get an arrest warrant for Schumaker.

She stayed behind Darnell as he drove past the guard's house and through the fancy gates. Two police cars pulled in after him.

When she parked behind one of the cruisers, Winter checked the façade of the grand home. There were no lights on. Everyone must have been asleep.

Out of his car in a flash, Darnell took the stone steps two at a time. Winter worried as the massive wooden doors got closer. The children were here. Did she want them to see their father getting hauled away in handcuffs?

She caught up and touched Darnell's elbow. "What about the kids?"

He raised his hand to the bell, avoiding eye contact. "I'm sorry for them. But I have a job to do."

Darnell leaned on the bell, letting the chime from the thick doors go on and on.

Winter almost expected a maid or the butler to answer, but when Schumaker himself yanked one of the French doors open, she fought to keep a smile off her face.

He stood wide-eyed with his shirt half unbuttoned, his hair in disarray, and the gleam of sweat on his forehead.

A petite young woman with a beautiful face smeared with makeup peeked over his shoulder. Winter got a glimpse of a wrinkled green dress all askew and twisted at her hips before the woman pressed into the wall behind the open door. As if she were trying to be invisible. If the wall had opened into the depths of Hell, Winter thought the young woman would have gratefully stepped through it.

"What the hell is the meaning of this?" Schumaker's shout carried across the entrance.

"My name is Detective Davenport with the Austin PD." Darnell showed him the paper in his hand, never taking his eyes off Schumaker. "Frederick Schumaker, you are under arrest in connection to the disappearance of Harper Glynn."

Schumaker's lips pulled back in an evil sneer. "Listen to me, Detective." He pointed at Winter. "I don't know what this woman has told you about me, but I had—"

"You have the right to remain silent," Darnell cut in. "Anything you do or say can be used against you—"

"Belinda!" Schumaker shouted. "Get down here."

Within seconds, every light in the foyer came on, blanketing the front of the house with a warm glow.

Darnell continued reading the suspect his Miranda Rights, but by Schumaker's red face, Winter guessed he wasn't paying much attention. The girl in green slowly shrank away even farther when Belinda arrived, wearing a baby-pink robe.

Schumaker barked orders at her, telling her who to call. Belinda didn't seem to hear him anymore once Darnell flourished his handcuffs. She stared daggers at Winter.

Her expression only shifted when she heard the click of the locks as they secured Schumaker's wrists together. Eyes wide with horror, she stepped toward her boss. "Do you have to do that?"

That was when Winter noticed Gabriella heading down the staircase. In very formal nightwear, the little girl stared as their father submitted to the humiliation of being arrested.

Carrying a stuffed unicorn, Gabriella ran to Belinda's side and threw her arms around her legs.

Her tears cut Winter in two. She'd never intended for this to happen.

"What's going on?" Gilbert shot down the stairs and was at Belinda's side in a flash, hands on his head, fingers deep in his hair.

Winter shook her head. "I'm sorry about this."

"How could you do this?" Belinda said between gritted teeth. Winter didn't have any trouble reading the hate and loathing that blanketed the nanny's face.

What could she say?

"Let me help you get them back in bed," Winter offered, guilt-ridden over what the children had witnessed.

Belinda glowered at her. "Haven't you done enough?"

Winter waited as Belinda guided Gabriella away, attempting to console her.

Gilbert remained at the door, pale as milk as a police officer placed his father in the back seat of his cruiser.

She reached to touch the young man, but he backed away from her. That was when she saw his forehead glow again with that odd crimson energy she'd noticed before. Only this time, it wasn't wonder that seized her but the icy grip of dread.

He shrank away from her, turned, and ran to the wide staircase, following his nanny and sister up the steps.

"What do I do?"

She turned to the young woman in the green dress. She'd remained off to the side in the grand foyer, looking pale and frightened.

Winter lowered her voice. "What's your name?"

"Rylee. Rylee Baxter." She fidgeted with her dress, smoothing it over her hips. "I had a, um, meeting with Mr. Schumaker."

Winter raised one eyebrow. "Let me guess. In the pool house?"

The woman lowered her gaze to the floor. "Am I in trouble?"

"Consider yourself lucky to be alive, Ms. Baxter." Winter took out her phone and typed the young woman's name into it. "We'll need to speak with you tomorrow. Give me your contact information."

After Winter typed Rylee's number and address into her phone, she offered Rylee a faint smile. "Go home and stay put."

"I'll…I don't have a car. I have to order one."

Exhausted, angry, and at the same time worried for the girl's safety, Winter told her one of the officers would drive her home. And if they didn't, she would.

Rylee's hands shook as she walked with Winter out the front door. "Was he going to kill me? He seemed so nice."

Winter took one last peek at the stairs. Grace was peeking around the corner from the second-floor landing, glaring down at her, wide-eyed and angry. Or was that excitement Winter saw in her eyes? A chill ran down her spine.

30

W*hoo-hoo. Whoo-hoo.*

Harper's eyes popped open at the sound, her hand snapping up to cover her scream. She scrambled backward, almost crying out as twigs and rocks bit into her palm.

Where am I?

Forcing her breathing to calm, she glanced around, attempting to get her bearings. She couldn't. It was simply too dark.

How was that possible?

She'd been running for miles when she'd stepped into a hole and turned her ankle. The sun had been shining through the woods as she'd lain there sobbing. She was so tired, and she remembered telling herself it was okay to close her eyes. *"Just for a few seconds."*

Now?

Clouds hovered over the moon, leaving her in nearly pitch-black darkness.

"Stupid idiot."

The scratches on Harper's hands and arms stung like a bitch, almost as much as the cut on her neck, but she pushed to her feet anyway. Testing her ankle, she decided she hadn't done much damage. Carefully pushing aside the thorny, low-hanging branches, she limped through piles of loose leaves and twigs. Her muscles screamed with fatigue, but she slogged through, praying for an end to her misery.

She didn't know how long she'd been in the thicket of trees, but it seemed like an eternity. Minutes became hours, and every step was a mile. Had she been running in circles? Her mind was playing tricks on her. She had to stay strong. She plodded on, one foot in front of the other, remembering her fate if she gave up.

They would come for her. Men like that didn't let good merchandise slip through their fingers. She had to remain vigilant.

How did I get here?

Flashes of her life before ending up in the madwoman's lair popped into her head. Her apartment, the steady stream of clients she catered to. Even the slice of strawberry cake she had wrapped in cellophane waiting to be eaten on her cheat day. She didn't have a terrible life or an evil one. It was a life, and though Harper knew she wasn't as pure as the driven snow, she was a good person. So why had God done this to her?

Ahead, she spotted a creek or river, a glistening dark ribbon between the trees. The closer she got, the easier she could make out details, and relief flooded her when she saw it was a highway. The moon reflected off the blacktop. A surge of energy gripped her.

She limped forward, using every ounce of strength she had to reach the road. Her lungs burned, and she pushed for as long as possible until her body finally ran out of steam. She collapsed on a patch of yellow prairie grass between the trees and a barbed wire fence running alongside the road, unable to go on. Exhaustion, dehydration, and the drugs in her system proved too much. Despite the terror coursing through her, Harper couldn't keep her eyes open any longer.

Just a few minutes, and then I'll push on.

She was back in that horrifically cold, damp place, and someone was screaming. She waved her arms in front of her face, attempting to fight off the witch who held her. The witch turned into bats, and Harper screamed as they fed on her, hurting her as their teeth sank into her flesh.

She bolted upright. Disoriented, Harper got to her feet again. Had to be a dream. A crazy dream brought on by the stress of her situation. She cleared her mind, pushing the horror of the bats away. She remembered the highway. Forcing back the thirst and hunger that hounded her, she willed herself to move.

Do it for Bridget.

The occasional whoosh of cars and headlights danced ahead in the darkness. She focused on the lights. All Harper needed was one car. One good Samaritan to pick her up.

She fell to her knees when an agonizing cramp shot up her leg like fire. She knew the signs. Harper needed water and food soon, or she wouldn't make it.

"Don't give up. Don't give up."

Harper concentrated on the highway, summoning every ounce of energy she had to stay focused. She crawled across a field filled with high grass and painful goathead burrs. Her nausea returned and her skin burned where they poked her, but she battled on. Spots danced before her eyes, and she feared she might pass out before reaching the road.

She dug her nails into the dirt, pulling herself along. She remembered the faces of the others whose lives depended on her, especially the children. She had to get help for them.

And the men who'd held them? The sick bastards who kidnapped and sold women. And that woman... She knew where they hid and saw a few of their faces. She could put them away, so they never did this to another woman or girl ever again.

After wriggling beneath the barbed wire fence, Harper didn't see the roadside ditch until it was too late. She stumbled down the embankment, wanting to cry when she rolled into pokey ditch weeds. Her hair snagged on a tumbleweed.

She caught her breath and rested, but the ones she left behind still haunted her. "Get up and get to the other side now."

Harper could rest later. Hurt later. Cry later.

She pulled herself up with shaking hands and freed her hair. When she resumed crawling, her fingertips touched the gravel shoulder of the road, and hope swelled in her chest. More cramps seized her, threatening her balance. She was about to fall backward when headlights approached.

Harper's vision blurred as the light intensified. She fought to raise her hand, wave, or call out. Just when she was about to conquer her weakness, a black curtain descended over her eyes, and the world vanished from view.

31

T he clang of the metal door opening into the holding
   area of the Austin jail, with its gray cinder blocks and
cement floor, sent a rare ripple of satisfaction through
Winter, knowing the man she was about to visit would spend
a good chunk of his life in places just like this.

The tall man walking next to her kept a stoic frown plastered on his face. "You've got ten minutes, and that's it."
Darnell Davenport lowered his head. "And watch what you
say. Everything is recorded back here."

She chuckled, wondering if he'd forgotten about her
experience as a federal agent. "Yeah, I remember."

Schumaker had lawyered up right away. But Winter
wasn't a law enforcement officer. She didn't have to follow
that code.

Darnell cast her a sidelong glance, his dark brown eyes
radiating concern. "Still don't know why you need to do
this."

Winter walked past a cell of men who appeared to be
sleeping off the effects of drugs or booze. They wore
rumpled, dirty clothes, and the cell stank of urine. "Payback.

The man showed up on my doorstep and threatened me after I took his ex-wife's case. It's my turn to tell him that his name and business will be ruined."

Darnell tugged on her arm. "He threatened you? Why didn't you call me? We could've put him on our radar way before today."

Winter put on a brave face, her go-to when things got difficult. She could never let anyone know how much certain cases bothered her. During her days at the Bureau, Autumn had served as the main outlet for her frustrations. Without her best friend, she'd returned to holding in every maddening thought, letting it nibble away at her core.

"Nothing I couldn't handle." Winter kept her voice calm and steady. "I've been threatened before, and I'm sure I will be again. What I do isn't exactly popular with criminals."

"Hell of a career you've got yourself, Black." Darnell walked ahead. "Just make sure you tell me next time an asshole gets too close." He went to the end of a row of square jail cells secured with the latest electronic locks and stopped at the last one on the left.

She smiled, thankful for the backup but doubting she would ever call him for something as silly as a pushy client. She had a gun for that.

Winter stood beside Darnell in front of the eight-by-eight room, which had a bench built into the wall, a toilet, and a sink. Instead of four men in this cell—its capacity—there was only one.

Wearing the sweaty, disheveled clothes he'd left his house in, Schumaker didn't seem so sophisticated or threatening with a perimeter of gray bars around him. The fluorescent overhead light gave his skin a yellowy hue, and he was nothing like the seductive predator she'd watched escort women to his pool house.

He sat on the bench, his head in his hands. Not an ounce

of remorse awakened in Winter. This was for all the shit he'd given Julia, the anguish he'd caused his kids. Freddie Schumaker was right where he needed to be.

When he saw her with Detective Davenport, Schumaker rocked his head against the wall and released a loud groan. "Why did you bring her here?"

How's it feel when the tables are turned, asshole?

Winter tucked her hands behind her back, struggling not to appear too smug. "You'll be officially questioned in the morning after your attorney arrives. You have the chance to make things right before then. Tell us what you've done. All that you've done. If it can lead us to Harper or her remains, you might receive some mercy from the judge."

Schumaker jumped from the bench and charged at Winter. His fingers wrapped around the bars, his knuckles turning white.

"I'm telling you, I didn't do anything to that girl, or any girl for that matter." The high-pitched panic in his voice was unexpected. "The only mistake I made was giving that girl a string of diamonds and a great evening in bed. I'd never met Harper Glynn before Monday night. We had dinner at a local restaurant and then returned to my place. After that, I got her a car and she left. I never saw her again."

Winter never moved from her spot in front of the bars. She could see every bead of sweat, the red capillaries in his eyes, and the pounding of the pulse in his neck. She wouldn't say the signs of distress filled her with any sense of gratification. That was never the case. His apprehension only confirmed what she already suspected about Schumaker. He was a guilty man.

"What about your watch? We found it in Harper's apartment."

His face turned a deep shade of red, and he slapped the

bars of his cell. "I knew it." Schumaker backed away, running his hands through his hair before resting them on his hips. "My watch went missing after our night together. I was certain the girl had stolen it. You'd think the diamond necklace I gave her would be enough. I should've reported it, but I didn't want to field questions about being with her. The watch was easy enough to replace, so I let it go. I don't have time for that bullshit. That's why I *hire* women. They're less trouble and take up less of my time than a girlfriend."

Winter inched closer, making sure to add a menacing tone to her voice. "If they convict you of killing Harper, you'll have nothing but time. You do realize that?"

Darnell touched her shoulder. "Take it down a notch, Black. You're not here to interrogate."

Schumaker stalked toward the bars again. "Convict me? Based on what? My watch at her apartment? So what? I don't even know where she lives. Dust for prints if you don't believe me. DNA, whatever. Isn't that your job? Go do it."

Winter lifted her mouth in a sly grin. "We've got blood at the scene in Harper's apartment. There was blood all over her sheets. Something went on there. What we need to know is where you dumped the body."

"I didn't do anything to that girl. You can't pin this on me." He glared at Darnell. "I want my lawyer. I'm not saying another word until I see him." He turned away and returned to his bench, never looking at Winter.

Winter wanted to press him further. She had questions about the kids. What had he done to them? What had they seen or, worse, experienced?

Darnell took her elbow, leading her away from Schumaker's cell. "That's enough. Let him stew before the Feds show up in the morning to question him."

Winter got a last peek into the cell, eager to memorize

Schumaker's sagging shoulders and sunken face. She grudgingly went with Darnell.

The detective escorted her down the hall toward the entrance to the lockup area. "Was that wise? Letting him know what we have?"

"I wanted his reaction." Winter stared at the metal door, ignoring the prisoners to her left. "He's scared."

"I would be, too, in his situation." Darnell sighed and lowered his head. "What we've got is damning, but we need more for a conviction. You know that."

"We'll get it." She put a hint of confidence in her voice. "Schumaker's smart, but he isn't that smart. We have to find out how he got rid of the girls. Then we've got him."

Darnell gripped her wrist, stopping her. "Why do you hate this guy so much?"

She lifted her chin. "I don't hate him. I just don't trust him. There's a difference."

He chuckled. "Not for you."

They arrived at the thick door, and Darnell punched a code into the keypad.

"Go home. Get some sleep." He opened the door after a loud buzzer rang. "I'll let you know what they get out of him."

She stopped inside the reinforced doorway. "The man's not going to say jack shit. We both know that. He lawyered up before he even got in that cruiser. Me talking to him for a few minutes was the best shot we had of getting anything from him tonight."

Darnell frowned. "Which we didn't."

Winter sighed. He wasn't wrong.

As she left the jail, she was afraid for Harper Glynn's family and Schumaker's children. They had all suffered enough. A long trial and conviction would only make matters worse for everyone.

Once in the parking lot, she breathed in the night air, clearing her head from hours of hectic activity. When she settled behind the wheel of her Honda, another disturbing thought seared through her. Why hadn't she heard from Noah?

Where in the hell is my husband?

32

The gray morning light coming through the blinds of Winter's bedroom forced her from bed. She'd slept fitfully, with her thoughts returning to Schumaker's insistence of innocence and her husband's unusual radio silence. Instead of giving in to the fatigue aching her bones, she climbed from the bed in desperate need of coffee.

She'd just fastened the tie on her robe and stepped out of her bedroom when a blinding pain shot across her temples.

Oh, no. Not now.

She turned, hoping to get back to the bed before the visions overtook her. Wetness trickled from her nose. She didn't need to touch it to know the flow was blood.

The agony in her head escalated, feeling like a vise crushing her skull. Stumbling, she dropped to her knees. The floor came up to meet her, and she couldn't stop herself. Winter collapsed onto the wood, her body like a heavy anvil.

A young girl with long legs and golden hair sat huddled on the floor in a walk-in closet with frilly dresses and a selection of shoes around her. Arms locked around her knees. Her eyes were shut tight as she rocked back and forth in a bleak picture of immense pain.

Winter recognized her blue school jumper with an eagle emblem on the chest. The same one Gabriella wore, but this child was taller and older than the little girl.

A younger Grace?

The oldest Schumaker child appeared distressed, but over what, Winter couldn't tell. She tuned into the vision, and soon, shouting filled her head. Angry, hateful voices that she knew all too well. Schumaker and Julia. They fought over something as their daughter hid in her closet, soothing herself.

The scene shifted. One image appeared over another, shuffling through Winter's mind. Winter remained in the closet, but the girl before her matured into a young woman. Grace sobbed uncontrollably while, in the background, Winter detected the same hurtful voices of Schumaker and Julia.

Winter braced herself, knowing there was more to come. She hated seeing the girl in such pain, but she was helpless to control her visions. The image changed, blurring in and out until she could see Grace again.

She remained in the closet, her head resting on her knees, rocking and staring at the ceiling. A young woman now, the years of listening to her parents fight had traumatized her. The blue in her eyes had dulled, and a lone tear raced down her cheek. Her face was a blank canvas, empty of any emotion. Her rocking, methodical and hypnotic, hinted at the pain beneath the surface.

The closet door opened, and a tall figure entered…

The image disappeared.

Winter opened her eyes. All she could see was the hard-wood floor of her hallway. Dust particles danced before her, and a small box, one she had left there intending to hang the framed pictures inside, came into focus.

She sat up, her ears ringing. How many times could she

hit her head before she did permanent damage, or worse, needed additional brain surgery? The blood on the floor woke her from her stupor, and she held her nightshirt to her nose, blocking off the flow.

Winter made it to the kitchen, where she grabbed a wad of paper towels and poured a glass of water. She took several gulps as she stumbled back to where her attack occurred. On legs that felt like jelly, she sank to the floor, eager to clear up the droplets of crimson staining her hardwood.

Once the panic of the vision eased, she tried to remember everything she'd seen. Grace's young face filled her mind, along with the profound pain she'd exhibited. The young woman had problems. Grace was the only Schumaker child Winter hadn't spoken to. Time to fix that. Otherwise, she might never find out what had happened in that family.

Grace was the key.

After dropping the blood-tinged paper towels in the trash and getting her coffee percolating, the trill of her phone's ringtone rolled across the kitchen.

Noah?

She ran to grab the phone out of her bag, eager to hear her husband's voice. Detective Darnell's name flashed across the screen instead, sending a swath of disappointment through her. Quickly followed by panic.

Please don't tell me they let Schumaker walk free on a technicality.

"What happened? Is it Schumaker?" she all but shouted into her phone.

"No, I got a call from Vaeda Smith after you left the station." Darnell's voice faltered as he took a breath. "She claims another of her girls, Bridget Augusta, who happened to visit Schumaker last Saturday night, is missing. Apparently, Bridget missed an appointment, which was unusual for her."

Winter's gut twitched. Almost the same as Harper. Was this Schumaker's M.O.?

"Does Ms. Smith suspect something happened to Bridget?"

"Vaeda panicked while checking over her appointment book after hearing we arrested Schumaker. When she saw Bridget's appointment with him, she thought it was too coincidental."

Winter stared at her coffee maker, willing it to hurry. She was no good when she was exhausted and operating without a hefty amount of caffeine. "What about Bridget's phone?"

"All calls go straight to voicemail. Vaeda got in touch with Bridget's landlord last night and got the super to check the apartment. Bridget wasn't there, and her mail hasn't been picked up in days. That's when Vaeda called me, freaking out."

Winter wished she had a clear head to think. That was the problem with her visions. They left her fuzzy for a bit. Until she got two cups of coffee in her, thinking would be spotty at best.

She rubbed her forehead, fighting to focus. "What's the plan?"

"I got a search warrant issued ten minutes ago to collect the security cameras from the Schumaker residence. I figured since this was originally your case, you might want to ride along."

A surge of energy revived Winter. She thanked providence for the man's thoughtfulness. "You bet your ass I would."

Darnell's deep chuckle resonated over the speaker. "I'll be by in half an hour to get you."

After he disconnected the call, Winter put her phone aside on the counter, the allure of her morning coffee fading. Images of Grace Schumaker remained, adding to her doubts about what went on in that damn mansion during and after Freddie and Julia's marriage fell apart. All breakups were terrible, but had Grace taken the end of her parents' relationship harder than the other kids?

Grace had suffered tremendously during their fights. The shaking girl huddled on her closet floor told Winter all she needed to know about her trauma, but how people responded to such trauma was key. She didn't see Grace going off the deep end.

Right?

Her reservations made her want to speak to the young woman as soon as possible, but with Schumaker in jail, Winter would have to tread lightly. Enduring the yelling and accusation of her parents was one thing but seeing a father she adored incarcerated would make any teenager angry and possibly hostile.

Winter remembered Gilbert's fury before she left the mansion following Schumaker's arrest.

Great. Another Schumaker child who'll blame me for everything.

33

I itched to be moving…running…driving…anything but sitting inside this damn house. But I couldn't leave. Not yet.

I needed another package before the next drop, and the girl I'd earmarked still wasn't in the bag. Rylee Baxter had everything the buyers wanted. She would fetch a top price, but I had to get to her quickly.

Once again, I'd timed everything perfectly. My partner would be with me for added muscle. We would sneak into Rylee's trailer, bypass her druggie boyfriend, which wouldn't be hard, and capture the girl. Thanks to the bug I'd planted, my surveillance let me know she was in her trailer, recovering from a hellacious night with *Freddie*.

The news was abuzz with his arrest. The vultures were already circling for an interview with the man to tell his side of the story. If they found out about the woman with him at the time of his arrest, reporters would flock to her trailer for an exclusive. From what my research showed about Rylee, she would do anything for a shot at fame.

I needed to grab her soon. If the reporters got wind of

who Rylee was and where she lived, I'd never be able to take her, and my entire plan might come undone. She had seen my face and would be sure to blab in front of any camera aimed her way. As if she deserved one second of notoriety, the little tramp.

No one was supposed to miss my packages. I made sure their miserable little lives were empty before I claimed them, and no one would think twice when they disappeared. Whores didn't matter, and these women were all cut from the same cloth.

"You need to slow down." Ken's pathetic face twisted into a mask of fear as he sat in the corner of the room like the baby he was. "You're gonna get us both killed."

One day, asshole.

"Stop worrying. I know what I'm doing. I've timed this down to the minute. I know exactly what time we need to leave and get back."

Ken crossed his arms, frowning. I was not fond of that sour face. It reminded me of everything wrong in our relationship. "Maybe you shouldn't plan on abducting your packages around biology exams."

The assistance my partner offered had become far more of a hindrance than a help. With each package we'd acquired, the constant bitching grated deeper into my skin.

"Unlike some people, I'm not losing my shit." I cast him a resentful glance. "I have a clear mission in mind. I sometimes wonder if you've forgotten that I'm the planner. You're expendable."

He actually laughed. "You might want to rethink that. What's gonna happen to you if this woman's boyfriend fights back? I won't be so expendable then, will I?"

There it was. The cocky attitude showed up when things got too heavy. The little idiot had never been reliable, but lately, the second-guessing made me question my partner's loyalty.

"I'll have my gun with me. If the boyfriend gets in the way, I'll shoot him. I might even shoot you, if you aren't careful. So stop whining. This package pickup and sale should be the culmination of my initial plans, and after that, who knows where the world will take me?"

Ken didn't offer any more pearls of wisdom. Thank goodness. The asshole had the intelligence of a gnat.

I glanced at my watch, wishing time would speed forward. My fingers tingled, knowing we were getting closer. A night abduction would have been better, but time was not on my side. I had to move everything forward before the cops closed in.

Closing my eyes, I retraced my route to get to Rylee's trailer park. I imagined the park itself, and my upper lip curled into a disgusted sneer. Trash, rundown trailers, open ditches filled with standing green water, and old, rusted cars were everywhere. Even the air took a more putrid turn once the trailers rose on either side of my car. I wasn't familiar with such places and wasn't sure if the stench and sense of malaise in the air were characteristic of all trailer parks. Who would choose to live in such squalor?

I'd read about the increased crime in these types of environments. Having seen one firsthand, I understood why criminals preferred such sites. It was a breeding ground for exactly the kinds of people most likely to commit crimes to begin with, the lowlifes and losers and whores like Rylee Baxter. And with most of them being criminals in one form or another, they wouldn't rat each other out.

Snapping the soulless Rylee out of the clutches of such a god-awful place would be doing her a favor. No more days stuck in her trailer, living her shitty little life. Even though where I planned to send her wasn't exactly paradise, at least she wouldn't sink any lower.

I smiled as I thought of what lay ahead for Rylee not long from now. I was her rescuer. Her savior.

I'm a frickin' Mother Teresa.

34

_____

Winter sat back in the passenger seat of Detective Davenport's unmarked car, waiting as the guard at the gate of the Schumaker estate read the search warrant. Darnell didn't have to share anything with the security detail. He'd wanted to ensure the man alerted the household that he was on his way.

She warmed her stiff hands in the heat blowing out of the vent, approving of Darnell's tactic. The guard would ensure someone greeted them before knocking on the front door, and anyone with something to hide might make a speedy exit from the premises.

She'd used the same approach when determining a family's involvement in a case. When confronted by search warrants, the guilty usually ran, leaving the innocent confused and having to answer all the questions.

The guard handed the paperwork back to Darnell and motioned to the gate. "I'll let them know you're coming."

Darnell chuckled. "You do that." He rolled up his window as the heavy black gates opened. "Keep an eye out for anyone leaving."

Winter nodded. "Somehow, I don't see his employees taking part in Schumaker's debauched lifestyle. And I know the kids are clueless. They're his victims as well."

"I didn't want it to go down like that." He put the car in drive after the gate fully opened. "But after what we found in Harper's apartment, did you want to sit around and wait to see who he hurt next?"

Winter glanced at the manicured fruit trees and thick shrubs along the road to the house. "Of course not. I just wish we could have spared the kids."

Darnell pulled his car into the circular drive.

Winter hadn't unfastened her seat belt when the massive doors to the entrance opened.

Belinda Merril walked out onto the portico, standing beneath the heavy copper lantern suspended by a chain. By the stiff way she walked and the sag in her shoulders, Winter expected she hadn't slept a wink. Of all the staff in the home, she would be the one most devastated by the arrest. The Schumaker's nanny had made her feelings about her boss clear from the first meeting.

Belinda walked down the stone steps to greet them. There was no smile on her face, and her eyes appeared red and swollen.

Winter and Darnell climbed out to meet her. Belinda's drawn features radiated contempt.

"I want to know what's happened to Freddie." The strain in her voice matched the fatigue in her face. "The police at your station refuse to tell me where he is or if he's safe." She eased right in front of Darnell's face, acting nothing like the diminutive nanny who cared for the Schumaker children. "He's not a criminal. He's hurt no one. When is he coming home?"

Winter slipped between Belinda and Darnell. "That's not true. He hurt you, didn't he? Tossed you aside when you became too old."

She examined the nanny's constricted pupils, rapid breathing, and the fluttering of the vein in her neck. Anger and fear caused the same responses in people. Belinda was angry about Schumaker, or maybe she feared something else. Something she didn't want the police to know.

Winter drove the knife in deeper, hoping to get Belinda to crack. "What can you tell us about what went on in the pool house?"

Belinda backed away, her demeanor changing in an instant. She calmed and waved toward the front of the home, showing none of the upset she'd displayed before. Her expression had turned into a stony mask. "Freddie's attorney called earlier and told us to expect the police with a warrant."

Darnell handed Belinda the papers to search the home. "This gives us access to every room on the property and the right to question the staff."

With a trembling lower lip, Belinda took the papers. "Mr. Schumaker isn't coming home anytime soon, I take it."

"No." Darnell hesitated before he walked to the front doors. "Where are the children? You should get them out of here while we conduct our search."

Belinda held her head up high. "Gilbert and Grace left for school a few minutes ago. Gabriella was too upset to go. She's in her room." She arched one eyebrow, adding a hint of impertinence to her sneer. "Unless you plan on ransacking a little girl's room to satisfy your witch hunt?"

Darnell shook his head. "No, that won't be necessary."

"Why are you letting any of the kids go to school after last night's events? Aren't they all upset?"

Belinda faced Winter. "They were, but they remained adamant. They each already missed a day of school this week and don't want to miss any more classes."

Darnell gave Winter a pensive frown. "Seems a bit harsh, considering everything that happened."

Belinda clutched the warrant in her hand, crumpling the paper. "Their private school has rigorous standards." She moved past them and stopped when she reached the doors. "If you need anything, call for Adams, the butler."

Darnell and Winter followed Belinda inside. The morning light coming through the large windows shimmered on the white floor and brought out the gold thread in the wallpaper.

Winter took in the room with a new understanding of the man who owned everything there. The emptiness reminded her of Schumaker. She'd compared it to a museum when she first set foot in the grand foyer. Now everything had a chilly, impersonal feel. Her wonder had tarnished, and she saw the home for what it truly was. A temple to a man whose ego outweighed his humanity.

Belinda slinked toward the stairs, but Darnell stopped her. "Where can we find the security room?"

She turned back to the detective. "Behind the kitchen. The monitors and remotes for the cameras are in a room there. The door is never locked." She set her foot on the bottom step. "If you don't mind, I have an upset little girl to care for."

Winter waited, watching Belinda take her time as she climbed to the second-floor landing and then disappeared into the upstairs hall.

"I don't think she likes you." Darnell rubbed his hands together. "So which way is the kitchen?"

Winter motioned to the corridor along the side of the grand staircase. "Back there? And what makes you think she doesn't like me? You're the one with the warrant."

Darnell held out his hand, urging her to move ahead of him. "But you're the one who cracked the case. Without your investigation, Schumaker might still be entertaining women in his pool house."

The mention of the den of iniquity behind the home sent a tingle along Winter's spine. She remembered what Gabriella had said about seeing her father and the women heading to the pool house at night, but why hadn't Grace and Gilbert ever mentioned anything? Couldn't they see their father's antics from their bedroom windows?

An image of Grace huddled in her closet, hiding from her screaming parents, flashed across Winter's mind. She needed to find out more about the oldest Schumaker child.

Now's your chance. Go to the scene of your vision.

"You hit the security room." She nodded at the stairs. "I want to check on something first."

Darnell's dark eyes became two slits, seething with suspicion. "What are you checking?"

"Just a hunch."

She could tell he was going to argue, but several officers and crime techs streamed through the front door, and he turned his attention to assigning duties.

She left him in the foyer without saying another word and hurried to the stairs.

Once she stepped on the second-floor landing, Winter checked for anyone else in the upstairs hallway. She didn't want to fend off questions from the overzealous staff as she searched for Grace's bedroom.

Tiptoeing along, she kept a keen eye out. She remembered Gilbert's room, the second door on the right. The hall held three more doors beyond that. One of them had to be Grace's bedroom.

She arrived at a partially opened door on her left just beyond Gilbert's room as Gabriella's high voice wafted into the hallway. "When is Daddy coming home?"

"Soon, sweetheart. Soon."

Winter had to give Belinda credit. She was doing her best to soothe the little girl.

Carefully, she stepped past the ajar door, praying nobody spotted her. She stopped at another thick door on the same side of the hall as Gabriella's room. Holding her breath, she gripped the brass knob and gently turned.

The door eased open without making a sound, and she slipped inside, closing it behind her.

Winter fumbled for the light switch, as the drapes were closed, so she could barely make out the room. The instant glow from the overhead chandelier bathed it in a warm light.

Walls covered with collages of lacrosse teams in action poses and photos of smiling girls wearing the same blue school uniform she'd seen in her vision graced the walls. A white dresser with an oval mirror had more pictures of a blond beauty with curious blue eyes posing with a lacrosse stick and a silver medal around her neck.

Winter recognized the younger girl in those pictures, verifying with certainty that it was Grace in her vision.

She checked the window. Grace had an unhindered view of the pool house entrance, so she could've seen her father's activities, along with the women he escorted.

Winter scanned the room, trying to see if she picked up anything. "What happened to you, Grace? Did it happen here?"

The dresser had a neat array of cosmetics, nothing too flashy or glittery. She didn't see any pieces of expensive jewelry. Only a strand of pearls sat atop the makeup table, along with a set of tortoiseshell headbands. Unexpected for a teenage girl.

She had a four-poster bed with detailed carvings of rice plants adorning the headboard and posts. The precisely made covers were so tight, Winter bet she could bounce a quarter off the beige linen.

What teenager makes a bed like that?

One with servants, Winter guessed. Or one afraid to do anything wrong?

A tall dresser, with all the drawers closed, showed no clothes peeking out. Even the bedside tables were spotless, bearing no lip glosses or scrunchies. One had a neat stack of books. The subjects ranged from chemistry to calculus.

Rows of shoes were perfectly arranged in the closet, and the clothes hung according to color and type, with pants on one side and dresses on the other. Even the handbags had an assortment of hooks. Fendi, Chanel, Kate Spade...the purses were pricey and stylish.

Just like her mother's.

The connecting bathroom had the same attention to perfection as the bedroom. A spotless shower stall and the towels on the rack in pristine condition looked as if they've never been touched by a soiled hand. The vanity counter didn't contain one hair, one toothpaste stain, or even a dash of dust from applying makeup.

Winter remembered what Julia had said about her daughter's fastidiousness but seeing it firsthand chilled her. Teenagers were impulsive, messy, and loud, but most of all, they hated rules. This girl seemed to thrive on them. Her sterile, organized environment reminded Winter of her days at the Academy, where structure was essential for training. This girl was no military brat, though, and her father was far from a disciplinarian expecting a perfect bedroom.

Or was he?

Neither of the other Schumaker siblings seemed fixated on a perfect appearance. Gilbert had a bedroom akin to one from a post-apocalypse novel. And Gabriella might have been obsessed with pink purses and cupcakes, but the way she smeared icing on her face told Winter that OCD didn't run through her young veins. Both children appeared normal. What had made Grace so different?

Pulling on gloves, Winter started with the young woman's hamper because, in her experience, trash cans and hampers were where she'd find the most dirt.

Hardy-har-har. There's more where that came from, folks.

A couple of school uniforms joined the stack of jeans, shirts, and underwear Winter sorted through. She wanted to berate herself, but common sense told her that clues could come from anywhere. She'd dug through enough dumpsters to know that finding clues was never glamorous. Whatever it took, she would do it.

When she pulled yet another shirt out, this one felt different. Heavier. Something cold caught on her finger, and she gasped when she found half a strand of diamonds dangling out of the breast pocket.

Oh my god.

A sinking feeling cramped her stomach while a million questions raced through her head.

She tilted the shirt and a Tiffany diamond necklace tumbled the rest of the way out of the pocket and into her palm.

"What the hell is a teenager doing with this in her clothes hamper?"

Or had the nanny placed it there?

Schumaker had said something while in his jail cell about diamonds. He'd given Harper a diamond necklace, but they'd found nothing like that in her apartment. Could this be the missing necklace? Or did Grace own so many that she tossed them casually around?

An icy wave rolled through Winter as a pattern emerged. Bridget had visited Schumaker and then disappeared. Harper had visited Schumaker and then disappeared.

Until that moment, she'd believed Schumaker responsible. That, or he paid someone to do the deed. He was a powerful man with lots of connections. Julia had admitted as much. But how long could Schumaker continue with such behavior without getting caught? He was a cunning businessman, but was he so vain as to think no one would find out?

Another unsettling idea surfaced. What if someone else was behind the disappearances? It would have to be a person who knew about Schumaker's late-night parties in the pool house. Someone familiar with the Schumaker estate and who had a motive for getting rid of the call girls Schumaker had hired.

Could that motive be resentment over a ruined marriage that dissolved a family? Or was it jealousy?

Or maybe the father had set up the daughter? Or the nanny had?

Shit.

Winter was seasoned enough to know she had to examine every theory.

Energized by possible new directions in the case, Winter dug through the rest of the room, eager to find more evidence.

She discovered a designer purse tucked behind several pairs of panties in a drawer. For most teenagers, the placement might not have been odd. But for Grace Schumaker and her immaculate closet, this was strange indeed.

Winter's fingers trembled as she caressed the beading. She hesitated before working the golden clasp open. Inside there was a lipstick case, some tissues, and a wallet.

The plain brown leather wallet, nothing as fancy as the purse, contained damning credit cards and a driver's license. Bridget Augusta's essentials were in that wallet. No one tossed away a bag with so much information left inside. There was no way Grace had found this, and if she had, why was it in her room? It must have been taken either before or after Bridget disappeared.

Winter sank to the floor, sick to her stomach, still gripping the purse, wallet, and diamond necklace. The evidence was overwhelming. As much as Winter wanted to believe that Schumaker was setting his daughter up, her gut knew better.

The young woman on the stairs, her wide-eyed expression after her father's arrest, took on a whole new meaning. Winter no longer questioned what someone had done to Grace, but rather, what Grace had done to others.

She closed her eyes, picturing Julia's devastation at the news of her daughter's crimes. She was sure Schumaker would show the same despair, because Winter was convinced that his daughter was framing him. How would the caustic asshole take that news?

Winter's heart rose in her throat as she remembered the young woman with Schumaker the night of his arrest. She'd sent her home, but was she still safe? How many more women had visited the house? Were they missing too? What sucked the air from Winter's lungs was the sinking suspicion that Grace was not finished with her evil deeds.

There was more devastation on the way for the Schumaker family.

Winter was sure of it.

But first, she had to get to Rylee Baxter.

35

E very bone in Noah's body ached as he drove along the highway back to his motel. Close to twenty-four hours had passed since he'd last shut his eyes, and he needed a couple of hours' worth of sleep before continuing the search.

Eve had passed out in the passenger seat as soon as they left the hospital. He wished he could talk to her more about the case, but she needed sleep too. After what they'd found at the traffickers' hideout, Noah doubted he would ever close his eyes again.

The raid, processing the two perps still alive after the shoot-out, and then tending to fifteen traumatized survivors took all night. Once the victims were safely in hospital rooms, he and Eve had split the duty of handling their statements and getting information to track down the next of kin.

Dealing with the three minors had been the hardest. The emaciated girls, dulled by the drugs, had sat lifeless in their hospital beds like mannequins. The victims even moved the hospital doctors and nurses to tears.

Noah took responsibility for the dead Jane Doe. Eve had fought to oversee her remains, but he'd taken charge. Guilt drove him. He hadn't done enough or acted quickly enough to save her. The least he could do was oversee the disposition of what was left of her.

The one who got away still haunted him. They'd found no trace of her in the woods, no signs of blood, a struggle, or a body. The trail had gone cold in a grassy field beyond, and the search party, worn out from the day's events, had called it a night. They needed fresher eyes to scour the woods. Everyone agreed that some shut-eye was in order before heading out to more thoroughly search the trees.

What if some of the traffickers found her first? That question ate at him. They could've killed her before law enforcement arrived at the property. Her body might be at a different location, making the chance of finding her remains impossible.

All his worries nagged at him, creating a burning in his gut so intense that no amount of antacid would offer relief. This always happened when loose ends lingered on a case. Noah wanted closure like any victim or their family would, and as the one tasked with bringing that closure, his unease festered when he didn't get it.

He knew of only one cure for what ailed him. Or more to the point, one person who could help. It seemed like months —not thirty-six hours—since he'd spoken to Winter. Her voice was what he needed right now, more than anything.

He checked on Eve again, amazed at her ability to sleep while traveling the bumpy roads. Removing his phone from his jacket pocket, he hit Winter's number on speed dial.

They'd been playing phone tag with each other. That hadn't happened since Justin had taken her. The terror and pain inflicted by her kidnapping resurfaced, creating a tidal wave of worry in Noah's gut. Whenever he couldn't contact her, those old anxieties returned.

Winter's dead, dull eyes as she lay in that hospital bed

following her rescue from the madman still filled his nightmares. Her cropped hair and the pain she relived, not from the gunshot wound she'd suffered but from what Justin had made her do. Killing two innocent people had torn her apart, and Noah still ached to help her put the past behind her. But no matter how justified the killing, no agent ever forgot the names or faces of those they had killed.

"Hey there." Her sweet voice filled the speaker of his phone.

The weight of worry on his shoulders eased a little. "How are you, darlin'?"

"I'm on my way with Detective Davenport to the home of an escort who may or may not have a psychotic seventeen-year-old girl trying to kidnap her."

Noah's eyes popped open. "Wait. Say that again?"

"It's complicated but related to my case. I can explain more later when I get all the facts in." She paused, and her voice gentled. "How are you?"

How was he? Noah didn't know if he had an answer. Processing a case, especially one as hard-hitting as his current one, took time. Days, weeks, even months to put all the pieces in the jigsaw puzzle together.

"I'm beat. Been up all night on a case, and I'm heading to the motel with Eve for some much-needed sleep."

"You won't sleep." Winter knew him so well. "You always get too wrapped up in a case to sleep."

He smiled, thinking of her inviting lips. "Now who's calling the kettle black?"

"When are you coming home?" The desperation of her tone moved him.

He glanced at his sleeping partner. "After we get some rest, we'll head back to Austin. Everything's in the locals' hands now."

"Did you find anything?"

Noah hesitated, trying to figure out how to answer her question. "We found a lot. Seventeen women waiting to be trafficked. We uncovered a stop on some sort of pipeline."

"You don't sound happy." Winter's voice dropped to a whisper. "What is it? What happened?"

He grinned, amazed by how well she knew him. Noah should have known that keeping anything from his intuitive wife was pointless.

"Three of the seventeen we found were children. *Children*, Winter. Number seventeen…we couldn't find her. I'm afraid she might have been caught, killed, or shipped before we raided the property. And one, who had tried to escape with the seventeenth victim, we found dead. I couldn't save her."

The silence on the phone let him know she'd heard every word. That was Winter. She never blurted out an answer, and carefully weighed everything he said.

"You need to take it easy on yourself. You can't save everyone. Save who you can, remember? If you can make a difference in their lives, you've done something right. That's the best you can do. You changed those women's lives today. You saved them. Concentrate on that."

He sighed, rolling his shoulders to ease the ache in his neck. "Yeah, but the two I failed won't leave me alone."

"What were their names?"

"Don't know yet. We've got them as Jane Doe One and Jane Doe Two. Jane Doe One was found dead not far from the traffickers' facility. She wasn't a child but was far too young to die. She fought back against those wanting to sell her off like livestock. And they shot her for it."

"You got a description?"

Noah knew all his wife's moods. Or he hoped he did. There was happy Winter, sad Winter, thoughtful Winter, snarky Winter, his favorite, and angry Winter. What he heard was curious Winter. She only showed up when his wife was knee-deep in a case, and the wheels in her head were spinning like bald tires on a slick road.

"Why do you ask? You think this has something to do with your case?"

She snickered. "I hate that you know me so well, but I'm just curious. Maybe I can help."

His tone became businesslike as he briefly described the corpse now lying in the hospital morgue. "She was a pretty brunette with long hair, blue eyes, and a trim figure. My guess is she was a dancer. She seemed the type."

"Any distinguishing marks? Tattoos?"

The rising lilt of her voice meant Winter's adrenaline had revved up. She was onto something.

Noah went over every detail he remembered about the dead woman. He pictured her lying atop an autopsy table, leaves still caught in her hair. A butterfly tattoo on her wrist appeared in his head. He'd only caught a glimpse before they covered her body, but it had been there.

"A butterfly tattoo on her right wrist. A little blurry. Like the cheaper ones that fade with time."

Winter gasped. "I've got to go, but I'll call you back. I love you." The line went dead.

Noah stared at the phone. "What the hell?"

Eve roused from her nap. "Everything okay?"

He returned his phone to his pocket. "Sorry. I was talking to Winter."

Eve sat up and wiped her eyes. "Yeah, I heard."

"I thought you were sleeping. After last night, you should be dead to the world."

His partner rubbed her neck. "FBI agents don't sleep. We catnap. I thought you knew that already."

Squinting at the windshield, Noah noticed something on the side of the road. A dead animal?

Eve pointed. "What's that?"

He leaned forward. "You see it too." He pulled the car over to the shoulder, his stomach churning.

"Is that what I think it is?" Eve opened the door before he stopped the car.

Hair. Clothes. Not an animal.

Shit.

Ramming the car into park, Noah was out of the vehicle an instant after Eve was. A woman, her clothes badly torn, her hands and knees covered with dried blood, lay motionless halfway in the ditch.

A zing of shock jolted Noah. *Son of a bitch.* This had to be number seventeen. Jane Doe Two.

He bent over the woman while Eve put in a call for help. His throat constricted with worry. Was she alive?

He touched her cool skin, and his hope crashed. His fingers found her carotid artery, and he held his breath, eager for the slightest flutter of life.

Thump, thump.

There was a faint heartbeat, and her breathing was shallow.

As Eve spoke to 911, Noah inspected the cuts on her cheeks, her swollen lips, and the tears on her clothes. He couldn't find any gunshot wounds and saw no patches of blood. Only cuts and scratches covered her exposed skin.

Noah lifted the woman out of the ditch and settled her on a patch of grass beyond the roadway while Eve gave the dispatcher their location. She had to have run from her escapers all day and night to have made it this far. Fear did amazing things to people. He removed a few strands of mahogany hair from her face. Her eyelids fluttered, but she remained unconscious.

Noah knelt next to her, thanking providence for helping him locate his seventeenth victim. Jane Doe Two was alive and hopefully would make a full recovery.

Physically, at least.

He recalled the dead girl on the cold, metal table in the morgue and forced her young face from his mind so he could focus on the living.

"She may not have made it, but you will. You've got a life to live, so keep fighting."

Noah held her hand, talking to her and encouraging her back from whatever darkness she inhabited. One day she would tell her tale, and when she did, Noah would be there, ready to take down whoever had done this to her and all the others.

36

R ylee sprawled on her back, staring at the rust spot in the ceiling, debating between making coffee or peeing. She needed the coffee. The crazy antics of the night before had left her nerves frayed. She'd believed her prince charming had arrived to rescue her from Jud and the trailer park. To see him hauled off in handcuffs was more than a letdown. It shattered her dreams.

Schumaker had been charming, funny, and all the things she'd wanted in a man. Especially rich, the biggest criterion. To think she'd been in the home of a criminal, one who could have possibly killed her, became too much. When she'd gotten home, she stole Jud's weed to calm down. That had helped a little, at least to fall asleep, but now all that circled her head was fear and shame.

With her hopes of a better life with Schumaker dashed, Rylee contemplated her next move. Staying with Jud wasn't feasible, but where would she go if she left their trailer? She'd have to get with Vaeda today and see what else was out there. Rylee would find a new ticket out of her depressing life.

Schumaker wasn't the only wealthy guy who used escorts to give him what he needed.

A renewed sense of purpose warmed her toes. She tossed aside the covers, beelined to the bathroom, and then stumbled toward the kitchen, putting the previous night out of her head. Rylee opened the fridge, her mouth drier than the desert, and decided on orange juice to perk her up before she started the coffee maker.

The damn thing takes forever.

When the fridge door shut, she screamed, nearly dropping the juice.

A woman stood in the hallway. A weird uniform clung to her petite figure. She moved forward, her arms outstretched, reminding Rylee of a lion tamer attempting to corral a big cat.

The weed from the night before left her mind muddled, but the woman's face awakened a sense of familiarity.

"I know you." Rylee's head cleared, and she planted her feet, wanting to appear brave. "I saw you at Mr. Schumaker's. What are you doing in my house?"

"Good thing you've got a pretty face." The stranger waved a hand down Rylee's figure. "God knows where you would've ended up without it. Waitressing? Fast food industry? I can see a slut like you slinging fries."

Rylee twisted her neck one way, then the other, searching the camper for Jud.

The intruder closed the distance between them. "Lucky for you, I have a perfect life waiting for you. Something you won't need a brain for. Hell, you won't even have to think. All you'll need to do is spread your legs and take it over and over again. Now be a good girl and cooperate."

Rylee bent her knees, bracing for a fight, just like Jud taught her. He'd wanted her to know how to defend herself.

He'd always said pretty girls should know how to throw a punch.

She put up her fists. "Get the hell out of my trailer, or I'll—"

The menacing laugh that interrupted her was colder than before.

Rylee tensed, sensing she was in big trouble.

"What are you going to do?" The maid took the last step. She was nose to nose with Rylee. "You can't stop me. No one can."

The warmth of the maid's breath had barely left Rylee's cheek when a flash appeared behind the dangerous woman. Either Rylee's quick glance gave Jud away, or this maniac heard him approaching. Either way, she pulled a gun as fast as lightning.

Jud skidded to a halt, his nostrils flaring. "You can't shoot us both. Fire and one of us will go after you, and I promise I won't let you live, bitch."

Rylee flinched as he yelled, afraid his anger might have heightened the situation. She'd watched enough cop shows to know you never confronted anyone with a gun.

She noticed Jud hunching his shoulder, as if preparing to rush the woman. Rylee wanted to tell him to stop, fearing what would happen.

The muzzle pivoted, settling on Rylee, aiming at her chest. "Do you want her to die first, then?" The woman's heartless voice weakened Rylee's knees.

A creak sounded from the hall closet door slowly swinging open. A shadow moved out from behind it, and Rylee's blood turned to ice as the realization hit her.

The intruder wasn't alone.

Her accomplice moved like a lynx, his gun directed right at Jud.

"See?" The woman's cocky attitude permeated the small

room. "I don't have to choose." She nodded at her accomplice. "Two people. Two guns. Too easy."

Fear made Rylee's muscles tremble, and her mouth went dry.

What's going to happen to us?

37

Winter shook as the information spun in her head like a tornado. The photos on her iPad of Bridget Augusta, Harper Glynn, and Rylee Baxter had not come together until she'd spoken with Noah. She glanced at Darnell, driving his cruiser along the highway at breakneck speed.

She'd been going back and forth, seeing no similarity between the women except their beauty and occupation. The only detail that stood out to her was the butterfly tattoo on Bridget's wrist. When Noah mentioned a similar tattoo on the wrist of one of his Jane Does, Winter knew it couldn't be a coincidence.

"You really think there's a connection between our cases?" Darnell demanded as he negotiated a turn on the highway. "We need to be sure before we go in."

"You've got to admit, two women missing from Austin with the same hair and eye color, plus the butterfly tattoo on one of their wrists, seems impossible. The odds are the dead girl is Bridget Augusta."

The only factor that made little sense to Winter was Grace. Why would she commit such heinous acts? For her to be involved in taking the women and selling them seemed too farfetched. That wasn't something teenagers did. This was a crime constructed by a psychopath. An older, more capable psychopath.

Darnell let up on the gas as he approached his exit. "If Noah hadn't busted that trafficking ring's holding house, we might never have known about Bridget's fate, if that was her."

Winter held onto the door as he zipped off the highway. "Right. If that was Bridget, she didn't get there by coincidence. And he said she'd been escaping with another woman. Jane Doe Two. What if she's Harper Glynn?"

"Then I'd say Grace Schumaker has much to answer for." Darnell held onto the wheel as the car skidded over gravel on the access road.

Winter let go of the door as the car slowed. "I thought something seemed off about that girl's weird stare last night."

Darnell gave her a sidelong glance.

"Just before I walked out with Rylee, she peeked her head around the wall from the top of the staircase. She had crazy eyes."

"Huh." Darnell arched an eyebrow.

"It makes me wonder what she's been through."

"Some people are born bad."

"There must be something in her past to explain her behavior."

She didn't bother to tell him about her psychic vision of Grace huddling in her closet. The impression was a clue about the trauma Grace had suffered, not the trauma she'd inflicted on others.

"I know trauma can explain a lot about deviant behavior,

but what makes some people adapt and others sink to such depravity?" Darnell refocused on the empty road ahead. "I think there's more than Grace seeing her father take hookers to his pool house in this situation. We just haven't found that smoking gun yet."

Winter had to agree with him. But in her experience, very few people were born bad. Their environment changed them. Emotions such as hatred and fear were the fire that forged new identities. These personalities wanted vengeance for their suffering.

Darnell drove through the entrance to the mobile home park. Winter examined the collection of rusty, dirty trailers, and her heart ached for Rylee Baxter. She was a young woman eager to escape the sad life she'd been born into. Bridget and Harper's lives didn't seem as desperate as Rylee's, but they had all ended up in the same ugly situation.

He parked the car a few trailers down from Rylee's. A black van sat out front. A Mercedes minivan.

"That's her place, all right." Darnell removed the key from the ignition and popped the trunk. "She lives with a boyfriend. Van might be his."

Winter didn't think so. "That specific van? No, I'm pretty sure I saw it outside Schumaker's." She'd seen a similar van when she was perched in the oak tree.

"Traffickers use vans for transportation. Our guys keep a watch out for them on the roads."

This was making more sense by the second, as a teenage girl couldn't materialize a black van for smuggling women out of thin air. That van had to be one of a dozen in Daddy's collection. That guy had so much money and so many toys, he didn't even notice when a vehicle went missing.

Rage rolled through Winter as she removed her gun from the holster.

Darnell stared at the weapon. "You should have told me you brought that along."

She checked the safety. "What do you want me to do if Grace is here? Stop her with my sarcasm?"

He shook his head and opened the door. "Just don't shoot her. I have enough to explain to my superiors already."

She bet he did. "Sorry."

Darnell waved a hand in front of Winter, like he was anointing her. "There, you're deputized to assist in any potential arrest *I* may be required to make." He gave her a stern look. "We're going to wait for backup, hear me?"

She grinned and waited as he grabbed a bulletproof vest from the trunk and slipped it on before calling it in. The screech of the Velcro easing into place was music to her ears. She'd lived with that unique crunching sound for so long that she'd forgotten how much she missed it.

He shut the trunk. "I only got the one vest, so you follow my lead. I can protect us both."

Winter smirked and allowed Darnell to go first, ignoring the detective's frown when she came up alongside him instead of staying in the back. She was grateful he didn't argue. She knew she would get crap for it later, but she still considered this her operation. Winter might have been a private investigator, but years with the Bureau made her more than capable in such situations.

They crept closer to Rylee's trailer, guns out and searching ahead. Winter needed to establish if anyone was holding Rylee inside. The last thing she wanted was a gunfight.

She moved past a few lawn chairs and a firepit outside Rylee's door. Her head down, eyes up, and ears attuned to every noise, Winter experienced that itch, the one she got whenever a mission got dangerous.

Voices rose at one end of the trailer. The thin walls made picking up the conversation easy.

"...I don't have to choose. ...Two people. Two guns. Too easy."

A woman's harsh tone brought Winter to a standstill. Schumaker had sounded the same way on her doorstep the night he'd come to intimidate her. It had to be Grace. She had her father's coldness down pat. And the voice was familiar. She'd heard it on a number of the young woman's social media uploads.

Winter heard a loud smack or a punch, followed by someone choking on tears. That had to be Rylee. That was followed by clatter and commotion.

"You shouldn't be too upset with your change in circumstances. You're already a sex worker, but the pay is considerably less where I'm sending you."

Grace's cynical laugh brought a lump to Winter's throat. What would Julia say, hearing her daughter speak such villainous words?

"Why are you doing this?!" Rylee's voice was strained, teeming with fear.

At least hearing her voice reassured Winter that they'd arrived in time. Rylee was still in the trailer. Somehow, she and Darnell had to get Rylee safely outside.

Crying erupted, even louder. Rylee had to be at the end of her rope.

A male voice screamed, "Shut the hell up!"

Someone other than Grace was in there, but was it an accomplice or another potential victim?

It was maddening not to know.

"We've got to go in," Winter whispered as the crying escalated.

Not looking happy about it, Darnell nodded. "I know. Shit. I don't like this."

Winter didn't either, but it was what it was.

Darnell moved ahead as the only one with the legal right to storm the home. But Winter had another idea. He nodded at the door to the trailer, signaling his intention to enter.

She raised a hand. "No. I'll go in," she whispered. "I can play it cool. If I treat it as a friendly call to check on Rylee, I can get a better idea of what we're facing."

He shook his head, his cheeks flushing a deep shade of red. "No, this is my operation. Let me handle it."

A sick feeling swelled in her stomach. Grace was a disturbed woman, and Winter guessed she had a fair amount of paranoia to exacerbate her declining mental health. That was a deadly combination when guns were involved.

She was about to urge Darnell to wait a damn second so she could get around back when he charged past her to the trailer door. "Don't!" she hissed.

He didn't listen.

With a kick as solid as hers had been the night before, he thrust his foot to the left of the door handle. But instead of the door opening inward, the trailer door opened out.

Aside from a loud rattle, nothing happened—nothing except alerting the criminals inside that they were surrounded.

This wasn't good.

Winter indicated the back. "I'm going—"

Bam.

A bullet passed through the door, whizzing within inches of her and Darnell's position.

Shit.

Winter ducked low, getting close to the ground. She checked on Darnell, relieved to see the bullet had missed him too. They had no choice but to take the trailer by force. Things would get ugly now that the kidnappers knew they were outside.

The annoying rush of fear tightened Winter's grip on her gun. She didn't have a bulletproof vest to protect her.

If their attempt to take the trailer and save Rylee went south, she might never see Noah again.

But to save a young woman from human trafficking? So be it.

38

The crack of two more gunshots ripping through the metal door had Winter crouching on her knees, wedged between the trailer and the metal tub used as an outdoor firepit. She searched the area for Darnell. He wasn't far away. His gun remained pointed at the trailer door as he knelt against the mobile home, his gaze locked on Winter.

At least he appeared sorry for his reckless move. Not that it would help them now.

He pointed, motioning that they should go around back. Winter shook her head.

That was what Grace would be expecting. That was where her attention would be.

She hoped.

After a moment of thought, Darnell nodded and indicated that he would take the right side of the door while she took the left. She nodded back. A few minutes ago, she was going to take the back while he took the front. That was no longer an option. The chance of crossfire was too great. They had to do this together.

She hoped.

Hope's not a strategy.

She knew that, but right now, Darnell had tossed them into a shitstorm that she wasn't sure they'd survive. Hope and muscle memory were all she had.

She took a deep breath and remembered her training. *"Analyze the vulnerability of your target and attack their strongest inadequacy first, saving their weakest for last."* Her instructor had drilled that rule into her from the first day of operational skills classes. She'd used that to help her take down serial killers and perps a lot more dangerous than a seventeen-year-old with daddy issues.

Grace might have had a gun, but she didn't have training. The girl also knew nothing about tactical planning in closed spaces. Winter had two advantages Grace had never counted on—experience and Darnell.

When they got into position, Darnell pointed to his chest, mouthing, *I'll go in first.*

Winter made a mental note to buy her own vest the minute this case was over. If she hadn't been so wrapped up in moving from Virginia and establishing a life with Noah, she might have thought about her safety before this moment.

She waved him to the door, mindful of her weakness without the armor. She wanted to get back home to her husband in one piece. Walking into a narrow trailer with a known hostile and no knowledge of the layout required her to give Darnell the lead.

Winter took position on the other side.

"We go on three," he whispered.

She nodded and checked her gun.

One...two...three.

Darnell pulled open the door this time, and Winter jumped into action.

She stuck close to his back, keeping her gun pointed ahead, checking for any movement.

The first room they entered was a small living area. The priority when entering any unknown situation was to clear your approach and find cover. Winter spun to check her inside corner, and dodged behind a breakfast table in the small nook beside the kitchen. Darnell went for a wall closer to a hallway.

She quickly scanned the layout, noting the kitchen just behind the living room, the hallway, and an open door in the hallway she assumed was a bathroom or closet. The hallway had the potential to end up as a bottleneck where she and Darnell could come under fire with no place to escape.

Darnell glanced down the hallway and pointed to his eyes while making a *V* with his fingers. She had a better vantage point to assess the hallway than he did.

A sudden flash of something at the end of the hallway kept Winter crouched low behind the table. Someone was coming from the back of the trailer. She motioned to Darnell to watch his six.

It didn't take long for Winter to identify Grace Schumaker. She had a gun pointed at Rylee's head.

Dammit. I've gotta keep her talking before someone gets killed.

"Get out of here or I'll shoot the bitch." Grace pressed the gun harder against Rylee's temple. "Don't test me, assholes. I mean it."

Where's the guy I heard talking earlier?

Tears streaming out of control, Rylee pressed her hands together, as if pleading with Winter. "Don't let her hurt me."

Grace smacked Rylee on the side of the head. Rylee cowered and ducked her chin.

"You're pathetic. All your kind are." Grace's voice cracked. "Lying whores who don't give a damn about the people you hurt."

Another critical lesson Winter had learned at the Academy was reading criminals, especially in tense situations like this one. A minimal amount of negotiation proved essential for hostage situations, but what Winter quickly understood about Grace was that she harbored resentment against Rylee and women like her. The crack of her voice and how she targeted these women proved to be the impetus for her crimes.

No matter how brave Grace pretended to be, she was a young woman suffering emotional torment. Winter could use that to her advantage. "You don't want to kill anyone, Grace. That's not why you're doing this."

"Bullshit," the girl fired back with a hefty amount of bravado. "You don't know crap about me."

Winter concentrated on her voice. Easy, soothing words were the best. "I know you're not a killer. I know your mother. She's been so worried about you and your siblings. She doesn't want to see any of you hurt. That's why she hired me. To protect you from your father."

"For fuck's sake, Barbie."

Barbie?

Winter knew that voice. Outside, she'd thought it was Rylee's boyfriend, but now, in these close quarters…

"This has gone too far. I did what you wanted, but it has to stop." A young man moved into the light, brandishing a handgun. "I don't want to do this anymore. And you can't keep bullying me. I'm done!"

Recognition worked its way through Winter. *Gilbert Schumaker? What's he doing mixed up in all this?*

Winter's insides twisted into knots at the realization that the siblings had been working together to kidnap the women. These were privileged kids, wanting for nothing. What did they get from hurting women, destroying their lives, and sending them to certain death?

"Don't you chicken out on me now, asshole." The vehemence in Grace's voice curdled the air. "We promised to do this together. To make him pay together. You were as sick of his shit as I was."

Schumaker. They had to be talking about Freddie Schumaker. Everything stemmed from their father's dalliances with call girls and the divorce.

Gilbert sniffled from somewhere behind Grace. "But I never wanted to hurt anyone. That was all your idea."

"You traitor!" Grace seemed as if she were about to crack.

Darnell flagged Winter and pointed into the hallway. He could sense things were about to get out of hand too. He was going to go after Grace and her gun. It was risky, but also their best shot at saving Rylee and de-escalating the situation.

"You were always a bitch!" Gilbert shouted. "Always hurting everyone…me, Gabriella, Mom. You loved bossing us around and spewing your lies. You wrecked our family. You're psycho, and I'm done!"

Winter's gaze stayed on Grace as Darnell maneuvered away from the wall and stayed low, hiding behind the partially opened hallway closet door so Grace and Gilbert couldn't see him.

Grace turned the gun away from Rylee and aimed it at Gilbert's chest. "What in the fuck do you know about what I did to our family?"

Gilbert did the same, putting the siblings at a standoff. "They were always fighting because of you!"

Winter raised her head from behind the table and gestured at Rylee. She had one shot at getting the woman away from Grace. She motioned her forward and mouthed, *slowly*.

Rylee gave a jerky nod and moved one foot out and away from Grace's side.

Thankfully, Grace never noticed. Her attention and anger stayed directed at her brother.

She raised her arm, directing the gun from his chest to his forehead. "Do you know what our dear father did to me? All the things I protected you and Gabriella from? The evil, ugly, disgusting things I had to endure so he would leave you two alone? You *owe* me!"

Winter's chest constricted as she listened to the young woman's words. *Oh, God. Please, no.*

Rylee took another tentative step away from Grace under Winter's watchful eye. The tension in the trailer escalated. Grace's hands shook and her gaze darted about. Winter now understood why she had gone this far.

Gilbert actually looked confused, and his gun lowered an inch. "What are you talking about? What did he do to you?"

Sweat trickled down Winter's face. She had to move quickly before Grace noticed Rylee inching away from her.

Grace stepped forward and *thunked* her brother with the barrel. "You think he's so wonderful. You said you wanted to be like him when you grow up, but you don't know him. How can you protect that man and abandon me when my mission is so close to—"

Rylee took a bold step back, lunging away from Grace.

Grace spotted the movement and spun. Her gun came around just as Darnell charged forward and yanked Rylee into the closet. Winter took advantage of the distraction Rylee and Darnell offered to take Grace down.

Bam.

Winter didn't want to kill the girl and was pleased when a circle of blood appeared on Grace's right shoulder. Her gun clattered to the floor.

As Grace screamed in pain, Winter leapt forward and kicked the gun away, her weapon on Gilbert. "Drop it!" She barely had the second word out before his gun joined his sister's.

Winter pinned Grace to the floor, knocking the other weapon out of reach.

Grace squirmed beneath her, fighting back. "You don't get it!" Grace shrieked. "He has to pay."

Soon, her shouts turned to sobs, and tears stained her cheeks.

Winter secured the girl's hands behind her back with the extra cuffs Darnell tossed her. He used the other set on Gilbert.

Winter glanced back to see Rylee cowering in the closet without a scratch on her.

Thank God.

Rushing to get a towel, Winter turned Grace over and put pressure on her wound. "What does Gilbert not understand about your father? What does he have to pay for? I want to know."

Now cuffed and compliant, Gilbert watched his sister. *He wants to know too.*

Grace stopped fighting the cuffs. She turned her angry gaze to Winter. "Daddy didn't always have hookers and strippers to play with." Her tone was as empty as her soul. "He had me. I was his special princess for years."

Winter's insides dissolved into a mass of fury. How could she not have seen the signs?

"One day, he stopped playing with me. He threw me away like the rest of the trash." Grace turned away, her blank stare fixated on a paneled wall.

Gilbert pulled against Darnell's hold on him. "Why didn't you say anything?" His croaky voice cleaved Winter's heart in two. "I would've helped you. We could've told Mom. We could've gone after Dad. You could have been—"

"Nothing! I would have been nothing." She bared her teeth at her brother. "I liked what he did to me. I enjoyed it, and I didn't want it to end. Do you know what that makes me?"

Gilbert sagged against Darnell. The muscular cop pulled the young man away from his sister. "Let's get you out of here." He met eyes with Winter. "Thanks for not getting your ass killed."

"You too." Once Winter helped Grace to her feet, she relaxed, glad everyone was in one piece. And that the sound of sirens was getting closer.

The young woman snickered. "You'll never find them. All the women I took. They're gone forever. Daddy will never play with them again."

Winter tried to separate her pity for this young woman from the twisted crimes she'd committed. Was she legally responsible? Could years of sexual abuse from Schumaker have warped her mind to the point that she no longer knew right from wrong? That was for the shrinks to figure out.

Rylee staggered to her feet, tears streaming down her cheeks. "They hurt Jud, my boyfriend. He's in the back, knocked out."

Winter felt pity for the woman who had almost joined the list of Grace's victims. *First come the tears. The nightmares will follow.* "We'll have an ambulance for both of you."

Winter was almost to the trailer door when a text pinged her phone. She kept one hand on Grace as she retrieved the device from her jacket pocket.

We found Jane Doe Two. She's alive. She says her name is Harper Glynn. We saved sixteen of them.

As she read Noah's words, a satisfying rush of certainty eased through Winter, like a cold drink on a hot day.

She lifted her screen in front of Grace's face. "Turns out you're wrong. We did find the women you've been abducting and trafficking. That means you may not be facing as many penalties. And once you tell a jury what your father put you through, he'll end up paying for what he did."

The girl sagged against her and broke into defeated sobs.

Winter felt for the girl…a little. In addition to ruining so many lives, she'd ruined her own. Maybe, someday, Grace might find a way to make peace with her past, even though it would likely be from within the walls of a psych ward.

39

The frigid air in the stark-white hall wrapped around Noah and chilled him to the bone. He hated the stench of death. No matter how much the hospital tried to mask the odor, he knew what was on the other side of the wall next to him. He'd spent so many years chasing those who loved killing, death had become part of the job.

Still didn't make moments like this any easier. Finding a body always seemed surreal. It never hit home that this was a person, a son, daughter, father, or mother, until he met the family. Like a soldier going to war, he had to know who he was fighting for. Some agents hated this part, but meeting the families of those who died kept him hungry for the fight.

The sign above the double silver doors with *MORGUE* in bold red letters almost made him turn tail and run. He reined in the desire when he spotted the woman up ahead. She stood at the viewing window, where a family could identify their dead relatives.

Eve had told him Evelyn Augusta had arrived to see her daughter. The plump woman with dark curly hair didn't resemble the dead woman on the slab whatsoever. Noah wondered if Bridget had favored her father. He suddenly felt guilty that he hadn't taken the time to get to know the dead woman's past. He wished he knew something besides how she died. Bridget shouldn't end up as a footnote in anyone's report. To always be *that woman shot by traffickers* didn't seem fair.

He drew closer, studying Mrs. Augusta's profile, noting the tears streaming along the curve of her cheeks and settling just under her chin.

"Missus Augusta?" He stopped at her side, wishing he could find some way to ease her pain.

She wiped her cheeks and turned to him. "Yes?"

He held out his hand. "I'm Agent Noah Dalton. I was with the party who found your daughter."

She nodded and sniffled. "And found so many others, I heard. I'm glad you could save some of them."

He kept her hand in his. "I wanted to tell you, ma'am, how sorry I am. How sorry we all are for your loss."

She let go of him. "Please call me Evie, Agent Dalton."

Noah cleared his throat, hoping his words might help her. "What your daughter did, well, she saved so many. If Bridget hadn't fought back, all those women might have died, or worse."

The tears reappeared, trickling down Evie's cheeks. "I never did know how to protect my Bridget. I tried best I could, but sometimes, you're so busy fighting to stay alive that you forget what it does to your kids."

"You taught her how to be strong." He gazed into her eyes. "You taught her how to fight, Evie. That takes an awful lot of courage."

She sucked in a deep breath and patted his hand. "Thank you. Her stepdaddy, Cyrus, wanted to come with me, but he backed out at the last minute. He loved her to pieces, even adopted her, but he couldn't stand seeing her like this." She turned back to the window. "I know men like to call us the weaker sex, but I think it's funny how women are the strong ones when things turn bad. We're warriors when we need to be. Just like my little girl."

And my wife.

Noah remembered how hard Winter had fought while at the Bureau, her determination to shine in such a challenging career. She was like Evie and her daughter, a warrior charging the toughest front line, determined to see the battle through until the bitter end.

Her desire to rescue others had led to Winter's rescue of herself.

He missed his wife more in that moment than any other over the past few days. He couldn't wait to get back, embrace her, and tell her how damn lucky he was to have her by his side.

Winter sat at a cozy breakfast table in a kitchen warmed by the morning sun, nursing a cup of coffee and listening to Julia's sobs as she tried to absorb the chaos of her new life.

Her heart went out to the mother of three. Two of her children sat in prison for kidnapping and taking part in a human trafficking ring, along with a host of other charges. Winter wasn't sure what weighed on the woman more, knowing her children had committed such heinous crimes or that their actions had led to the death of an innocent woman. And then there was the matter of her husband, who'd abused her oldest daughter for years.

Julia lowered a tissue from her eyes and sniffled. "I still can't believe it. Gilbert and Grace?" She closed her fist around the tissue. "And Freddie…? I knew he and Grace were close, but I never…why didn't she come to me? I would have protected her. I would've *killed him* if I'd known. How could I not have sensed it? I'm a mother, I'm supposed to have that…" She broke down again.

Winter tapped her finger against her coffee mug, struggling to find the right words. *Are there any right words?* So often, when one parent was an abuser, the other was just as likely to ignore the obvious signs as to mistake them for innocent behavior.

"When did you notice her behavior change? Did she change her appearance? Seem more preoccupied with her looks?"

Julia shook her head, lost in her thoughts, her eyes going in and out of focus. "When she was about thirteen, she became obsessed with her weight. She stopped eating for a while, and I threatened to send her to a therapist who deals with eating disorders. The need for the perfect outfit and hair started then. Pearls and perfectly primmed ponytails, even on Sundays. I thought it strange but better than begging for tattoos like her other friends do. She was always a neat freak, and I blamed it on puberty. I blamed it all on puberty. I was so blind. Why didn't I see it? I thought it was just a teenage thing."

"Accepting that sexual abuse is happening under your own roof is one of the hardest pills for a parent to swallow. And we all develop defenses that prevent us from seeing what looks obvious after the fact." Winter's guilt crept up her throat, sending a bitter taste to her mouth. "Victims deal with the scars of their trauma in many ways. Grace had the classic behavior of an abuse victim. Her fastidiousness, attention to detail, and even her hunger for control. Everything you describe is what we look for. Maybe if I'd been able to see more of her behavior firsthand, I could have spotted something was off. But I might just as easily have mistaken her attitude for typical teenager behavior."

Julia sat back in her chair, her red eyes swimming with heartache. "As if the divorce didn't already make me feel like a terrible mother. Now this?" She scrubbed her face with her hands. "Is that really why Grace did those horrible things? Because of what Freddie did to her? Or was she trying to get back at me?"

"By her own admission, it was all about making Schumaker pay for what he did. Even though she claimed to feel jealous of the women he brought into the house, Grace suffered at her own father's hand. She wanted them to feel the same abandonment and torment he had inflicted upon her."

Julia wiped her eyes. "It's not totally my fault? You're sure of that?"

She might have contributed to Grace's desire to destroy lives by constantly fighting with Schumaker, but the guilt she would carry for the rest of her life—knowing her daughter was a monster—was something no mother should have to bear.

"I don't think any of us can be sure why Grace chose human trafficking as her means of communication. Abuse survivors act out in different, often self-destructive, ways to call attention to their suffering."

Julia ran a fingertip around the rim of her mug. "I don't know if I can ever forgive myself for ignoring her situation for so long. When she and Freddie grew closer, I...I took it personally, at first. I felt I'd been thrown over by both of them, and that sounds like such a red flag now that I say it out loud."

"What about Gilbert? Did his personality shift at any point?"

"Gilbert? No, he'd leap off a skyscraper or set the house on fire if Grace told him to. Hell, he'd set himself on fire."

A blind follower. There were too many of those in the world, unfortunately.

Winter rubbed her palms along her slacks, uncomfortable with going on but knowing she had to help Julia find some way to release herself from this prison of guilt.

"Grace wasn't working alone, you know. She was supporting an existing ring of traffickers run by adults. Well, by men over the age of eighteen."

"Who were they? How did she get mixed up with such people?"

"Once Grace admitted to kidnapping Bridget Augusta and Harper Glynn and attempting to abduct Rylee Baxter, she spilled about the rest of the ring, giving up names of people higher up in the trafficking organization. It's like she was desperate to tell someone the truth, which also checks out with younger criminal offenders. They enjoy the rush of what they're doing but harbor a deep desire to tell someone, *to tell anyone*, about it."

"What for? Why would she want anyone to know she was doing these things?"

"To get their attention, which she couldn't get when Schumaker was abusing her."

"You mean *my* attention, don't you? I knew it was her way of getting back at me." Julia's sobs started up again, progressing into full-blown wails within seconds.

Winter reached out a hand and placed it on her client's shoulder.

"She wanted to make it stop, so she could get back to what used to be normal. Julia, it wasn't about getting back at you or blaming you for anything. You weren't the abuser. If anything, you were an earlier victim, given what we've learned of Schumaker's behavior with women in general. We think his abuse of Grace started after he ended things with your nanny,

Belinda, and it stopped about a year before the divorce. That's when Grace found out about Ike Huddlesworth and his involvement in human trafficking rings."

"Ike? We had dinner with the man on several occasions. I never imagined in a million years that he would run such a filthy business. He seemed like…like such a decent guy."

Winter's eyes danced about the kitchen, from the shiny, stainless appliances to the white marble countertops. There was an almost gawdy gold and crystal chandelier centered on a pale blue ceiling framed by thick white crown molding, giving it the illusion of a clear, blue sky. The lovely room should have been the focal point of Julia's home, a place where the family gathered at dinnertime, but Winter doubted she would ever see it as anything other than a confessional for all the Schumaker sins.

"Grace told us she overheard Ike on a phone call outside the pool house. He was talking with a consort, revealing his activities. Grace put together a scheme to kidnap her father's escorts and sell them into Ike's pipeline as a way of punishing him for breaking things off with her. She used the old storm shelter off the estate's garage as a holding area and recruited Gilbert to help. With her plan in place, she seduced Ike. And in exchange for sex, he introduced Grace to the traffickers he worked with. He claims she blackmailed him, using his 'lapse in judgment,' as he called it, to her advantage."

"And where is he now?" Julia ran her fingers across her forehead. "Skipped the country, I bet."

"No." Winter shook her head, carefully choosing her words to not betray her involvement. "The authorities were able to keep the raid on the trafficking camp and Grace and Gilbert's arrest quiet long enough to surprise Ike with a raid on his home. The Feds took him into custody, hoping to get him to tell them more about the traffickers. He has connections to several rings, and, with any luck, we'll take down more of his operations."

Julia closed her eyes, appearing so exhausted that Winter didn't know how she remained upright. There was a point in trauma when extreme fatigue never registered. A person ran on stress, and when they finally crashed, they needed help. Julia and her family would require years of therapy to find their way out of the darkness, but Winter remained confident they would.

"Could there be more women out there?" Julia asked in a frail voice.

Winter sighed, wishing what she was about to say wasn't true. "There are always more. For every pipeline that gets shut down, two more pop up."

Julia folded her arms, peering down at her untouched coffee. "I keep searching for a silver lining in any of this, and the funny thing is, I found one with Belinda." She lifted the side of her mouth in a half-smile. "I hated her for the affair with Freddie, but after everything that's happened, me getting full custody and her out of a job, we've found some common ground."

Winter leaned on the table. "What's that?"

Julia dropped her tissue on the table. "Grief. She had no idea Freddie was abusing Grace and wanted to kill him when she found out. Misery loves company, I guess."

Winter recalled the devoted nanny and recognized her as another victim in Schumaker's wake. The man was evil and had instilled that disregard for others in his daughter.

"Grace and Gilbert doing such horrible things astonished her. She thought she knew the kids. Without them, she's been lost. Her entire world came tumbling down in a day too. I, at least, have Gabriella to comfort me. She has no one." Julia cradled her head in her hands. "Who am I kidding? My life had already fallen apart. But this? Where did I go wrong? I could have stopped this if I'd only been paying attention!"

Winter reached for Julia's hands and gently pried them away from her face. She picked up the tissue box on the table and held it up. "You're bargaining, Julia. It's a natural stage of grieving. But think about it. You *did* stop this. You followed your instincts and hired a P.I."

Julia wiped her nose. "I can't thank you enough for all you've done."

"Yes, you can." Winter put the tissues aside. "You can stop spending the rest of your days wondering where you went wrong. That will accomplish nothing. Focus on where you went right and never look back again. Your children will need you. Grace and Gilbert have a long road ahead of them, especially Grace, but you *can* mend your relationship with her. You can show her the right way to face trauma. After all, you faced it with Freddie." She softened her tone. "All the fighting, the affairs, and the unhappiness. That was abuse too. You just didn't realize it at the time."

Julia's shoulders relaxed as she examined Winter with a newfound glint of curiosity in her gaze. "How did you know about all that?"

Winter flashed back to the images of Grace cowering in her closet while her parents argued. There was more than a little girl being torn apart in that closet. A family was crumbling.

"When Schumaker visited my home, I got a taste of how he must have been to live with. He had rules. Break them, and things became heated. I have a feeling the last years of your marriage were pretty rough."

Easing back, the clouds briefly lifted from the other woman's features. "When I first married Freddie, we were happy. I'm not sure when things fell apart, but I remember waking up one day and thinking this was not how I saw my life playing out. I was miserable." She shuddered. "I just never imagined him doing the horrible things he's done."

Winter's chest heaved as she remembered the eager recruit she had once been at the Academy. She pictured an illustrious career in the Bureau, chasing criminals and keeping the streets safe. Then she discovered her idyllic dreams were far from reality. "Nothing ever goes according to plan." She offered Julia a tepid smile. "That's the one thing you can count on in life. It's as certain as death and taxes."

40

T hough he was smiling, the child sitting on the couch across from Winter elicited pangs of guilt, and she had to work to control her breathing.

They all sat in the inviting living room, with a wall of bookshelves and paintings of open fields crowded with buffalo. But the quaint home, with its views of floral gardens, did little to assuage her resurfacing trauma as she gazed into Timothy Stewart's dark brown eyes, fighting to forget what she'd done to his parents and what he'd done to her husband.

Before Timothy had ended up in custody, he'd attacked Noah while disguised as a little girl. She often attributed the outburst of rage to Justin's twisted influence. She had moments when she blamed herself for what happened. Maybe karma wanted to pay her back for what she had done to the boy's parents. No matter the cause, the guilt would always be there, making her feel lower than the scum she used to send to prison.

"It's good of you to come." The deep voice of the older man seated next to Timothy settled her. "He's been wanting to talk to you."

Winter glanced at Guy Fuller, Timothy's uncle, amazed at how the two shared the same dark eyes. The wealthy recluse gained custody of the boy when his parents left the guardianship of their son to him. Winter learned he wasn't keen on having custody but honored his deceased sister's wishes. Like others in Timothy's family, Guy had demons, but Winter was glad to see the boy thriving in his care.

Winter returned her attention to the little boy who had been through so much. "Your uncle said you requested to see me. So here I am."

The nine-year-old brushed some shaggy bangs out of his eyes. "When I was at therapy last week, I learned about forgiveness. My doctor says it's important. We can't move on until we forgive." He squirmed on the sofa. "I wanted to tell you that my mom, dad, and sister forgive you. They were good people, and good people forgive." He glanced at his uncle. "That's right, huh?"

Guy patted the little boy's head. "You bet."

The words settled into Winter's center, creating a mixture of relief and anxiety. That was not whose forgiveness she needed most. "What about you?" She hesitated, finding her nerve. "Can you forgive me for what I did?"

Without missing a beat, Timothy bobbed his head. "Sometimes, good people have to do bad things, don't they?"

This wasn't the answer she needed, but it would do. Winter figured forgiveness was a process, like building a house. Many elements needed to come into play to create a foundation capable of withstanding the fiercest storm.

She watched Timothy, his playful grin ebbing, concerned about what bothered the boy. "You look sad. What is it?"

He slapped a hand on his leg, appearing frustrated. "I wish I could wipe away all bad people with a wave of my magic wand."

Bad people.

The worst person she knew, Justin, hadn't started out as a psychotic killer. He'd owned a stuffed giraffe he loved named Raff and had a funny lisp because of his missing teeth. She'd teased him mercilessly, something she still regretted, but his evil came later, encouraged and spawned by the grooming he'd received from Douglas Kilroy.

She knew the time Timothy had spent with Justin had twisted him, so when he spoke of bad people, she wondered if he thought of her brother. He was the one person in the world they both wanted to disappear with the wave of a magic wand.

"What do you mean by wipe away?" she asked, pushing Justin back into the darkest corner of her mind. "Make them go away forever, or are you talking about sending them to prison?"

Timothy's soulful eyes took on a glow that made him appear far older than his years. "I don't see why they're alive, is all. They seem like a mistake. A big one."

Winter's skin prickled, and that familiar pain throbbed in her temples.

No, not now.

She took a few deep breaths, praying it would pass. Soon, the pain faded, and Winter relaxed, grateful to avoid a vision, especially in front of the boy.

Her head cleared, and the boy's words came back to her. She couldn't help but side with him. Deep down, beneath the responsibility of the badge, she'd often wanted to wipe the bad people from the planet so they could never hurt another living soul.

You're right, sweet boy. Why does evil have to exist at all?

"The important thing to focus on is good people," she told him, wanting to remain encouraging. "I know you're one of them, because you've worked so hard to get better. Between your schoolwork and therapy and your kind uncle, I know you're doing so well. And that makes all of us very proud of you."

Timothy grinned, warming her heart.

Despite all the loss and pain, he was here, and so was she. It wasn't over for either of them, but they had forged ahead despite their emotional wounds. Healing was a process they understood. It wasn't a race, but a long walk up a very steep hill.

One day, Winter would reach the top. Today, one year and one day after her abduction, they were doing as well as expected. In the meantime, she would work on waving her magic wand and saving the world, one bad person at a time.

The End
To be continued...

Thank you for reading.
All of the Winter Black Series books can be found on Amazon.

ACKNOWLEDGMENTS

How does one properly thank everyone involved in taking a dream and making it a reality? Let me try.

In addition to my family, whose unending support provided the foundation for me to find the time and energy to put these thoughts on paper, I want to thank the editors who polished my words and made them shine.

Many thanks to my publisher for risking taking on a newbie and giving me the confidence to become a bona fide author.

More than anyone, I want to thank you, my reader, for clicking on a nobody and sharing your most important asset, your time, with this book. I hope with all my heart I made it worthwhile.

Much love,
Mary

ABOUT THE AUTHOR

Mary Stone lives among the majestic Blue Ridge Mountains of East Tennessee with her two dogs, four cats, a couple of energetic boys, and a very patient husband.

As a young girl, she would go to bed every night, wondering what type of creature might be lurking underneath. It wasn't until she was older that she learned that the creatures she needed to most fear were human.

Today, she creates vivid stories with courageous, strong heroines and dastardly villains. She invites you to enter her world of serial killers, FBI agents but never damsels in distress. Her female characters can handle themselves, going toe-to-toe with any male character, protagonist or antagonist.

Discover more about Mary Stone on her website.
www.authormarystone.com

facebook.com/authormarystone

twitter.com/MaryStoneAuthor

goodreads.com/AuthorMaryStone

bookbub.com/profile/3378576590

pinterest.com/MaryStoneAuthor

instagram.com/marystoneauthor

tiktok.com/@authormarystone

Made in United States
Troutdale, OR
11/06/2024

24515940R00155